girls just want to have fun

The COSMOPOLITAN Book of Short Stories

D1650151

girls just want to have fun

The COSMOPOLITAN Book of Short Stories

Edited by
Mandi
Norwood

COSMOPOLITAN

HEADLINE

Off Your Trolley © Cathy Kelly 1998
Rude Awakenings © Sarah Harvey 1998
Another Fine Mess © Isla Dewar 1998
Loving You © Laurie Foos 1998
A Dip in the Gene Pool © Jo-Anne Richards 1998
Love, Lies and Other Delusions © Val Corbett, Joyce Hopkirk and Eve Pollard 1998
The Stench of Rotting Love © Sophie Parkin 1998
Popping Out © Jill Mansell 1998
Topaz Dreams © Alison Joseph 1998
Fiorella la Bella © Vida Adamoli 1998
Cold Turkey © Carole Matthews 1998
Bad, bad Girls! © Tyne O'Connell 1998
Quiero Ba . . . Ba . . . © Cynthia Rosi 1998
Similar Tastes © Emer Gillespie 1998
A Feng Shui Romance © Julia Stephenson 1998

First published in 1999
by HEADLINE BOOK PUBLISHING

Collection © 1999 Headline Book Publishing
Published in association with *Cosmopolitan* magazine and Hearst
Communications, Inc. *Cosmopolitan* is a trademark of Hearst Communications, Inc.
The use of this trademark other than with the express permission of
Hearst Communications, Inc. is strictly prohibited.

10 9 8 7 6 5 4 3 2 1

ISBN 0 7472 6186 5

Typeset by Avon Dataset Ltd, Bidford-on-Avon, Warks

Printed and bound in Great Britain by
Mackays of Chatham plc, Chatham, Kent

HEADLINE BOOK PUBLISHING
A division of Hodder Headline PLC
338 Euston Road
London NW1 3BH

Contents

Introduction

As the world's bestselling magazine for young women, *Cosmopolitan* has a unique and accurate eye for what grabs the attention of its readers. Month after month we deliver great ideas, brilliant writing and fabulous photography... in fact, everything bright, ambitious young women need to enhance their careers, their friendships, their love and sex lives. It's the only magazine that truly celebrates being a woman and encourages you to be the best you can be!

Cosmo women love to read which is why we regularly review the hottest new books on the market. Inspired by their popularity, we've commissioned some of the brightest young writers around to put together a collection of feisty short stories. Inspiring, joyful, bittersweet, fun... one thing's for sure, each one will touch your heart. I know you'll enjoy them as much as we did.

Mandi Norwood
Editor, *Cosmopolitan*

girls just want to have fun

The COSMOPOLITAN Book of
Short Stories

Cathy Kelly is a feature writer and film critic for the *Sunday World* newspaper in Dublin, where she also writes the 'Dear Cathy' agony column. Her first novel, *Woman to Woman*, spent eight weeks at number one on both *The Sunday Times* and *The Irish Times* bestseller lists. Cathy Kelly lives in Dublin. Her second novel, *She's the One*, is published by Headline in spring 1999.

Off Your Trolley

Cathy Kelly

Purple was not my colour. Not even a subtle, iris-hued cobwebby cardigan that was supposed to drape delicately over the shoulders, revealing elegant collarbones before ending in fragile scallops around a Scarlett O'Hara-sized waist.

That's what it would have looked like on Chloë, my older sister: a girlie confection of silk that made the wearer look part-water fairy/part-supermodel.

On me, it just looked like something I'd knit myself, *without* a pattern. The tiny, elbow-length sleeves made my own solid forearms look as if they belonged to a sheet-metal welder, while the tiny mother-of-pearl buttons were stretched in a too-small rictus with the buttonholes as they strained against extra-enormous, PMS-variety boobs.

In the cardigan and a slithery lilac skirt, I resembled nothing so much as a bruise in full colour. A big bruise.

Not the elegant, lissome girl I wanted to transform myself into before the ten-year school reunion. Which was only six days away, so I didn't have much chance of transformation, not unless the Junk Food Diet had a dramatic cumulative effect; Eat Chips and Burgers for Ten Years and in the Week of Your Choice, Lose Two Stone Instantly!

'Come out of the cubicle, Sarah,' ordered Chloë. 'We want to see you.'

I came out gloomily.

Chloë and the assistant looked at me for a moment, matching bird-like blonde heads at an angle, mascara-ed eyes narrowed as they took in the purple ensemble.

They looked more like sisters than Chloë and I did: both petite, fine-boned and capable of giving admiring men in passing cars whiplash.

Six foot tall with the sort of athletic build that meant I was always being begged to sign up for the female soccer team in the TV production company I worked for, the only way I'd ever give a man whiplash was if I banged into him at full tilt.

Men just weren't interested in me. I mean, I was the only female researcher in Reel People TV who'd never been chatted up by the Head of Marketing, although my colleague Fiona reckoned this was because even Slimy Ted didn't have the nerve to flirt with a woman who could look down on to his bald patch. It wasn't that I secretly longed to feel his sweaty paw on my backside in the secrecy of the executive lift. I just wanted to be one of the girls for a change, instead of Amazon Woman.

'Perhaps the green one?' suggested the sales assistant.

Green! If purple made me look like a female boxer after a title match, green was even worse. Green made me look sea sick, bilious, second-stage of bruise.

'I mean,' the assistant continued helpfully, seeing as I wasn't saying anything to the contrary, 'with your auburn hair, green would be lovely.'

'Green doesn't suit her,' Chloë announced in a bored voice, studying perfect acrylic nails for flaws.

Sometimes I hated Chloë.

'Don't worry about me. I'll have a wander around the shop and see if there's something else I'd like,' I lied, obviously convincingly enough, as the assistant drifted off to flog more Tiny Tears-sized clothes.

'I don't think there's anything else here that would suit you and we don't have much time,' Chloë said crushingly. 'I have to be back in the office in half an hour.'

God forbid that she didn't get back to PR Solutions in time, I thought crossly, wrenching the curtain across the cubicle.

I mean, who else would be able to organise all those crucial details for the latest society launch she was involved in – like making sure the Page Three stunna who was guest of honour didn't end up sitting beside the footballer she'd kissed and told about the week before, or checking they'd got the right sort of non-sparkling mineral water so that the ladies who lunched wouldn't be belching through the speeches.

I carefully inched my way out of a hundred and fifty quid's worth of purple cobweb and simmered. Why did my only sibling have to drive me insane every time she opened her mouth?

Catching a glimpse of myself in the mirror as I reached for my T-shirt, I remembered why. Because Chloë was gorgeous and I wasn't. Because she had attractive men falling over themselves to take her out to dinner while my last date had been with a systems analyst named Humphrey who'd brought me to a sports pub in Clapham and had run out of cash after buying me two vodkas. And because, at the age of twenty-seven, I was sick and tired of being 'the clever one'.

Just a year apart in age, we were a million years apart in everything else. All through school, Chloë'd had endless boyfriends and everyone loved her. She'd actually been voted the most popular girl in the school in her last term. My claim to fame was winning the fifth-year physics prize, not an achievement guaranteed to make you a member of the cool gang. Chloë wasn't just a member of the gang; she *ran* it. And I still wasn't allowed in.

Ten years after leaving school, it still rankled. I still felt like the clever one. The invitation to the reunion had seemed like the ideal chance to redress the balance, to prove to the old girls of St Agatha's that I was different from the Sarah Powell of old: glamorous, successful, thin and chased by scores of men . . . Except that I wasn't any of those things. Well, I was successful enough. I'd just been given a promotion – *without* the help of the Head of Marketing – and I'd saved up enough for the deposit on a flat of my own. But the 'glamorous, thin and chased by men' bit was a non-starter. You couldn't be glamorous with unruly long red curls, freckles and size eight feet.

So I'd drafted Chloë in to help purchase the perfect outfit. If anyone knew how to wow the St Agatha's Old Girls, it was Chloë. But that hadn't exactly panned out either. I suppose you couldn't expect a size eight nymph to know what would suit a hulking six-footer with no discernible waist.

We hurried along the Old Brompton Road together. Me stomping along in my TV researcher's uniform of black jeans, black leather jacket and white agnès b T-shirt. Chloë immaculate in a white Whistles trousersuit, killer stilettos and more MAC than Ru Paul needed for a photo-shoot.

I was too disheartened to talk but she chattered away like a canary on acid.

'We're running the Jacob Kelian exhibition at Jo Jo's on Friday night and everything's been going wrong,' she fretted, half-running to keep up with my long strides.

'Who's Jacob Kelian?' I asked, wondering if he was that bloke I'd seen on TV who made sculptures out of old vodka bottles. If it was the same guy, he'd go berserk with delight when he saw all the raw materials he could dredge up from the drinks cupboard at my place. We never got round to cleaning out the old bottles and when we were manless – most of the time – myself and my flatmate, Jessie, went through quite a lot of vodka.

'Honestly,' huffed Chloë. 'Don't you ever read the arts pages? He's only the hottest young artist around. He paints the most amazing nudes in oils.'

'Oh,' I muttered, keeping an eye out for taxis as I was now very late for work.

'He's gorgeous, you know, Jacob. I met him yesterday. Real he-man stuff, American-football shoulders,' Chloë said dreamily. 'You can come along on Friday if you want,' she added off-handedly. 'It'll be fun.'

Since my usual Friday-night plans involved waxing my legs or getting plastered with Jessie and our pals down the Duke's Head, I accepted. Beggars couldn't be choosers. There were bound to be cocktail nibbly things to eat too, so I wouldn't have to cook that night. Although it did cross my mind that Chloë wanted me there so I could hand out the cocktail nibbly things.

On Tuesday, I left work early and hit the shops,

desperately hoping that the perfect reunion dress would leap out at me, screaming 'Buy me! Buy me!' Nothing leapt out, apart from a grey fleece jacket that would look great with jeans but would hardly cut the mustard in Brighton's poshest restaurant among sixty Prada-clad high-fliers.

Dejected and ravenous, I hiked over to Marks & Spencer's food hall and proceeded to trawl the aisles for dinner. Forget the diet, I thought savagely, as I threw a brace of full-fat chocolate dessert things in my basket along with a tub of ice cream.

The reunion's on Saturday, my conscience reminded me, so I put it all back and took two low-cal mousses instead.

'I can never make up my mind either,' said a deep voice with a faint American twang. 'I love the fatty stuff but you've got to really work it off.'

I wheeled round and found myself staring up – yes, *up* – at a dark-haired man in denim who was holding a shopping basket crammed with fruit. He was undeniably good-looking, with short, wavy hair brushed casually back, glittering black eyes and enough five o'clock shadow to make him a dead ringer for the Diet Coke bloke. Broad-shouldered and lean in a white cotton sweatshirt worn with faded black jeans, he was one of the few men I'd ever met who dwarfed even me. He certainly looked like he worked out. All he needed was the Harley Davidson, I thought with a gulp, noticing the biker boots and the chunky diver's watch on one massive tanned wrist.

'I don't usually do this but I couldn't help noticing you,' he said, dark eyes appraising me coolly. 'Would you like to go for a drink when you've picked up your groceries?'

I stared at him the way you would stare at a strange, admittedly gorgeous man who'd just chatted you up in the supermarket. My mind raced. This had to be a joke. There was no way he was for real. Men like this went for beautiful girls like Chloë. They didn't eye up women like me over the low-fat yoghurts, even when I was wearing my favourite pinstripe stretchy trousersuit and had recently washed my hair.

I peered around him, convinced I'd see someone from Reel People TV hiding behind the cheese, giggling hysterically at the idea of having set me up so marvellously. I couldn't see anyone but I knew they were there. It had to be Fiona's idea. Another researcher, she loved practical jokes and had just started dating some American bloke. They'd probably spotted me coming into M&S and had decided to play a wicked trick. It wasn't going to work.

'Are you on day release, by any chance?' I asked, trying to sound supercilious. 'Is this Care in the Community Week?'

'No.' He looked a bit surprised at this. One dark eyebrow went up in a look that was almost genuine. Probably an out-of-work actor, I thought. Fiona loved actors.

I marched off towards the vegetables. Nobody was going to make a fool out of me. He followed.

I picked up some celery and stuck it virtuously in my basket. Whoever he was, he wouldn't be able to tell Fiona that I was a glutton who ate the wrong things, anyway. I dumped another packet of celery in for good measure. The fact that I didn't like celery was immaterial. You could use it for Pimm's, couldn't you?

'I didn't mean to give you a shock but I really would like to buy you a drink,' he said, standing very close to me so that I could smell his aftershave, a musky scent I didn't recognise.

New York? I wondered. I'd never been very good at American accents. *I'd rilly likta buy y' a drink.* Great accent, great voice. Dark, rich and treacly. Great-looking guy. I sighed. Why couldn't this be happening for real?

To take my mind off him, I stared at the avocados. I loved them with vinaigrette, onions and some black pepper. But they were anti-diet items and I only bought them in moments of complete piggery.

Mr America expertly squeezed a couple of avocados with one tanned hand and stuck them in my basket. I stuck them back on the rack with their friends.

'Avocados are full of protein and their nutritious qualities outweigh their calorific content,' he pointed out calmly, putting them back in my basket.

'What are you telling me that for?' I demanded, eyes glinting dangerously. 'Are you telling me I'm fat or something?' This joke was going too far.

'I think you're lovely. I like curvy girls.'

'Yeah, right!' I stuffed his bloody avocados at him crossly. 'And Cindy Crawford would look better with another stone or two on.'

'Probably,' he said evenly.

'Anyway, what are you doing in the vegetable section?' I pointed accusingly to his basket where a head of lettuce and two giant cucumbers nestled in the middle of a large bunch of bananas, a honeydew melon, several lemons and a net of oranges. 'You've got enough fruit and vegetables for a vegan orgy. Are you following me?'

'Yes.'

'Are you a friend of Fiona's?' I snapped.

'Fiona? Who the hell is Fiona?' he asked, his accent becoming even more pronounced.

He couldn't have faked that much surprise. Not unless he was a very good actor, and a very good actor would have been rehearsing for some play or other and wouldn't have time to play games with Fiona.

'You mean you're not doing this for a joke?' I asked, in a less strident voice.

His eyes, which were very intelligent for such a handsome beefcakey type, sparkled. 'You think I'm doing this for a joke? I'm not. I wanted to buy you a drink. If you're not interested, say so. But I am.'

I loved the way he said 'interested'. *Innerested*.

'I didn't say that,' I mumbled.

'Great.' His face was creased into a huge grin, a gloriously sexy grin with gleaming white American teeth in a mobile mouth which I had a sudden vision of being glued to.

Control yourself, Sarah! I ordered. Being manless for a few months shouldn't turn you into a complete sex-mad nympho.

'OK. Let's have a drink.'

We sat in Callaghan's Irish bar in Piccadilly, bags of shopping clustered around our feet. Jake – that was his name – had obviously been there before because he led me to a cosy little snug in the back bar, pushed the revolving stained-glass windows shut and ordered drinks from a chatty barman he knew by name.

Unlike Humphrey, he didn't run out of money in 2.5 seconds. He bought me as many vodka bulls as I wanted while he stuck to Guinness.

We talked about the oddest things, things I'd never discussed on a first date – well, not that it was a date, exactly. When he asked me why I'd thought he was joking when he chatted me up, I explained. I told him about being the 'clever one', about Chloë the PR queen, and about the reunion that was hanging over me like the Sword of Damocles. It was strange for someone so physically blessed, but he understood.

He explained that his elder brother was a doctor and his younger sister was a teacher: steady professionals. He'd been the wayward one who'd run off to Europe to follow his dream and it hadn't worked out quite the way he'd planned. After years of waiting on tables by night, he still hadn't got anywhere. It had hurt like hell admitting to his family that he'd failed.

'What was your dream?' I asked softly.

He grinned boyishly. 'To be an artist.'

'I'm afraid I don't know anything about art,' I said ruefully. 'I'm a philistine. But what do you do now?' I asked quickly, not wanting to labour the point that he obviously wasn't an artist if his dream had failed.

He looked down at his hands, large hands that had a smattering of yellow paint on one thumb. 'I'm a decorator,' he said abruptly.

It was a wonderful evening. He was funny, charming, clever and seemed so interested in me. We both loved *Frasier* and *Cybill*, hated Britpop and adored Billie Holiday. His favourite movie was *Some Like It Hot*, which was certainly in my top ten, and our birthdays were exactly six months apart, although he was three years older.

After five drinks, we meandered over to Compton Street

and ate enormous chicken sandwiches in a jazz-filled bistro.
Our knees touched under the table. It felt electric – to me,
anyway.

At half ten, he said he had to go.

We stood outside the bistro door, shopping bags knocking off each other. He stared down at me, dark eyes in
shadow.

'I've really enjoyed this evening, Sarah,' he said. 'You're so
different from the women I've met recently – they're all so
uptight and they think I'm something I'm not,' he added, a
bit confusingly. 'You're not like that. You're an original.'

I blushed, and was so busy wondering if I looked horrible
and red that I didn't notice his lips coming down to meet
mine. As kisses went, it was gentle, his lips firm but not
probing. But the effect it had on me was incredible. My
stomach muscles clenched involuntarily and I felt as if a
million fireworks had been set off deep inside me. I didn't
know how good he was with a Laura Ashley floral border
but he could certainly kiss for America in the Olympics.

'I'd like to see you again,' he said when he stopped kissing
me.

Like a shot, I dumped my shopping, rooted a pen out of
my pocket and gave him my number. (It's obvious that I
only got as far as page three of *The Rules*, isn't it?)

He stuck it in his jeans pocket. 'See ya,' he said, waving.

I waved back happily.

He wouldn't call. I knew it. It was one of those rules of
dating: the sort of bloke you wished wouldn't call always
did, and the one you dreamed about every night for a week
never remembered your number. Or at least that's what
he'd say the next time you bumped into him by accident

and he had to come up with an excuse rapidly. Jake had no excuse for not remembering my number. But he wouldn't ring because no matter what he said about liking big girls, I probably wasn't his type. I was Humphrey's type; Humphrey, the two-vodkas-and-I'm-broke type.

At least wondering if Jake would call took my mind off the reunion for the rest of the week. I'd stopped caring about what devastatingly sexy little outfit I'd turn up in to stun the old girls into awed silence. Nightmares of looking like hell in my old school uniform had been replaced by hot, sweaty dreams of being kissed by a giant American with meltingly beautiful eyes, a cheeky grin and arms that could crush you to death.

Chloë called round on Thursday night in time to see me open a bottle of rosé in Jake-didn't-phone depression. Unusually, she seemed depressed too. From the train of the conversation, you didn't need to be Einstein to figure out that some bloke was the root of the problem.

'Men like you,' Chloë said sadly. 'They don't like me.'

'But that's not true,' I protested. 'Guys love you, they fancy you rotten . . .'

Chloë looked at me pityingly. 'Sarah, if you don't know the difference between lust and like at your age, there's no hope for you.' She adjusted herself on the sofa and took a deep slug of her rosé. 'Men fancy the knickers off me,' she announced, 'and that's generally what they want to do – get my knickers off. They want to *talk* to you. I couldn't tell you the last time any man wanted to talk to me.'

I looked at her fine-boned face, the silky blonde hair rippling artfully around her shoulders and the slim legs curled up under her, legs I'd have killed for. Chloë had

14

never eaten a Ryvita in her life, only had to open her handbag in the pub for ten guys to proffer lighters and hadn't spent a single New Year's Eve without a date since she was fifteen.

'I don't have the knack, that's all,' she said. 'It's so easy for you – you just talk to them, you speak their language,' she added, almost accusingly.

I thought longingly of Jake, gorgeous Jake who spoke my language and who still wasn't interested. She hadn't a clue.

'We've this new client,' Chloë was saying. 'He's into opera and we're organising an event for him. I had to take him out yesterday and he just looked through me all during lunch. He wasn't interested, I could tell. I tried *everything*. I was even wearing my Karen Millen suit,' she wailed.

I poured her more wine.

'Welcome to the club, Chloë,' I said.

I wore my stretchy trousersuit again. It seemed the right thing for an art gallery do and anyway, everything else was still at the dry cleaners or the bottom of the laundry basket.

I'd just wolfed down three baby quiches and half a glass of red wine when I saw him. He was talking to Chloë, still wearing his biker boots and faded black jeans but this time with a white cotton shirt that was open at the neck, revealing the tanned throat and the cluster of dark hairs I'd admired just a few days before.

Even across the room, I could hear Chloë's voice as she introduced a couple of grey-suited men to him.

'Meet Jacob Kelian, tonight's star,' she said brightly.

I felt a lump in my throat. Jake. Jacob. Decorator, huh? I had been conned, but not by Fiona. By a man. A handsome, bored artist who thought it was fun to pick up women in supermarkets and chat them up. Maybe it was for a bet, a variation on the 'see who can screw the ugliest woman' game played by holidaying lager louts in Torremolinos. The lump threatened to become an all-out howl of misery.

Glancing around for somewhere to put my wine glass, I heard my name being called.

The base of a sculpture would have to do. It was better than all over his shirt, which was where I really wanted to dump it. I'd made it to the gallery door before he caught up with me and grabbed my arm with one large hand.

'Get off,' I hissed, wrenching my arm away. 'You bastard. You lied to me.'

'I'm sorry.' He looked it. 'Please give me a chance to explain, Sarah.'

'You couldn't explain this,' I said angrily.

People turned to look at us. Jake pulled me into the foyer, his face anxious. 'Please listen, Sarah,' he begged.

I couldn't resist those dark eyes. 'Why didn't you tell me who you were?' I asked quietly. 'Was that a joke?'

'Why do you think everything's a joke?' Jake asked in exasperation. 'Do I have a funny face or something?'

I couldn't help smiling, even though it hurt. 'No, I do.'

He took my face in his hands. 'You don't. You have a wonderful face, a face I'd like to paint. I'd quite like to paint the rest of you too . . .'

I went puce, knowing that the walls were covered with Jacob Kelian nudes. Nudes of big women. Suddenly it all made sense.

I faced him, eyes blazing. 'Why? Because you need another heap-of-the-week model? How many do you go through per exhibition?'

'In fact,' he said calmly, 'these are all pictures of my last girlfriend. We split up a year ago and I haven't painted a new subject since. I need to feel connected to someone to paint them and I haven't. Until Tuesday.' He paused. 'I lied because I was sick of meeting people impressed by what I did and what I was becoming. I wanted to meet a normal person who'd like me for being ordinary Jake Kelian from Queens instead of media darling, award-winning Jacob. That's all.'

He looked at me earnestly, one hand still caressing my arm through my jacket. 'My cleaning lady washed the jeans and I couldn't read the matchbook any more.'

Yeah, right, I thought sourly.

'I've rung every TV production company in London looking for you,' he added. 'I finally tracked you down today and a woman named Fiona told me you'd gone early to a hush-hush meeting, you were then going to a journalistic seminar and you wouldn't be back.'

I gazed at him open-mouthed. That was exactly what I'd told Fiona to say in case our boss, who was on holidays but constantly rang to check up on us, phoned after I'd skived off early.

He *had* rung after all.

'I was crazy to see you again. I couldn't believe it when I saw you here and I knew what you'd think. I want you to trust me, Sarah. Please say you'll stay here for the evening, I'd love to have you with me.'

'And will you ring me tomorrow for a date,' I asked tartly, 'or will you lose my phone number again?'

'I thought you were going to a reunion tomorrow,' he said.

My heart fell. 'Oh yeah, I'd forgotten.'

'Tell you what,' he said, pulling me closer and kissing my forehead. 'How about if I drive you down and stay over. Brighton's not that far. We can make a day of it, have lunch in a pub along the way. If the party's boring, you can always meet up with me . . .'

'Drive down in what?' I asked.

'On my bike.'

'Don't tell me,' I said. 'It's a Harley.'

'How did you guess?' he asked.

I didn't answer. A vision of myself in leathers, clinging to Jake for dear life as we pulled up outside the restaurant, all my old school pals gazing out admiringly at my hunky, clever and successful escort, fluttered into my head.

'Perfect,' I breathed. 'That would be perfect.'

Sarah Harvey is a freelance journalist and has contributed many short stories to *Just Seventeen*. Her first novel, *Misbehaving*, was published by Headline in spring 1999.

Rude Awakenings

Sarah Harvey

The origin of telephone.
Tele – meaning far off.
Phone – from phonetic, meaning element of
spoken language.
The origin of hangover.
About two bottles of Soave to one person.
There's an incessant ringing in my ears.
The origin of the ringing?
I don't think it's the hangover, I think it's the
phone, but I'm too weak to answer it.

I think it was the last drink that did it. Up until then I'd
felt relatively sober. Well, not so much sober as con-
trollably and pleasantly drunk. You know, the couldn't-
give-a-toss-any-more everybody's-your-new-best-friend
stage of drunkenness? That dangerous time towards the end
of the evening where you're in danger of losing either your
handbag or your inhibitions, where you buy strange food
that you wouldn't normally dream of feeding to your dog,
from greasy men in greasy catering vans. The point where

you're most likely to meet the most awful man on this planet, and decide he's the best thing since Greg Wise in period costume.

Looking back, I should have left that last large glass of wine well alone and hung on to the lovely drunken happy feelings whilst they lasted, but no, the party animal in me had been well and truly unleashed, like a rampant hippopotamus on heat, and I knocked it back with all the reserve of a dusty desert traveller hitting an oasis for the first time in a week.

Looking back, I should have just stuck to Plan A and had a night in with the entire contents of my bathroom cabinet. Just me and a few cosmetic friends for a little beautifying party of our own.

Then again, everything would be so much easier with the gift of hindsight, wouldn't it? If I'd got hindsight, I probably would never have got into such a state in the first place.

If I had hindsight I'd still be with Matt. Wouldn't I?

Matt Davidson, short, blond and handsome. Love of my life, future father of my children, co-driver in a turbo-charged zimmer frame for two.

Or so I thought.

'It's all Matt's fault.'

I state this very loudly to myself as I attempt to prise open my eyelids – mentally, of course, because my mouth is stuck with the same hangover-produced ultra-glue that's gumming my mascara-matted eyelashes so very firmly together.

It's Matt's fault that I hit the town last night with the devastating impact of a hydrogen bomb, it's Matt's fault that I now feel my head's stuck in one of those gruesome machines that squishes cars into tiny metallic boxes, it's Matt's fault my tongue's growing more green fur than a month-old Danish blue lurking at the back of the fridge, it's Matt's fault that I'm desperately dehydrated and trembling like an Eskimo in an Arctic nudist resort, and it's Matt's fault that my emotions have been boil-washed, spun and hung out to dry over the past few weeks, culminating in last night's wild frenzy of hard partying.

I'd been with Matt for nearly two years when he announced, completely out of the blue, that he wasn't sure if he loved me any more.

Four weeks ago yesterday. I remember the exact moment perfectly. It's like a picture freeze-framed in my head – *The Scream II*.

We were sitting at the dining table in the corner of my living room, having just consumed a rather large lasagne followed by Cookies and Cream ice cream. I was wearing my extremely well-fitting size twelve jeans in an effort to look slim and sexy, and was just wondering if I'd ruin the effect by surreptitiously undoing the top button to fit in a second helping of dessert.

'Ali, I don't think I love you any more.'

Just like that.

One simple sentence.

The spoon that was snaking oh so surreptitiously towards the ice cream tub clatters on to the table, closely followed by my bottom lip.

Without giving me a moment to recover from the first blow, he nips in quickly with a few more verbal jabs, and finally an uppercut which sends my jaw swinging shut with the rapidity of a snapping mousetrap.

Not only does he not think he loves me, but he's not sure if he's ever really loved me, thinks he's only stayed with me out of habit, wants some time on his own to think things through, and is therefore buggering off to India for a while in order to collect his thoughts.

I personally normally collect my thoughts along with my loyalty points whilst manoeuvring a trolley round the vegetable section at Sainsbury's. But not Matt. Oh no, twenty minutes wandering amidst the courgettes, aubergines and organic potatoes isn't enough for him. He has to take a more dramatic and infinitely more distant route, and head off to the Taj Mahal to find himself. Leaving me at home, alone, miserable and suddenly feeling like I'm the one who's completely lost.

The irony of it is that I was so blind to it all. He'd been nervy all week, kind of edgy, short when I called him, not calling me, then over dinner he just announced that he was going, just dropped it into the conversation, then got up and left. Like a reckless teenager chucking a firecracker through someone's letterbox, then legging it down the street away from the explosive consequences of his actions.

And to think that I'd even, in one of my madder moments, thought he might be working up to asking me the ultimate question. No, not would I like the last scoop of ice cream, although I was beginning to drool a little and wouldn't have said no, but that all-important, get-down-on-one-knee-for-it question.

Couldn't have been more wrong, could I?

Instead of being perched on the edge of an emotional

precipice waiting to throw himself into the ultimate commitment, he was poised for escape, ready to spread his wings and fly off into the sunset on board an Air India jet!

'Er . . . there is one more thing . . .' He turns as he reaches the door and kind of smiles nervously at me.

'Yes.' I look up hopefully.

'You haven't got any sun tan lotion I could borrow, have you . . . ?'

I just managed to resist the urge to throw the rest of the ice cream at him, knowing that I'd probably need it for emergency comfort eating once the door was actually shut behind him, wandered dazed into the bathroom, squirted half a tube of Immac into a bottle of Factor 15, staggered back out, knees suddenly feeling rather trembly, and handed it to him.

So Matt buggered off to India to find himself, with a rather feeble 'I'll be in touch', and promptly got lost. Well, as far as I'm concerned anyway.

Four weeks and nothing, not even a postcard.

Then again, if he had been in touch, how would that have made me feel?

Dear Ali, Wish you were here? Hardly.

Ever since he went, my moods have been swinging faster than a hyperactive child in a playground. One minute I think I want him back, the next I'm hating him with a terrifyingly ferocious passion for the way he just walked out on me. If he came back through that door right now, I wouldn't know whether to hug him, or hit him where it hurts with the hardest object I could lay my hands on. Pick up the door stop and swing it crotchward . . .

Unfortunately, the only thing that's been hit for six at the moment is me, heavily, by the varying stages of après-relationship break-up.

The initial numb shock wears off after twenty-four hours and I'm flung into après-relationship break-up *Stage One*: desperately depressed, soggy as a bowl of leftover cereal, forming an overdependence on your duvet, and a strange addiction to daytime TV, as you convince yourself that you're far too upset to go into work.

Looking back, those first few days are just a blur of tears, tea cups, sympathetic best mates and as much junk food as a single woman can consume within a seventy-two-hour period without exploding – just.

Day Four. On to *Stage Two*: hopeful.

Matt only said he didn't *think* he loved me any more. That means there's hope, doesn't it? I've let myself go. Given in too many times to dessert. Allowed chocolate to become the centre of my life instead of my man. I'm going to spend the time that we're apart getting my life and my libido sorted out, reminding my stomach muscles that they did once hold themselves taut and together instead of sagging tiredly against my clothing, like a fat, weary donkey leaning against a palm tree.

Matt is going to come back to a wonderful new me. A sexy, slim, toned and taut, svelte and lovely, completely irresistible me. He's going to walk back through my front door and be completely knocked out. He'll be down on his hands and knees simply begging me for another chance.

This phase fortunately only lasts for about five days, during which time I nearly kill myself jogging, swimming, eating vast amounts of salad, drinking buckets of water, and cleansing, toning and moisturising as though my very life depends on it.

The next phase is far more mellow and much easier – for both me and my rapidly despairing friends – to cope with.

Stage Three: philosophical.

It's for the best. (To be repeated frequently in very calm voice.)

I'm not surprised that things fell apart, in fact I'm surprised we managed to limp along together for as long as we did. I mean, when was the last time we went out and just acted crazy together? When was the last time we really had fun?

Despite the fact that we didn't actually live together, we'd become like a boring old married couple – never talked to each other, never had fun together, went out on the same night every week, stayed in on the same night, made love on the same two nights every single week . . . if you could call it making love. Let's just say I'm far too familiar with the cracks in my ceiling to ever claim to have had a healthy sex life with him . . .

If Matt had been girding his loins in preparation to pop the question, would I actually have been prepared to don something diamond and sparkling and rent a few lines in the *Times*? Or would I have done exactly the same as he's done and sprinted off into the sunset as fast as my now slightly more toned legs could carry me?

I can't really blame Matt for wanting some time out.

I can, however, blame him for the way he did it . . .

Welcome to *Stage Four*: anger.

Matt is a complete and utter coward. Scum of the earth, dirtbag extraordinaire. I'm not saying that he should have stayed with me. Bastard. If he doesn't want me any more then that's his choice, but why the hell didn't he tell me sooner, why spring it on me only the day before he left for India? Bastard. It must have taken him weeks to organise, he'd have had to book time off work, sort out the tickets. I know he nicked my sun tan lotion – bastard – but there would have been other things to buy. And shots. Anti-malaria or hepatitis-whatever-it-is you have to have before you go. Don't you have to have them at least a couple of weeks before you leave?

He left it till the very last minute so that he got the least possible flak.

If you love somebody, you don't do that to them, do you? Then again, he doesn't know if he does love me any more, does he . . . Nobody loves me any more, sob wail boo hoo . . . and so back to Stage One again.

A dizzying, wearying roundabout of pure, raw, sore emotion.

The bells! The bells!
   Something's ringing again.
   It's not my alarm clock, because I threw that at the wall earlier, so it must be the bloody phone again.
   Internal Memo: Ears to Brain: The phone's ringing.
   Return Memo: Brain to Ears: Fuck off, I'm still asleep.

Week Three. I try a new tactic: instead of mooning around gazing at old photographs, listening to sad songs and dribbling unhappily into a rather large glass of something alcoholic, I decide to focus on everything I didn't like about Matt.

I enlist my best mate Imogen's help with this one. If I'm going to get past the beautiful-blue-eyes stage, then I need a severe kick in the right direction, and although she wasn't keen on joining in the jogging, I know she'll be more than happy to put the boot in on this occasion, never having liked Matt very much.

'I never did like Matt very much,' she announces, marching through to the kitchen and beginning to unload a bulging Marks & Sparks food hall bag.

'Face it, Ali, he was a total jerk, and he's just gone and proved it, hasn't he?' she states, piling wine, pasta and three different kinds of desserts on the counter. 'You're far better off without him.'

Good. This is what I need. The 'he was never good enough for you anyway' speech, especially designed for occasions such as these to convince the dumpee that she is a dumpee not because she's fat, ugly, stupid and boring, but because the dumper didn't have a single brain cell in his moronic head.

I help myself to a glass of wine and settle back against the counter whilst Ims begins to hurl cartons into the microwave.

'He took you totally for granted,' she says, peeling the hot cardboard lid off a tray of steaming tortellini. 'He treated this place like a hotel that provided free board, laundry services and sex thrown in on top, and never once thought about what you wanted. Face it, Ali, you weren't a real person to him, someone with feelings and needs; you were a convenience, something to be used when he felt like it, then just thrown away when he got bored.'

I take another gulp of wine and slump a little further. I don't know if this is having the desired effect. My self-esteem's already taken a total battering, and now I'm being likened, by my best friend, to a disposable nappy: dumped on, then discarded with distaste.

Fortunately, just as I'm slumping so much my arse is nearly hitting the lino, she moves on to the bolstering part of the speech, the bit about how wonderful I am, how bright, intelligent, sexy and vital, how I'll have a horde of gorgeous men knocking down my front door in the stampede to ask me out.

I can't exactly hear the thunder of size eight Cats heading towards my flat, but by the time Ims leaves for home, she's fired all of the abusive adjectives in the English language in the direction of the absent Matt – or Prat, as he has been rechristened – and my poor squashed ego has been bolstered so much that I now feel like I'm a better catch than Claudia Schiffer. I'm on to my second bottle of Frascati, and am sporting a smile for the first time since Matt – sorry, Prat – left.

Friends – love 'em! I toast, falling into bed still clutching a half-full wine glass.

Matt – *arse!* Don't miss him at all . . .

There's always a brief moment, when you wake up in the morning, when you are immune to everything. Just the slightest whisper in time where everything is all right with the world. And then your memory kicks in.

Back to *Stage One.*

* * *

Please, no, not again!

Whoever invented telephones should be forced to drink eight buckets of vino collapso, strapped to a heavy-duty pavement drill for half an hour – which I would imagine is the equivalent of three hours' frenetic disco dancing – and then left comatose in a dark room for four hours before having a loudly ringing handset inserted into each ear – and all other orifices for good measure!

Never again!

How many times have I said that before?

I try to lift my arm to pick up the handset by my bed, only to find that a gremlin with a staple gun has pinned it to the mattress.

I didn't even want to go out, but you know what it's like when your best mates decide that something is good for you. They nag and nag and nag until it's easier to give in . . .

When Imogen and Barbie had finally poured me kicking and screaming into an outfit they felt was suitable for a night out on the town and I felt was suitable for a night out on the game, pinned me down and painted my face a rainbow of colours from Lancôme, and coaxed my hair into something resembling a style, I actually looked pretty good.

It's nice to know that the 'turn myself into an ultra-babe' section of the depression roundabout has had some effect.

In fact, I have a sudden burst of a completely new stage in the après-relationship break-up thing – Optimism.

Not loads, mind you, but enough to get me out of the front door and into the waiting taxi. Unfortunately, by the time we reach the end of my road, the euphoria of actually fitting into my size twelve hipsters without my stomach crawling over the waistband like an escaping prisoner has worn off, and I'm as agitated as a dog who just knows it's on its way to the vet to have its bits seen to.

'I want to go home,' I moan after five minutes of petulant pouting which is pointedly ignored.

'Don't be silly,' the girls chorus in unison, like they've been rehearsing it.

'What if Matt phones?'

A synchronised incredulous raising of eyebrows is enough to silence me on that extremely vague possibility.

Twenty minutes later, I'm parked on a stool in a packed bar, two bottles of wine on the table in front of me, face like a bashed crab.

I don't know who's the more determined, me not to enjoy myself, or the girls that I will enjoy myself.

It's at this point that Imogen decides the best course of action is to fill me with alcohol as quickly as possible.

That can't be the phone again, it must be my hangover.

Or tinnitus from too much loud, pounding dance music.

I can't believe I feel this bad.

How much exactly did I have to drink last night?

One glass: not much different, still feeling pretty morose, not really enjoying myself, thinking back to the last time that Matt and I were in this place, when we were still together, miserable face on.

Second glass: alcoholically emotional, slightly tearful, how could he do this to me when he said he loved me? No, I forgot, he doesn't know if he loves me, does he? What have I done to deserve being treated like that? Bastard.

Third glass: perhaps this wasn't such a bad idea after all, it seems like ages since I went out with my mates for a proper girlie night out, I'd forgotten what fun it is, just me and the girls, and by the way who's the guy with the nice arse over by the bar in the light grey Ralph Lauren polo shirt?

Fourth glass: stuff Matt, he didn't deserve me, life's too short for just one man, he was a complete git anyway, this place is full of men, lots more drinking like a fish ... no, that's not right ... plenty more fish in the sea, that's the one.

Fifth glass: who the hell's Matt? I love everybody, especially the guy with the nice arse in the light grey Ralph Lauren polo shirt, and wouldn't it be a good idea to dance on top of the table instead of on the dance floor?

My dysfunctional answer machine decides that it actually has a purpose in life, and picks up the next call.

It's weird listening to your own voice played back by a machine.

'Hi, it's Ali, I'm sorry but I can't make it to the phone right now because I've passed out in a drunken stupor.'

I know I'm hungover, but I know that's not my

voice. Not unless I underwent a drive-in sex change last night.

I finally manage to prise open one eyelid as a voice that is extremely familiar begins to fill the air.

'Ali, where the hell are you? I've been trying to reach you all morning. Look, we need to talk, I'm coming round . . .'

Matt!

For a moment my heart leaps up into my throat, like a bungee jumper on the rebound swing, and then I feel a blast of overwhelming anger.

Where the hell am I? Where the hell am I? How dare he? He's the one that's been lost in space for the last four weeks . . .

Reality starts to filter through the rage.

Matt's back.

He's back and he's coming round.

A sudden surge of adrenalin gives me the propulsion I desperately need to detach myself from the duvet.

Why do I suddenly feel so angry. This is what I wanted, isn't it, Matt back?

Then again, I peer with my one open bleary eye into the dressing table mirror, I wanted to seduce him back into my arms and back into my life, blind him with a vision of loveliness, not scare him off with my impression of Dracula's little sister.

I've got the hangover of the century. I look like death on legs, ghostly pale skin, eyes like

Neapolitan ice cream, equal shades of brown, cream and bloodshot pink.

Black coffee, lots of black coffee. Shrugging on my robe, I stagger out of the bedroom and head for the kitchen.

It's only when I hit the living room that I remember the strange male voice on my answer machine, and realise, with a lurching stomach that has nothing to do with the acid swirling round inside, that there is something, or rather someone, on my sofa. I edge gingerly around the coffee table.

There is a man on my sofa.

He's fast asleep, long light brown lashes curling against his cheeks. He's snoring softly, but it's a pleasant sound, like the purring of a great cat.

Matt will be here any minute and I have a man asleep on my sofa.

Why have I got a man asleep on my sofa?

Unfortunately a major proportion of my brain still thinks it's slumbering happily under a duvet and doesn't offer an immediate answer.

Well, you don't get cat burglars pausing for a quick nap mid-robbery, so I suppose I must have invited him in.

A half-drunk bottle of wine sits on the coffee table, along with two wine glasses, one of which bears the incriminating print of what is definitely my lipstick . . .

How on earth am I going to explain this?

Hang on a minute, I'm not the one who needs

to give explanations here, I'm not the one who sods off for nearly a month, then expects to come back and find me sitting at home waiting for him, exactly where he left me, like my entire life can just be put on hold, like he's just popped out to the shops for a pint of milk or something . . .

I look down at the peacefully sleeping body.

At least he's on my sofa fully dressed, instead of in my bed completely naked – now that would be a hard one to wriggle out of . . .

He's rather attractive.

Sleeping Cutie.

I wonder what he looks like naked . . .

I give myself a very hard mental slap around the face.

I should be thinking how to get this stranger awake, off my sofa, and out of my flat before Matt turns up, not gazing at him like he's a cute cuddly sleeping puppy, and wondering what he looks like with his kit off.

The figure on the sofa stirs and the duvet falls back to reveal a creased light grey Ralph Lauren polo shirt.

Ah, a small number of memory cells are yawning, stretching, throwing off their duvets and complaining bitterly about their hangovers.

Fifth glass: who the hell's Matt? I love everybody, especially the guy with the nice arse in the light grey Ralph Lauren polo shirt, and wouldn't it be a good idea to dance on top of the table instead of on the dance floor?

I seem to recall being joined on top of that table by a man with merry blue-green eyes, who couldn't dance for toffee but was enjoying himself too much to care. I also have vague memories of being given a piggy-back down the King's Road, hurtling along at breakneck speed, my hair flying behind me, arms clutched around his neck and broad chest, hanging on for dear life, and laughing like a drain.

So that's how I got home.

Another memory cell wakes up. Declan. His name's Declan.

I think I chatted him up.

I am astonished to find myself beginning to giggle at this.

I've got better taste when I'm drunk than when I'm sober.

This must also be the mysterious voice on my answer machine.

The door bell rings, the harsh sound making me jump and jolting me back to reality.

Matt!

It's weird, you'd have thought I'd be racing to that door with the speed of a greyhound out of a trap, but I suddenly don't even know if I want to speak to him. Anyway, how can I with Sleeping Cutie in residence?

I suppose I could always pretend he's not there, that he's a figment of Matt's imagination. That Matt's caught some strange tropical disease that's making him hallucinate that there is another man asleep in my flat.

I can just see us having a polite conversation, with Declan curled up on the sofa between us, snoring softly.

The door bell rings again, at which point Declan slowly cranks open his eyelids to reveal aforementioned blue-green eyes, which light up as a slow, creased and tired smile spreads across his face.

'Morning, Ali.'

I should feel awkward, especially as the memory of a long, lingering kiss in the lift floats gently into my mind, but I don't.

I even manage to smile back at him.

'You changed the message on my answer phone,' I say rather lamely.

He grins, attempting to look sheepish but failing dismally.

'This jerk's been phoning all morning. For some reason he wouldn't take sod off for an answer . . .'

I'm laughing again. Why am I laughing? Matt finally gets in touch only for a strange man to tell him where to go, and all I can do is grin and laugh about it like an idiot.

The door bell rings again, an impatient, lengthy ring, finger pressed firmly on the buzzer.

Declan lifts his eyebrows in question, as I make no move towards the intercom.

'Don't you need to answer that?'

I hesitate for a moment.

Do I need to answer that?

I think the dense fug is finally clearing from my brain, and I'm actually waking up.

'No,' I reply, a slow smile beginning to spread across my face. 'It's nothing important.'

Isla Dewar lives in Fife with her husband, a cartoonist. Her novels, *Women Talking Dirty* and *Giving Up On Ordinary*, were both high on the Scottish bookseller lists for several months. Her latest novel, *It Could Happen to You*, is published by Review.

Another Fine Mess

Isla Dewar

There was Molly standing naked with the Chelsea line-up just before kick-off in their match against Arsenal. One of her paintings – her honesty period. They all showed Molly naked and ashamed. Molly, unclothed as always, on the sofa of a breakfast programme, drinking coffee, chatting to some made-up presenter, cameras around her beaming her nakedness out to millions. She never flattered herself: every roll of fat, every dimple of cellulite was carefully daubed in for people to view.

Alice didn't understand why she would want to reveal herself like this.

'It's real,' Molly told her. 'I'm trying to reach into my soul. To reveal my inner truth by showing the outer grim reality. I have to find out who I am.'

'But you don't have to let the world know what you find,' Alice said.

'That's art,' Molly told her. 'You're a businesswoman. You know nothing of truth and art. In fact, you know nothing about life.'

'Do too,' said Alice. 'There's more life, nastiness,

wheeling-dealing, backstabbing, friendship and downright good laughs in business than there is in art. In the age we're living through, business is where life happens. Not art.'

'Rubbish,' said Molly. 'At least I have fun. You have no concept of fun.'

'I do,' said Alice. Though she had a feeling Molly was right. She used to have fun. But now? She thought not. 'What is fun anyway? Tooters and funny hats? Running amok like those deranged women in Tampax ads?'

'It's when you don't remember who you are. And you don't want to be any place other than the place you are and you are having series of moments you don't want to ever end. It's when you're smiling and smiling and thinking this is a fine ol' mess I'm in. But you don't mind 'cos it's naughty. And you have a ball getting out of it. It's when you don't know where your life's taking you, but that's OK 'cos you're enjoying yourself. That sort of thing. You're useless at fun. Look at your bloke, ex-bloke. A married man. A suit like you. Your idea of fun is to own a coloured mobile phone.'

Alice thought about her new toy, her pride and joy. A natty Nokia with interchangeable coloured faces in her handbag said nothing. She worked for J.J. Sanderson, in Marketing. She was a team leader, whatever that meant. 'Sounds like I'm a professional hockey player,' she said. She liked her job for the most part, even if she knew she spent far too much time in meetings. Yet there was a certain rigidity about the organisation that always made her ill at ease. Oh yes, people used first names, but with a certain stiffness, and only if you were in the same management echelon. And even then they might as well have been addressing each other more formally. The walls were all pale yellow. There were no plants. Screens flickered. Employees went on courses, spoke jargon. There was a strict, if unspoken, dress code. Men in business suits, white shirts, no sports jackets. Women in management wore the same, except with blue or pink shirts. In fact Alice remembered an intense conversation she'd had with Joanna Wilkinson in Sales. 'I'd never wear a cardigan to work,' Joanna said. 'It's too, too flippant. I need to be taken seriously.'

Alice sighed. People came to J.J. Sanderson for eight hours a day (at least), five days a week. But there was an undertow of office existence, that their real lives started when they left the office. It was then they came alive and became the people they dreamed they actually were. Then again, they all seemed relieved when the stress of the weekend was over and they could return once more to their sheltered routine. Here at least they knew what was expected of them.

Molly lived in the flat below Alice's. But whereas Alice's flat was an indication of where she imagined her life was heading – upwards, with matching white sofas, polished floors, an unopened copy of the *River Café Cookbook* on the coffee table, the right sort of kettle and toaster in the kitchen – Molly's was a mess. The statement it made about her life's direction was: I am going not going anywhere. So what?

'It says everything about me,' Molly would say, looking blandly round. 'It's existential. I believe in nothing. Not cleaning. Nothing.' She did not have the money to decorate. In an effort to create a certain flow from room to room, she'd removed all the doors. Visitors could now view Molly in bed, in the bath, wherever. She didn't mind. 'What is there for people to see that they can't see just looking at walls?' Molly naked, that's what.

Molly looked like an artist, hair henna-ed and cropped, paint-splattered jeans. She had an intricate tattoo on her shoulder blade. She behaved like an artist, or at least how she'd decided she wanted to project her artistic image. She smoked. She drank pints. She swore. Six A levels, four years at Glasgow School of Art and a spell at the RSA, she still had only one adjective. Good, bad or indifferent, fuck said it all.

The latest painting showed Molly in the future, eighty years old, flabby-armed – dinner lady arms, she said, have you ever noticed dinner ladies' arms? – folds of flesh drooping round her belly, thighs raddled with cellulite, a scrubby patch of grey pubic hair. She was standing on the pavement between a dusty confectioner's shop and a grubby-looking pub, weeping as she ate a Snickers bar. This last effort had shocked her so much she'd gone blank. For the past year the only thing Molly didn't do as an artist was paint. Now she was seriously broke.

Money was not a problem for Alice. It was the every-dayness of things that got to her. The comings and goings. Seven forty-five every morning on the tube to work and six thirty going home again. Strap-hanging; there was never a seat. She felt her face fall into that expressionless traveller's glaze. A kind of mournful blank. Then there were the predictable business clothes she wore, the regular hours she kept, the food she ate – Marks & Spencer's meals for one. She felt her life was so routine it almost disappeared.

Today, standing on the platform at Leicester Square, she saw a rat, black as soot, black as the rails it darted under. It scuttled back and forth. She was the only person in the waiting crowd watching it. She hated rats, but sympathised with this one.

That was how she felt these days – she scuttled. She moved through the corridors going from meeting to meeting, shoulders hunched, carrying papers, notebook, wondering what the hell she was doing. She hated meetings. They worried her. She fretted before she went to them. What should she say? How to project herself? What if she farted? What if she missed important points? She fretted again after them. She'd forgotten what she'd meant to say. She'd drifted off and doodled when she ought to have been chipping in with important points. She'd yawned. Sighed. Fidgeted. She'd stared round at her colleagues, wondering how they coped with all the meetings. Were they as fed up with them as she was? She couldn't remember anything that was said.

It was hell. Today, after her sixth meeting, she sat before her computer. She spread her fingers over her keyboard, ready to type *Details of the Meeting Between Publicity, Sales and Marketing Concerning the Jones Account.* She went blank. Who had been there? What had they said? She got out her notebook. Squiggles, doodles, including a fairish drawing of the morning underground rat, and a note to herself reminding her to make an appointment at the hairdresser's. Shit. She should have paid more attention. She shouldn't have volunteered to network details of what had been agreed on the inter-departmental e-mail.

She put her head in her hands, drifted off. Recently, when she should have been busy with workaday things, memories would flood over her. She did not invite these thoughts into her head, they just arrived. Precious moments, visions of things she'd thought she had forgotten. Standing, six years

old, in a snowstorm in the suburban garden of her childhood, flakes swirling about her, a half-formed snowman on
what months ago had been a green, Wimbledon-perfect
lawn. She was staring at the little knobs of snow that had
formed on her mitten. The taste of ice and wool when she
sucked at them. The creases in her grandmother's face, and
the feel of her skin, soft, too soft, when, up on tiptoes, she'd
touched it. The old lady standing in her kitchen spooning
Angel Delight, strawberry flavour, into perfect crystal glasses
three days before she died. Other moments flew into Alice's
mind. Herself at seventeen. Meeting mates in the pub, that
sweet tingle of illicit drinking. What a grown-up she'd been,
so sophisticated. Back then she'd known exactly what she
wanted from life. A career, a flat and a bloke. Well, two out
of three wasn't bad. There was no bloke now Jack had left
her. She remembered Jack in the morning, surfacing from
sleep, hair tousled. The smell of him: fresh sweat, yesterday's
cologne, soap-scented skin. Alice would sigh. Another
woman would have that now. His wife.

It was now, when the memories stopped swimming
through her, that she'd notice she was sitting at her desk,
reaching out, clenching, unclenching her fist. Grabbing
for something, snatching air. Then she'd fish inside her
drawer, bring out a KitKat. A small comfort – sweet,
soothing, a certain texture on the tongue. But it was hardly
life-fulfilling.

Today, in the few seconds after the memories, before the
KitKat, she typed. *Fucking meetings. They are effing awful.
I fucking hate them. They are the thief of time. They ought
to be banned*. There, she'd written it out loud. She signed it
with her full name, Alice Georgina Kaseby. That was good, a

release. Not enough, she thought. There's still some bile in me. She loaded a CD from a picture gallery, found *The Scream*. Pasted it on to her screen. Repeated it and repeated it till she had a whole gathering, a meeting-full, of anguished, wide-eyed, despairing faces, mouths agape. She grinned; that had got it. She reached for her KitKat. Groped around in her drawer. Nothing. Shit, she'd forgotten to buy one.

She slumped instead. She hadn't intended to do the full forward fall that she did. She'd only meant to indulge in a mini-slump with sigh. But somehow she tumbled – if a woman can tumble whilst sitting at her desk – and her head crunched against her keyboard, pressing several keys as it landed. But the relevant key, the key that took, was the Send button.

Alice's little outburst went winging through the building. And networking its way across London to Kensington, to Mr Sanderson's three-storey, eight-bedroomed home, to his study, to the screen of his brand new G3 power book. He was a man for new technology.

He was sixty-two. Didn't go into the Sanderson building more than once a fortnight. But he kept in touch, faxes, inter-departmental e-mail, mobile phones. Wasn't modern gadgetry just marvellous? He loved that word, used it a lot. Marvellous.

He phoned his managing director. 'See that memo? What does it mean? Who is this Kaseby person?'

'Alice Kaseby?' answered Nicholas Jasperson, looking at the tortured message. 'Never heard of her.'

'Just a second.' He pressed the button on his phone that communicated with his PA. 'Who is Alice Kaseby, Helen?'

'Never heard of her,' said Helen.

'We employ her,' said Mr Jasperson. 'I want to know who she is. So does Mr Sanderson.'

It took seconds. Alice Kaseby's working life came rattling out of Helen's printer. She took the information though to Mr Jasperson. 'Miss Kaseby,' she said, putting it on his desk.

'She's in Marketing,' read Mr Jasperson. 'A team leader. Been with us two years. Couple of years in advertising before that. BA Hons. Newcastle, 1989 to 1992. A year out, travelled, Africa, South America. Fairly unremarkable.'

'Yet she wrote that message,' said Mr Sanderson.

'Appears she did.'

'It isn't the message that's remarkable.' Mr Sanderson knew that meetings were hell. He was sure that everyone who'd read the note agreed with it. 'It's the way it's put. And the actual boldness of sending it. The honesty.'

'Yes.' Mr Jasperson shrugged. He knew very well what she meant. Had he not been to four meetings today? And could he tell what they were all about? No he could not. Recently he'd been feeling that that was what he did for a living – he attended meetings.

'Well,' said Mr Sanderson. 'Is she right? Do we have too many meetings?'

Mr Jasperson huffed and puffed. Yes they did have too many meetings. But he wasn't going to be the person who said so. Better let the onus for that suggestion fall on a lesser head than his. Alice Kaseby's, for example.

'What should we do about it?' asked Mr Sanderson.

'Well,' said Mr Jasperson. He drummed on his desk. Manicured fingers. 'Call a meeting?'

'Yes,' said Mr Sanderson crisply. 'We shall have a meeting to decide if we have too many meeting. Kaseby to attend. In fact, Kaseby to take the meeting. I shall be there.'

He rang off. Unremarkable, Jasperson had said. But Alice Kaseby did not sound unremarkable to him. He was constantly on the lookout for remarkable people. He considered himself to be in that category. He had arrived in London forty-four years ago. All he'd had to his name was a crumpled suit, two shirts, fraying at the collar, thirty shillings and a heartful of blind ambition. Now look at him. Head of an empire. He'd houses in Monaco, New York and Hampshire, fifty million in the bank. That was not the catalogue of an unremarkable man.

Alice was leaving the office when the call came. She would take the meeting about too many meetings tomorrow. Mr Sanderson would be there, and all the heads of department. Alice said, 'Right.' And, 'I see.' And, 'I'll look forward to it.'

Alice switched off her computer. Put on her jacket, picked up her briefcase and handbag. Left the office. Into the lift. Down into the foyer. Through the huge plate-glass doors. Along the street. Into the tube station. Down, down the long stairs. Jostled through the evening crowds. On to the train. There was a seat. Praise be, the day wasn't a total disaster then. She sat. Then it hit her. Tomorrow she would have to account for her message. She threw her head back and cried, 'Oh God.' Out loud. The carriage was crowded. Nobody looked round. Nobody reacted. Anyone who yelled a lament at that time of day on the sweaty homebound train was speaking for everybody. They all knew what she meant.

Alice closed her eyes. Settling down for a thirty-minute worry. But her mind filled with more moments. Swimming in the sea off Cornwall, water so clear she could watch the sand and rocks below her. Face burned by the sun. Then wading to the shore, dripping, pushing her hair from her face. The sudden warmth on her body, drops of water, goosebumps, tiny hairs raised on her arms. The scent of hot sand. The sweetness of it. There was only smells and sounds. Gulls, waves. And she was smiling.

She did not go straight home. She could not face the silence or the Markies meal for one. Also she feared if she was alone she'd just worry and drink. She went instead to Molly's.

'You've brought it on yourself,' Molly said, handing Alice a vodka and tonic. Alice took it. She hadn't wanted to comfort herself with alcohol alone in her flat, but here, in Molly's, with Molly, alcohol was acceptable. 'You have bottled your emotions. Like I keep saying, you're constantly stressed out. You have no fucking concept of fun,' Molly went on.

'Rubbish.' Alice poured herself some more vodka. Held the bottle up to Molly, who held out her glass. 'Stress is good for you. Keeps you going. Makes you inventive, creative. I need stress. Anyway, it's all your fault. I swore on that memo. I never swore before I met you. You do it all the time and it's infectious.'

'Of course you swore before you met me,' Molly said. 'You just didn't do it out loud. You swore inwardly. Bottled it up like you do everything else.'

Recently Molly had been looking for new longings to put on canvas. She was finding this business of not painting extremely stressful. Indeed, had considered stress counselling, but couldn't afford it. Instead, stepping up her search for new yearnings, she did the quick crossword in the *Guardian* every morning whilst sprawling on her sofa watching Richard and Judy. After that she had time to nip down to the pub before being back on the sofa in time for *Neighbours*. 'I'm immersing myself in popular culture,' she explained. 'I want my art to be an expression of the times I am living through. Accessible. I want people to look at it and say, "That's my life. That's my pain. That's my joy. These are my moments." That is what I strive to put on canvas.'

'You need actual stress,' Alice told her. 'You need to be shoved headlong into the art marketplace. You need deadlines.' Actually, she thought Molly's desperate reaching for new inspiration a wonderful excuse for watching trashy telly, and wished she had thought of it. 'I'm sorry I can't come into work today. I'm doing vital marketing research. Keeping up with popular culture watching *Oprah*. Someone's got to do it.' She refilled her glass.

'Have fun with your meeting tomorrow. Go on, I dare you,' Molly said.

Three huge vodkas down, Alice was up to any challenge. 'What do you mean exactly?'

'Well, they say you're team leader. I dare you to go in dressed like the leader of a team. Wear a football strip. The Chelsea one I bought to get the detail right in my painting. And trainers.'

'I couldn't.' Alice shuddered. 'People would stare. It's just not done. People at work are very conservative about what they wear.'

'I dare you,' Molly challenged again. 'And walk round the table bouncing a ball. Tell them they're a bunch of stuffed shirts who've created a load of stifling rules that are inhibiting exciting, innovative ideas.'

'I couldn't do that.' Alice was appalled.

'Chicken,' said Molly.

'No I'm not.'

'Are, too. Difference does it make? You've lost your job anyway. It'd be a hoot. Make your name.'

Alice considered this. Go out with a bang. No whimpering for her. She was drunk enough for this to seem logical, sensible even. 'OK.' She set her shoulders, jutted her jaw. Alcoholically brave. 'But you have to do something too. A challenge. A fun contest.'

'OK.' Molly nodded. Hah, a wimp like Alice couldn't ever come up with something really challenging. She was safe. 'What?'

'Dunno yet. Wait and see.'

'OK,' said Molly.

'OK,' said Alice. They glared at each other, nodding fiercely, drunkenly, saying OK over and over, brazen OKs.

Next morning Alice, wearing the Chelsea strip carefully concealed under her coat, and bashed trainers, strode through the foyer of the J.J. Sanderson building. She carried her normal office outfit in a holdall. There was an awesome silence when she revealed her outfit. 'Special get-up for a special meeting,' she explained. She did not meet any astonished eye. She removed the ball from her bag. Sat at her desk, slowly turning it round and round. People were staring at her legs. She wished she'd thought to spray on her Estée Lauder fake tan. She felt more than stupid. More than vulnerable. An arse of a sacrificial lamb setting herself up for the slaughter. She cursed Molly. She cursed herself. She cursed vodka. Vowed never again to touch a drop. Still,

Chelsea wasn't so bad. Blue, she suited blue. Thank God it hadn't been Arsenal. Red did nothing for her.

The boardroom was thirty feet long. A huge gleaming table in the middle, a conference video screen. There was a drinks cabinet and bookshelves. The heads of department (HODs) sat round the table. All in grey suits, white shirts and ties so uniformly knotted they looked like their mummies had done them before they left for school. Only Mr Sanderson stood out, in black trousers, pink shirt with navy and gold striped braces. His jacket was draped over the back of his chair.

Casual wear was frowned on. Smart casual was almost, if laughably, acceptable. But this nonsensical football strip was *not on* – even on a Friday. The HODs were too shocked to register shock. They looked, instead, immaculately baffled. Mr Sanderson grinned. He liked this. He leaned over to get a proper eyeful of Alice's legs. A rebel, he thought. All the discreet businessmen who surrounded him bemused him. He never could tell what they were actually thinking because they usually agreed with him whatever he said. But rebels were different. You could either mould them or fire them. You knew where you were with rebels.

Oh, Jesus, Alice thought. This is a fine mess you've got me into, Molly.

She bounced the ball. What'm I going to say? Hurry, hurry, think of something. She had nothing prepared.

She'd been drunk when she got home last night. She'd gone straight to bed, sunk into blackness, which she'd woken from at three in the morning with a hangover, and hadn't been able to get back to sleep. But then Alice was used to sleeplessness. She knew the night well. Its colours and deepnesses. She could tell the time by how the dark lay in patches in her bedroom, black here, paler there where the streetlight seeped through the blind and shaded it to grey. Night after night she woke at three or four in the morning and lay staring into the dark, willing herself back into unconsciousness. She never succeeded. So she'd get up, make coffee (though she knew she shouldn't, it'd only make her more awake). Then she'd sit, legs curled, on the sofa and worry. She worried about work, about tomorrow's meetings, and about Jack. She doubted she'd see him again. He was in New York now. In Manhattan. 'Got an apartment,' he told her. 'Tiny place no bigger than a shoe box.' He was sharing it with his wife. That'd be cosy. She missed him. Though she'd only seen him Mondays and Wednesdays and the occasional weekend. She missed waking up Mondays and Wednesday knowing that tonight, for a while at least, he'd be in her bed beside her. That was over now, so it was the grey-dawn sofa for her and her thoughts and yearnings. 'Life's a bitch,' she said. 'And then you die. Then you realise you're not going to die after all. And that's a bitch too.'

She bounced her ball. Considered the dumbfounded group before her. There was something about horrifying men *en masse*. Something liberating.

'Gentlemen,' she improvised, 'this is me. This is who I am. Member of a team.' She bounced the ball. 'And when teams find out who they are, discover their team identity, they reach heights of innovation and creativity.'

Nobody spoke. So she threw the ball to Mr Hendry, Sales. He caught it. Looked horribly embarrassed. Tossed it back.

'Are our teams finding any real truth about themselves and what they want to achieve in the meetings we hold?'

said Alice importantly, she thought. She was feeling a tad sweaty. 'Some meetings are undoubtedly necessary. New clients courted. Contracts discussed. Details thrashed out. I'm not taking issue with all that. I'm against the other ones. The ones where we lie. We lie with our silence, our disinterest, our eagerness to get away. The ones where we get together to come up with exciting ideas and go away frustrated.' She held her arms out, displaying the strip. 'Are we stifling innovation? That glorious moment when the team comes together, works together, getting closer and closer to their rival's goal, and scores.'

'Good point,' said Sanderson. 'Interesting.'

Encouraged, Alice threw the ball to Mr Jacobson, PR. He was a man of the world. He was nonchalant at all times. He'd worked at it. He bounced the ball on the table a couple of times before returning it.

'I worry,' said Alice, 'that people are afraid to make fools of themselves. Like this.'

Everyone laughed. Mr Sanderson said, 'Marvellous.'

'People are afraid of individuality. They feel safe in their silence. Are we missing that dash of craziness, the sort of ideas that will make us market leaders? I want us to be unafraid of how we look and how we act and what we might say.'

She threw the ball to Mr Jasperson. That'd do it. That would get her fired. He took it, looked at it, and threw it back.

'I'm in search of blankness,' said Alice. 'We fret and we fuss. But it's in the moment of blankness when the ball is coming to us, when we reach out for it, that greatness comes. And along the way, in pursuit of wonderful moments, we should have fun. We shouldn't be afraid of fun in the workplace. Fun is good.'

'To me, to me,' shouted Mr Sanderson. 'I want the ball.' He was glad he'd come. He was enjoying this. Alice threw the ball to him.

'Here, Nicky,' shouted Mr Sanderson, throwing the ball across the table over the bottle of Badoit. His eagerness made getting the ball acceptable.

'OK, Jonny,' shouted Mr Jasperson, standing up.

'To me, to me,' shouted Mr Hendry.

'Come and get it, Charlie,' challenged Mr Jasperson, making off round the table, bouncing the ball.

Charlie tackled. Won the ball.

'Over here,' shouted Mr Robertson, Accounts, jumping from side to side to avoid Mr Jacobson, who was on his feet, working his way to a clear spot, away from Sales, PR and Marketing.

'Billy,' said Charlie, throwing the ball to Accounts.

'Room,' said Mr Sanderson. 'We need more room. Help me move the table. Use these chairs for goals. Teams, Kaseby's on my side.' He was keen to associate with the mastermind behind this nonsense. They removed their jackets. Decided upon rules. Set up a field of play.

Alice joined Mr Sanderson's team. My God, what had got into them? And why was it that all these high-powered men had reverted to nursery names? The ball flew about the room. 'Goal,' shouted Mr Sanderson. They were shouting, shoving and really, Alice considered, behaving very badly.

'Bollocks,' replied Mr Jasperson. 'That was offside.'

'A penalty,' shouted Mr Jacobson. 'A penalty if ever I saw one.'

Alice got caught up in the game. She won the ball, dribbled sweetly up the room, swerved past Publicity, Personnel and Accounts and scored. 'Yes,' she shouted, jumping up and down, fists aloft. 'Yes. Yes. Yes.' She and Mr Sanderson hugged in triumph.

'We win. We win,' Mr Sanderson shouted. He was a businessman. He was ahead. Time to quit. 'Wonderful,' he said. 'Best meeting I've ever attended.'

'Innovative,' said Mr Jasperson. 'Exhilarating. I can see what you mean, Alice.' It was first names now.

'Brilliant,' said Mr Jacobson. 'This woman is to be congratulated.'

Alice had slunk off to her meeting about too many meetings an embarrassment, a shock, and had returned a hero. She noted with triumph the small looks of envy. She sat back, put her trainered feet on her desk and gloated. The boys, her mates, the HODs, were talking of promotion, a rise, an office to herself, a new title – Executive in Charge of Creative Policies. All that, and she had more glee in store. Her challenge to Molly. Her revenge.

She couldn't think of anything quite vile enough. She gazed ahead. Moments came to her. Six years old, crawling into next door's garden to steal strawberries. Eating so many she was sick. That had been fun. Getting caught in the school cloakroom, a fag between her fingers and her tongue down Raymond Cuthbertson's throat, by Miss Halloway, her guidance teacher. Three weeks' detention for that. She grinned. She did not notice Mr Sanderson coming across the room towards her.

'Basking in your glory, Alice?'

Alice, he called her Alice in front of everybody. She

gloated. The whole office would be dressing down tomorrow. Jeans, T-shirts and exhilaratingly honest naughty inter-departmental e-mail.

'You forgot your ball.' Mr Sanderson tossed it to her.

She'd been right about the moment of blankness. It was at that moment of reaching for the ball that it came to her. The vile idea. The thing she could get Molly to do.

'You have to become your art,' she said, pointing at her chum. 'I challenge you to be a giveaway in a packet of cornflakes.'

'What?' said Molly. 'That isn't art.'

'It will be when you do it. I dare you to make a giant packet of cornflakes, fill it, wrap yourself in clingfilm and give yourself away. It'd be a statement about modern life. The free plastic human being.'

'What will I be wearing under the clingfilm?' Molly wanted to know.

'Your artistic usual. Nothing.'

'I can't.'

'Of course you can. You must. It's a dare.'

'Where?' asked Molly.

'Sainsbury's car park. Mid-morning, Saturday.'

It took Molly a month to construct the giant box of cornflakes – ten feet high, six feet wide. Huge cockerel on the front. Meantime, Alice settled into her new job. She took brainstorming sessions, she encouraged people to toss balls at one another. 'Free your mind,' she said. 'Let go. You are with friends. Discover where your thoughts will lead you and others round you.' She feared inside that all this was leading nowhere and at some point someone would point this out. Nobody did. Everybody wanted to be thought innovative. Alice wore T-shirts under her new business jacket, which was soft-shouldered and checked instead of her usual black, a sign of her new image as corporate insubordinate. She noticed that her new position consisted of taking meetings.

Now she was a full-time professional meeting-taker, but not too busy for KitKats. And not too busy for secret moments to come to her on the tube, in the lift, in the loo. Watching a Cup Final in a pub in Battersea with a bunch of mates, bawling at the team, drinking pints of London Pride. Hiding in the boys' changing room at school, stifling giggles. A lot to discuss afterwards. Lying about her age in the Star and Lion when she was sixteen, buying her first vodka and coke. Changing the flags on the local putting green. Sleeping with Duncan Robertson in his mother's bed when she was away for the weekend. What did it all mean, these thoughts? Was she longing for a purity of moment? Was happiness a collection of perfect moments rather than a state of being? Or did she just have a secret yen to be naughty? 'It means,' Molly said when Alice asked her, 'you're just wanting more fun. Nothing wicked. Just naughty. Naughty's good. It's your ego dancing.'

Alice nodded: yes, she thought it was.

Molly had a friend fretsaw out hundreds of giant corn-flakes to fill her giant packet.

'Why can't we use real ones?' asked Alice.

'Because that isn't art,' said Molly.

They hired a van to set it up. Placed it bang slap in the middle of the car park but were moved to the space beside the bottle bank. Molly, wrapped in clingfilm, lay on a bed of giant cornflakes in a perspex box at the bottom.

'What's she wearing under that clingfilm?' the super-market manager wanted to know. 'We have children here.'

'Dunno,' Alice lied and went back to the hired van to watch.

People gathered, children kicked the box, demanded the free giveaway. A couple of lady pensioners stopped, their combined block of hips seeming to take up all the space in front of the box, and stood, staring, saying nothing. They moved off, still wordless. A dog peed on the corner then shuffled off, mindlessly. The local press came. Molly emerged, sweating and stiff, and declared herself to be a free plastic human being. That was the state of art today. Nobody wanted to pay for it. Life had become a thoughtless fucking hurtle from birth to grave in pursuit of material possessions, nobody thought any more. Philosophies came from DJs and pop songs. In the nasty, wheeling-dealing, backstabbing business world there was more friendship and downright creativity than there was in art. She was an artist. She declared herself to the business world – a free plastic human being.

She made the tabloids. She lost two pounds from the sweat inside the film. Alice was jealous. 'That's not fair, losing weight. You should do an extra dare for that.'

Molly said, 'Pah.'

Her stint was discussed on the radio. She appeared on an arts programme on Channel Four, smoking, drinking a pint and swearing at the presenter. The manufacturer of a famous brand of baked beans wrote to her asking if she'd like to do something similar for them. They'd contribute the giant can if she'd immerse herself in the beans. They offered her a huge sum of money.

'They want me to do it for an advert. On telly,' Molly said. 'I'd be rich. This is my fifteen minutes,' she declared, 'and I'm having a ball. I'm going to make it last as long as I can.' She peered at Alice. 'What else can you think of? Since your piece of art got me a lot more attention than any art I ever thought of.'

'Well, your office antics got me promoted,' said Alice. 'Perhaps we should swap.'

They stared at each other a moment. Considering an exchange of lifestyles. Then said a mutual, 'Nah.'

'I dare you,' said Molly.

'Daring's over,' said Alice.

'No it isn't. It'll go on and on. I'm hooked. You're hooked. You've never had so much fun.'

It was true. Alice was feeling naughty again. Six again, stealing strawberries. In that cloakroom again sneaking kisses.

'OK,' she said. 'What? There's nothing you can do to me. I'm up for it.'

'Kiss Mr Sanderson. Outside the office, five o'clock when everybody's leaving. Feel his bum. A proper tweak. Make him jump. Then kiss him.'

'I couldn't. He's ancient.'

'It's a dare,' said Molly. 'You have to do it. Your honour as a new convert to fun is at stake.'

Five o'clock Thursday night. Mr Sanderson was standing on the steps outside the building. Alice came up to him. She slipped her hand round his bum. Lifted her middle finger, just so his underpants would tighten round his balls. It was a trick of hers. She leaned forward, whispered, 'Kiss me, Mr Sanderson.'

He turned. Smiled, oh horror. She hadn't expected that. She thought he'd fire her for sure. He took her to him. She could feel his ardour rising. His lips on hers. His hand sliding over her bottom. His tongue slipping into her, stroking the roof of her mouth, then shoving down into her. Oh God, she thought. This is another fine mess you've got me into, Molly.

Laurie Foos earned a Master of Fine Arts degree in creative writing from Brooklyn College, New York, where she won the MacArthur Scholarship for Fiction. She teaches creative writing and lives with her husband in Boston, Massachusetts. Her latest novel, *Portrait of the Walrus by a Young Artist*, is published by Review.

Loving You

Laurie Foos

Ma has set me up on a blind date with Jesus. It will be purely platonic, she assures me, as if I might have thought otherwise. We'll have dinner and break bread, take a walk on the beach and have some meaningful discussion, which is certainly more than I've been getting from Evan, a confirmed bachelor from the apartment downstairs who likes to sing Stevie Nicks songs while making love and once had his dryer privileges revoked for folding a woman's panties in order to avail himself of the machine. Since I'm thirty-five – and pushing it, as Ma likes to say – my hopes of meeting the perfect man have all but been dashed.

Until now.

She called this morning while I was flossing my teeth, having awakened late after a long night of discussing the pros and cons of Stevie Nicks' hair with Evan over a bottle of sangria and the *Bella Donna* album playing over and over. Evan prefers the frizzle-permed Stevie of old with her black shawls and feathered bangs, while I maintain that her blow-dried straight hair gives her a softer, more sedate look. If the truth be told, I'm an Elvis fan, and no singer's hair has ever matched the blue-black fullness of the King's. But I join in the banter regardless. What else have I got to do?

'Besides,' I said, after three glasses of sangria and the fifth rendition of 'Edge of Seventeen' (needless to say, I personally have not seen this side of seventeen for a long, long time), 'in the nineties less is more. Women know these things.' I downed the third glass with a dramatic flip of my neck and blurted, 'Everyone knows that perms are passé.'

I could have gone and pulled rank on him – I am, after all, an aesthetic consultant at the Clinique counter at Macy's – but I just wanted to get on with the business at hand, which as far as I was concerned meant finishing the sangria, going to bed and then retiring upstairs early enough to allow enough time for proper exfoliating and a good application of a new cream we'd just begun selling. I could feel my pores clogging with every minute that passed.

Finally, to get him into bed, I agreed to sing 'Leather and Lace' to him in only my bra and panties. I didn't know half the words, but he made me sing it anyway, while he lip-synched and pumped his hips on the bed. I mumbled the phrases I did know about being in the moonlight or some such. Twice he urged me to take a drag of his cigarette to give my voice the husky vibrato that Stevie's has. I finally gave up when he started singing the Tom Petty parts in my ear and begged me to stop dragging his heart around while he thrusted above me.

'Call me when you're ready to lay off the solo albums,' I said on my way out the door, careful to scoop up my black lace panties before making my exit, lest I find them in the laundry room the next day smelling of fabric softener and sitting among a pile of lint on top of one of the dryers.

'Everyone knows her work with Fleetwood Mac was unsurpassed by any of her later efforts.'

And then I went upstairs to watch *Aloha from Hawaii* until four a.m., weeping all the way through 'American Trilogy'. I sang to my mascara-stained face that all my trials would soon be over. To hell with Evan, I thought, wiping my eyes. I'll bet Stevie Nicks has never even been to Dixie.

This morning I was thinking of how I might explain my lateness to my boss, Mavis, a woman with pores the size of walnuts who knows foundation better than any woman I've ever met, when the phone rang.

'Delia, do you remember how I promised I'd find you the perfect man?' Ma squealed through the receiver as my gums began to bleed with the force of the flossing I was putting my teeth through. Flossing was meant as a means of self-torture; I'd been convinced of this for years. Even my hygienist, Georgia, agrees that there is no better way to punish yourself after regrettable sex than shoving nylon into your gums and spitting blood in your porcelain sink. It may be done in the name of cleanliness and tartar control, but that's the trick to all self-torture, isn't it? It's supposed to be good for you.

'Yes, Ma, I remember,' I said, half-listening as I swiped beige concealer under my puffy eyes. 'And this means you've found him, I assume.'

She sighed heavily in my ear.

'Him,' she said, meaningfully, 'and yes, I have.'

I spat one last trickle of blood into the sink and patted the concealer with a white wedge.

'Well?' I asked. 'Who is he?'

She let out a long breath and then held it.

'The King,' she said, in a high, breathless voice. I could feel her smiling through the receiver.

I pulled the floss around my fingers so tightly that the tips turned a terrible white. I imagined a red, white and blue spangled cape, swirling over the audience's heads, the King's arms spread out, head thrown back, hair perfect.

'You got me a date with Elvis?' I shrieked. 'How in the hell did you manage that?'

My mother has long been rumoured to have communicated with the dead, or so my friend Gladdie claims, as do several of Ma's friends at St Anne's, where she plays bingo every Wednesday. Maybe this was finally proof of it, I thought. Or maybe he's flown in from Kalamazoo or Timbuctoo or wherever the hell he's supposed to have been all these years. I'm not fool enough to believe he's alive, really, though Mavis once nearly convinced me, during a particularly rough spot with Evan, that he was lying in a vegetative state upstairs in Graceland after a dose of bad Seconal. At the very least, this latest idea of Ma's signified a recognition of my love for the King, which touched me, I must say. Ma never thought much of the younger Elvis's sneer or swivelling hips, I'm afraid, and even less of the older, bloated King with his enormous gold TCB pendants pressing into his hairy heaving chest. But I loved the King in all his incarnations, a fact which has always unsettled Ma to her core.

Gladdie (who was named for Elvis's mother Gladys by Gladdie's mother, a rabid fan) swears Ma channelled the spirit of Burl Ives in the grocery store last year and sang

'Holly Jolly Christmas' in perfect pitch from one of those old seventies specials where all the figures are made of clay, while her bingo pals insist they've received letters from their dead husbands with Ma's return address. To me there's always been a strong connection between Ma's Lithium dosage and her contact with the dead, though Gladdie will hear nothing of this theory. She says the Burl Ives thing gets her through her days, though I think her life isn't half bad to start with. And after my Stevie Nicks overdose, a date with the King, even an imagined one, seemed worth hearing about.

Ma paused on the phone and took a swallow of water. I wondered if she were popping a pill as we spoke.

'No, not that King,' she said with just a hint of impatience in her voice. 'The King of Kings.'

And that was when I knew she was talking about Christ. Of course I was ready to hang up after that, but I decided to let her go ahead with the delusion, making a note to call Dr Schwartz on my break and tell him the Lithium had upped and quit on us again. After years of dealing with Ma I'd learned it was best not to argue with her when she had an episode, that if I just let her talk her way through it, it would pass like most of the others – like the time she thought the Tooth Fairy had got trapped in our basement when I was seven and had been smashing all the light bulbs in her attempts to escape, or when she insisted the superintendent of our building had been possessed by the spirit of Lawrence Welk. I did catch the old man conducting on the steps one day and dancing with some of the other tenants amidst a host of floating bubbles, but as I later told Gladdie and the psychiatrists, that proved nothing.

I waited for her to launch into a full-blown account of how she'd met Jesus and arranged for Him to take me out, how He'd lifted her hand from her bingo blotter and said, 'The Lord will see your daughter Delia through' – Ma's delusions were nothing if not impeccably detailed – how she still had the ink stains on her palm like stigmata to prove it.

Instead she said only, 'He'll pick you up at seven sharp, and don't keep the Good Lord waiting,' and hung up before I had the chance to protest.

At work I put on my white jacket and head straight to the counter, where I busy myself wiping the glass shelves down with Windex. Mavis spots me and clicks her way across the sales floor to lean on the counter I've just cleaned. Her lacquered nails don't prevent her from leaving finger marks over the glass.

'You're late,' she says, crossing past to dab her nose with powder in front of the lighted mirror. I stand up to offer an excuse, but the minute she sees me, she pushes me into one of our high posh stools and starts brushing my face with pale pink blush.

'Good God, Delia,' she says, globbing more concealer under my puffy eyes, 'you look like hell.'

I don't miss a beat.

'And that's just where I'm going, if Ma has anything to do with it,' I say, but Mavis doesn't laugh, just keeps powdering until I have that gaunt look the fashion models have, all high cheekbones and sunken eyes. If anyone knows about self-torture it's the models in the magazines and on runways, yanking out their back molars and starving themselves for the good of all womanhood. It's what we all strive for, needless to say.

'There,' Mavis says, pronouncing me finished and dusting off my white lab coat. 'You look fit for a king,' she adds, and I stifle my laughter with my coat sleeve, leaving pale pink rings all along the seams.

I tell no one about the date, of course, except for Gladdie, who drops by on her lunch break to the food court for a salad with fat-free dressing and sparkling water. If Jesus does show up, I think, the last thing I want is to look bloated. Gladdie is somewhat heavy-set, the curse of being named after Elvis's mama, she says, though I'm fond of telling her that she is merely big-boned. Besides, I say, there are worse things you can do to a child than name her after the King's best girl.

'Like what?' Gladdie asks between forkfuls of her salad, and I press my hand into hers and wait for her to swallow so she won't choke when I say it.

'Like set your daughter up with Jesus,' I say, feeling my eyes brimming with tears at the thought of another year of Ma struggling to find the right Lithium balance, all the family sessions and in-patient treatments shot to hell and Evan playing 'Sara' over and over again as an attempt at consolation. I dab my eyes with a napkin and wait for Gladdie to say something soft and consoling to me, but instead her hand flies up to her mouth and she spits out a forkful of iceberg lettuce.

'The Good Lord be praised,' she says, pulling her chair in close to me. 'I knew she could do it.'

Gladdie is not a religious woman. Her outburst scares me a little, and I feel the fat-free dressing burning the back of my throat. I think of Evan above me last night while I choked out the lyrics, how I thought of getting a bad perm. Am I desperate enough to go out with God? I ask myself. I hear the theme from *2001* thundering in my head.

'It's the Lithium again,' I say, trying to keep the conversation on track. 'I've got to call her shrink.'

Gladdie shoves aside the salad and produces a large chocolate chip cookie from her coat pocket. Without even bothering to ask me if I'd like any, she takes a bite and smiles, her teeth flecked with crumbs.

'What time is He coming?' she asks.

Her words reverberate in my ears.

'Seven,' I say, feeling faint. 'I've got to get back.'

Before I'm able to walk away, Gladdie takes my hand and squeezes.

'Don't wear so much lipstick,' she says, 'the Lord likes things natural, and don't worry if your eyes look puffy.' She stands and gives me a cookie-stained kiss. 'By the way, the cheekbones look fabulous, haunted and desperate, just the way He likes them. Or so I've heard.'

As I move through the food court with the salad churning in my stomach, I can hear Gladdie humming the tune to 'Holly Jolly Christmas', the song echoing in the open space.

'Didn't Burl Ives sing that?' someone asks me, but I don't answer, just make a run for the nearest payphone to call my mother's shrink.

After leaving several messages on Dr Schwartz's voice mail, I give up and head for home. I sneeze on my way out of the store and Mavis shouts, 'God bless you!' from across the sales floor. I don't bother to thank her.

At home I make a tray of fish sticks in the microwave and eat them next to the phone, waiting for Dr Schwartz's call. Twice I call Ma's house, but then I remember it's Wednesday, her bingo night. It was at bingo that Ma claims she was 'saved', when she won the full card jackpot on I33.

'We've got a bingo under the crucifix,' the caller said, and then Ma swears Christ sat down right next to her and smiled while the man counted out twelve twenty-dollar bills into her hand. She later donated it all to the church, even though she couldn't pay her phone bill that month.

'The Lord loves a cheerful giver,' she said on the phone to me, just before they shut off her service.

I'm about halfway through the fish sticks when there's a knock at the door. It's Evan, I'm sure of it, come to apologise for getting so caught up last night. He'll wash my panties for a month as a penance, he'll say, as he has so many times before, and he'll sit through Elvis's comeback special without once mocking his black leather suit, as he's so often been known to do. He won't mention Stevie unless absolutely necessary which, where Evan's concerned, leaves a big enough window of opportunity to throw himself out of.

I wipe the crumbs away with the back of my wrist and open the door with one hand on my hip.

'It's about time,' I say, but then shock runs through me when I see it's not Evan at all but my Lord and Saviour – or at least a reasonable facsimile – standing there with His tanned and sandalled feet on my welcome mat.

At first He just stands there looking in at me with His blue eyes and crucify-me cheekbones, long, flowing hair right out of one of the velvet paintings Ma did long before the Lithium. I've always been something of a secular

Catholic, my teachings coming more from *Jesus Christ Superstar*, my favourite musical, than from the Scriptures, though I did take catechism up until the sixth grade and made my Holy Communion. Ma let me quit when she suspected my father of having an affair with the religion teacher – a fact which had later come true with a vengeance – but at this moment I regret more than anything not having made my confirmation. When you come face to face with your Maker, there's no telling what you'll think of.

'Delia,' He says finally, in a voice so soft I have to lean forward to hear Him, 'how nice it is to finally meet with you.'

I swallow hard and try to think of something to say.

'And also with you,' I say. Those catechism lessons die hard.

He smiles and nods, looking down at His feet. His sandals are the colour of driftwood.

We stare at each other for several more minutes until I realise how rude I must seem.

'Please, Lord,' I say, opening the door wider, 'won't you come in?'

He steps over the threshold and glides across the carpet to the living room. I follow behind Him, noting that his sandals leave no impression on my freshly vacuumed rug. I steal a quick glance in the mirror in the hallway and wipe off the lipstick that lingers at the corners of my mouth. As I approach Him sitting on my living room sofa, I think I hear Burl Ives crooning in the background.

By the time I make it to the sofa, the plate of fish sticks I've been eating is full to overflowing. He lifts the plate to offer them to me, and I eat several hungrily while He looks around at my apartment with that beatific smile of His that never quits.

He points to the plaster cast of Elvis I bought at a second-hand store some years ago and shakes His head.

'I see you're a fan of the King,' He says, his hair falling softly over one shoulder.

I swallow the fish sticks and try to keep from choking.

'Yes,' I say, 'but I was raised a Catholic,' and He laughs so hard He slaps one hand against His knee.

'That's a good one,' He says.

It's a comfort to know He has a sense of humour.

When the fish sticks are gone, I sit trying to think of all the questions I might ask Him if given the chance, but He seems absorbed by the Stevie Nicks video that comes on television. It's an old one, 'Gypsy', with Stevie in a white chiffon gown and blond children following her. My cheeks flush with embarrassment as I think of Evan and me on his bed last night, wondering if in His omnipresence He had watched me warbling in my black lace panties. I reach for the remote, but He lays a hand over mine and stops me before I can change the channel.

'She looks much better with her hair blow-dried, don't you think?' He asks, his blue eyes shining.

My heart flips over on itself. Am I flirting with the Lord?

I'm about to ask Him if he's ever been to the land of cotton when the phone rings in the kitchen. Stevie twirls around and around, her curly perm shifting softly in the wind. I feel the flush in my cheeks at the thought of Evan on top of me, the way I'd sucked down sangria in nothing but my panties.

'Forgive me,' I say, and He nods, but then I realise

he means for me to excuse myself and answer the telephone, that His forgiveness has nothing to do with my bad behaviour of the night before.

'Hello?' I say, out of breath.

Dr Schwartz's voice booms at the other end.

'Delia,' he says, his voice low and full of concern, 'tell me about your mother.'

I try to sound casual, laugh and tell him she's fine, that I've overreacted the way daughters sometimes do.

'But what about all this talk of God?' he asks. 'You know what this might mean?'

Jesus gets up and heads towards the door. He holds it open and beckons to me with a long white finger.

'Can't anyone talk about the Lord without being called crazy any more?' I say, and then hang up before he has a chance to respond.

The Lord waits for me in His sandals. For a moment in the shadows, His hair looks black. I don't even bother to check my reflection on my way out the door.

We walk along the beach at sunset, the waves crashing in the distance. I take off my shoes and hold my pumps in my hand, feeling the sand squish between my toes. The beach is deserted except for a few wayward seagulls and a procession of white doves that follow us at every turn. He smiles when I look back to see the one set of footprints we've left behind.

'That's an old trick,' I say, and I can see He's amused. 'I expect more from God.'

'But not from men,' He says, and then we're quiet for a long time, the only sound His long robe swishing in the wind.

When we reach the boardwalk, He spreads out a blanket and spins tuna fish from a soggy loaf of Italian bread He's kept hidden under His robe. I ask Him if He minds being addressed by title.

'Should I call you Lord or Lamb, or is Jesus good enough?' I ask.

He picks bits of tuna from his teeth and says that Jesus will do just fine.

Later, as the stars begin to appear, I think of the questions most people would ask about the afterlife and heaven, how it felt to be nailed to a cross, what God really looks like. As a little girl I imagined God looked like Desi Arnaz, though why, I have never been sure. Maybe it was the way he sang 'Babalu'.

'You can ask me anything, my child,' He says in that way He has. When you're the Lord, condescension becomes an occupational hazard, I suppose.

So I ask the two things I really want to know.

Yes, Elvis is doing fine and dead as a doornail, despite the rumours in Kalamazoo, He says, and yes, the King's version of 'How Great Thou Art' never fails to make His hair stand on end.

'I've always thought he never quite surpassed "Peace in the Valley" in 1956.' He says, though He admits the trumpeting 'Glory, glory, hallelujah' in 'American Trilogy' is a showstopper.

It's just what I've always thought He might say.

When we shake hands at the door, I thank Him for a lovely evening. Of course I'm not presumptuous enough to invite Him in this late, and it seems rather silly to ask Him for His phone number. What would I do, dial 1–900-God? He tells me to be good to Ma, that all she wants for me is to be happy.

'I may be perfect,' He says somewhat sardonically, 'but I'm still just a man after all.'

I nod and squeeze His hand with both of my own. Despite myself I find I'm getting teary at the thought of His leaving. I swallow hard and pull my chin up, feel the foundation cracking on my face, my gums so sore they might bleed at any minute. Without even so much as a kiss good night, this is the best time I've ever had.

As He starts to walk away, I call out to Him before turning back to my apartment door.

'I have a confession to make,' I say.

He turns around slowly, his palms upward as He closes His eyes and nods to me.

'Go ahead, my child,' He says, the long sandy hair hanging down His back.

'I hate Stevie Nicks,' I say, and He just nods, moves forward to brush a strand of hair away from my forehead.

As I'm about to close the door, He calls, 'Tell Gladdie that Burl Ives sends his best,' which leaves me sitting on the floor against my closed door and thinking about Ma screaming out 'Bingo!' beneath the crucifix. It seems there are worse things in life than being on Lithium, like pining over Stevie Nicks and painting women to look emaciated in a white lab coat.

Before I go to bed I break the last of my Stevie Nicks CDs over one knee and throw my lacy black panties in the garbage. And when Gladdie calls later to ask how everything went, I tell her only that it was the best I could hope for from any man. We sing 'Holly Jolly Christmas' and 'See See Rider' over the phone to each other and eat chocolate chip cookies until we're about to burst. I'm thinking of dyeing my hair black. I could say much more some other time, I tell her, but right now I have nothing else to confess.

Jo-Anne Richards comes from the Eastern Cape and now lives and works in Johannesburg as a journalist. Her first novel, *The Innocence of Roast Chicken*, was an instant South African success, topping the bestseller list for fifteen weeks; her second, *Touching the Lighthouse*, is currently available from Review.

A Dip in the Gene Pool

Jo-Anne Richards

There was nothing else to be done. It was two in the morning, you see, none of us had had any sleep and my housemate wanted me out of his bed.

It was time to make a list. Mark – that's my housemate – suggested it in that long-suffering tone he affects in the middle of the night. His partner, Paul, scrabbled on his nightstand and produced paper and pen without actually opening his eyes. I wrote:

REASONS NEVER TO GO OUT WITH MEN AGAIN

They both sighed. I couldn't do that, they told me, while I argued and wheedled and cited examples. I just couldn't write a list like that. It wasn't right. This was one of life's great decisions, Mark said. And at least, muttered Paul, hand over still-closed eyes, I should be able to approach it with adult sensibility or at least some objectivity – I was a TV researcher, after all.

I maintained a hurt silence. Mark sighed again. 'OK, who're we kidding, doll?' He swept his eyes heavenward and started with the high-pitched hum which always signalled the emergence of his high-drama-queen persona. Finally it was decided we would settle for at least the appearance of neutrality.

MEN

PROS
Good for making braais
Sex
Love and cuddling
Babies

Mark sighed again. He does it so well, that sighing thing, especially when it's attended by the little hum. OK, that's a start, he said in the annoying tone of encouragement he used to exhort me to do my best. But for a small accident of birth, Mark could've had an outstanding career as a Brown Owl.

'OK, OK, so I know the *braai* thing is a little romantic ideal of mine.'

The truth was that no one ever shaped up to my father in this. There he was in my head, squatting beside the open fire. If need be, he could create a *braai* from nothing but a strand of wire and a pair of pliers to fashion the grid, and his penknife to turn the meat. He and his fires were all sort of sepia-coloured by memory.

'Well, if you meet anyone sepia-coloured, doll, avoid him at all costs. He's likely to have a serious alcohol problem,' said Paul, while Mark pointed out that boys didn't carry penknives nowadays. *Très* uncool, he said. Not to mention the fact that my last three boyfriends could probably have burnt their fingers on a microwave.

We moved on to the sex issue. They both began to laugh so hard they lost their breath. It was difficult for Paul to maintain his languid air in the circumstances, but through sheer skill and experience he managed it somewhat.

'You told him,' I accused Mark.

'No,' said Mark at last. 'But it wasn't hard to pick up the state of your sex life, darling, when The Boy told us that joke, remember? The one about how do you find a clitoris? And the answer's "Who cares?" He was all a-twitter about why you didn't laugh, and going on at you for sense-of-humour failure. And then you . . .'

'Ja, well, I was irritated.'

'. . . You said you hadn't realised it was intended as humour, since it was so close to home.'

The Boy was my recent ex-boyfriend. Very recent. In fact he had attained his ex status about six hours before. It was still painful, somewhere in the region of my ribs. And I could guess the state of my eyes. Mark had just suggested that before I moved from the house in the morning, I should borrow his Estée Lauder eye-mask.

The next entry on my list caused so much laughter that I decided unilaterally to move on to Babies. They stopped laughing. Hmm, they both said.

'We'll come back to that,' I said. 'Let's get to the cons.'

CONS
Destruction of self-esteem
Atom-blasted equanimity
Misery
No olives in your fridge
More misery

'Oh my God.' That was Mark. 'It's just occurred to me: you broke up with him over the olives. Because he ate the olives. I cannot believe you broke up with someone for eating all the olives.'

Paul sat up suddenly and stared at Mark with patent disbelief. Paul was a chef. Paul took olives very, very seriously.

'Please, please,' I implored, 'don't break up over the olives.'

The Boy, as they had named him, had an attractive quiff of blond hair which tended to fall over his forehead when he was trying to be artful or boyish. It was the most attractive thing about him.

No, that's not true. He did have a few attractive qualities. When he wasn't around his chinas, he could be . . . well, vulnerable even, though Mark would scoff to hear me say it. Sometimes on a Sunday, when no one else was around, he'd park off with me, bringing his well-thumbed collection of poetry from long-ago English I.

We'd sit outside in the shade, he with his head in my lap, and he'd read that 'Kisses are a better fate than wisdom'. And then, as the sun glanced gently through the jacaranda, anointing his stomach with light, where his T-shirt rode up, I'd dare to hope.

But then he'd somehow forget to phone for a week. And he'd be flippant and offhand when I met him for breakfast, because his chinas were there. And they'd be laddish and discuss some game or other. And possibly women. Not quite offensively, but in that tone. Then I'd begin to wonder if hope could ever be a viable alternative to wisecracking for women in the nineties.

Anyway, the four of us – Mark, Paul, The Boy and I – had decided to have a dinner party to mark the fact that we'd all made it past the mystical three-month barrier, where most relationships seemed to founder nowadays. It was all to do with this sex-in-the-nineties thing, and tedious stuff like the threat of death.

You see, if you spoke seriously to a man about dating and kissing, about wanting to know him better before opting for sex, he generally thought he was being given Rejection Number One – where you dump him with a compassionate smile and a gentle hand on the shoulder. And where you say things like: 'You deserve better than me.'

If you did sleep with him, you weren't supposed to dump him the next day because of the state of his toothbrush or his foreplay. This was the nineties. You were supposed to be monogamous. So you'd slide into this state of mini-marriage, during which he'd drink all your beer, eat all your olives and suggest you stay in. Then he'd fall asleep on the sofa, or worse: invite his appalling friends around. After a respectable three months – with obvious relief on both sides and before your CDs had mingled too much – you'd break up.

The Boy lasted three months and three days. The night before our dinner party he had taken me out. He hadn't told me we were to meet his chinas, but I should have guessed when he vetoed my suggestion of quiet and chatty. Perhaps a small dinner at Sam's? Anywhere we could sit on the pavement, before winter hit us with chapped lips and free-floating despondency, as it always did? But oh no, we had to go to this roof place, where exotic people danced sinuously. The less exotic, like me, stood about nodding in time and saying, 'Hey,' in a meaningful way.

He and his chinas all danced briefly and wordlessly with a Nigerian beauty, before devoting much of the evening to the useful and exclusive discussion of how cool they were, and how other people didn't realise where the real heart of Johannesburg was. And how su-bur-ban those people really were who didn't come here.

Eventually we all joined a table of silent Ethiopians in dreadlocks, who nodded and said: 'Hey.'

'You see,' they congratulated themselves, 'it's only in places like this you'll get to meet, like, the real people of the continent.'

I don't think the Ethiopians could speak English, but they silently offered us some little sticks to chew. I declined. I like to identify my little sticks before I chew them. After the little sticks, the little minds went zi-ing, and I astutely discerned that I could expect nothing further of value from them.

I sat gazing down at the street, with its small, squat shops which sold records or second-hand clothing. And at the clots of people who gathered in the pavement flow to trade in wallets or belts or wire sculptures, or to score drugs.

Or just to greet each other with a 'Hey, Bra,' and a three-phased shake. 'Sharp,' they'd call, car radios bawling rap.

I think they let themselves into our house at eight in the morning, when I lay listening to the clamour of coffee and the serious assuagement of the munchies. But I never dreamt they would dare ... It was only when Paul, who took olives very, very seriously, donned his apron to make the chicken Marengo at seven last night ... it was only when he opened the fridge with a flourish and I heard his shriek, and saw his hand flutter to his cheek in horror . . .

Later, I had crept self-pityingly into Mark's bedroom and moaned about men, to which they'd uttered things like, 'Mm,' or, 'I kno-ow.' When I'd crawled under their duvet – you could smell the coming winter in the chill nighttime soil – they'd both just sighed and shifted to accommodate me.

It wasn't so much that The Boy was so special or anything. ('I kno-ow.') Deep down I suppose I had known, only I hadn't been ready to face it yet. ('Mm.') You know? Like a small secret you kept buried in your gut and hadn't wanted to look at yet? And it hadn't really been about the olives. You know? But olives could be a sign, couldn't they? They could be a symbol. ('Mm-hmmm.')

But suddenly I didn't know if I could bear it all again. I was so tired of the tedious run of it all. ('Mm.') I mean, the whole process: the searching, the sussing, the sex thing. The endless dispiriting round. And winter was nearly here, with frigid Highveld mornings and the frost which yellowed the grass and withered hope. ('Oh my God.')

So it had occurred to me that, with our empirical conclusion that men's only advantage was babies, perhaps I should just circumvent the whole process by having one. (Silence.) I mean, the only reason women in their thirties rushed around desperately seeking Sam was that. Wasn't it? (Silence.) Then I could contemplate the Ticking Time, when it came, without despairing. I could be a whole person who didn't need a relationship. Couldn't I? I was still young, there shouldn't be any problems . . . (Absolute silence.)

* * *

I think I realised that Mark and Paul were getting into the idea when Paul arrived home with a fluffy hyena. He said babies shouldn't grow up prejudiced, simply because hyenas had suffered a bad press over the years.

'Oh my God,' muttered Mark, with the hint of a hum. 'Next thing our baby'll be sleeping with a vulture.'

'Whose baby?' I asked.

So they told me my baby needed male figures, even if they were, you know, a little bit camp. Well, OK, as camp as a boy scout jamboree. And that they, who were unlikely to have their own, were the perfect protectors, the most doting of uncles . . .

'So we think of this baby as ours too,' concluded Paul.

I pointed out that the first step would be to locate the father of my unconceived child. So we made a list.

Bruce
That boy who plays guitar at the Bassline

They didn't like Bruce. Bruce was a press photographer, one of those Old Africa Hands who wore a flak jacket and had white lines around his eyes from screwing them up in the sun. He said things like: 'Hey, babe.'

I pointed out that Bruce, besides being tall and having perfect eyesight, was actually rather bright.

'No one bright stands up to take a picture when bullets are flying at him,' said Mark.

I mentioned that he was creative and had nearly won the Pulitzer Prize.

'No one nearly wins the Pulitzer Prize,' said Paul. 'They win it or they don't.'

'Well, he's macho,' I said. 'Don't you think we need a little balance around here?'

But they declared that being macho was not genetic. We'd hire a Sumo wrestler as a child-minder. The boy from the Bassline they dealt with by pointing out that not knowing his name was a small impediment.

That was when I suggested Mark. There was silence, before they both started with the humming thing.

'Wait, wait,' yelled Paul. 'Our baby can't be conceived just like that. He or she needs to be welcomed into existence with a salmon soufflé.'

They had just tenderly taken my temperature and told me to relax with my feet up. I had pointed out that I was not yet pregnant. Soberly sitting down, they had also told me coyly that, in preparation for all this, they had taken themselves off for joint AIDS tests.

'It was so romantic,' Mark said. They linked hands and gazed at each other. I became a little resentful.

Anyway, the preparation took a long time. Paul went shopping – a tortuous process, filled with disappointments (at the poor quality of the salmon) and rekindled excitements (at the thought of crayfish instead).

Then there were the tarot cards to be read. We were to expect a newcomer. A male newcomer. Mark sighed and Paul produced a book of names.

'Aaron?' suggested Mark, starting at the beginning.

'Let's get on with it,' I muttered.

'Wait, wait,' said Paul, and he rushed off to the incense-fogged shop down the road for a crystal . . . wait, wait, and some scented candles too. The crystal was for balance and serenity, he said. I needed both.

'Do you want a hot-water bottle for your back?' asked Mark. I pointed out calmly, with only slightly gritted teeth (hey, these crystal things work), that I wasn't actually giving birth. And never would at this rate.

After the crayfish soufflé and champagne, followed by herbal tea . . .

('Coffee's bad for pregnant women.'

'I'm not pregnant.'

'You soon will be.')

. . . we repaired to my bedroom.

'Aren't you going to leave, Paul?' I asked hopefully.

'Why? How're you going to get this done? I thought perhaps I could help.'

Mark and I gazed at Paul until a kind of startled recognition, quickly followed by horror, overtook his features. He shrieked, his hand fluttering to his cheek.

This was how we came to be rushing into old Mr Nathan's all-night pharmacy and begging for syringes. Old Mr Nathan, who has known me all my life, enquired after my acne problem, as he always did.

'That was adolescence, Mr Nathan,' I enunciated. 'Ad-o-lescence. I'm grown up now.'

'Oh, are you, dear? And what do you need the syringe for?'

'Well, um . . .'

Humming noises in the background. Mr Nathan looked severe and explained that, because of something called peer pressure – and here he threw a grim glance behind me – people would sometimes try to get me to take things that would get me into trouble.

At midnight the three of us were sitting disconsolately and syringeless on the kitchen floor. We had finished all the olives in the fridge.

'Well,' I said, 'it's back to the list then.'

'Perhaps it's just as well,' said Mark. 'You know they say there's a gay gene.'

'So what?' I said archly.

'Well, since this is our only shot at this child thing, I thought perhaps I'd like to bank on a couple of grand-children.'

'Hey, babe.'

Bruce spread his hands before him and added: 'No problem.' I had been right to call him in for a job like this, he said. When the assignment needed just the right touch, it was best to brief the man who knew the terrain.

I got a sudden flash of my baby swaggering down the birth canal, a pack of Camels in his tiny flak jacket, camera at the ready.

'Ja well no fine. What can I tell you? When I was in Nigeria . . .'

'Yes, that's just riveting, but have you been tested?'

'Hey, babe, sure. Don't worry, I don't shoot blanks . . . Oh, you mean that other thing? That too.'

I spent a long time considering underwear that evening. I mean, he'd seen quite a bit in his time. I didn't want to disgrace myself with the old pair which had turned grey in the washing machine. On the other hand, the new satin pair I'd bought . . . it must be just over three months ago now . . . they were a bit frivolous for the task. And then, he was so macho. What if he threw me on the bed and ripped them off with his teeth. I'd have to say: 'Wait, wait, these are imported. Let me get the old pair.'

Paul answered the door in his apron. He was making another soufflé, with salmon this time. Through the open door, I just caught sight of him behind Bruce, running his hand from the top of his own head in a vaguely horizontal line to the middle of Bruce's neck somewhere. He never believed me. I'd told him he was tall.

I was still trying, without mortal injury, to push Mark's evil-tempered Siamese from my lap before they came through. I liked cats, but surely nothing could be sadder than the sight of an unattached woman of a Certain Age with her cats. Not that I had reached a Certain Age, but then I had just invited an almost stranger over to impregnate me.

He declined the soufflé, and I nearly called it all off. I mean, how could one breed with a man who had the sensitivity of a bluebottle fly? How could anyone refuse such a consecrated offering? The three of us repaired to the kitchen for a team talk. Paul turned all selfless on us – I suppose I'd thought I might use him as grand justification for changing my mind. This whole thing . . . I wasn't sure any more . . . But they seemed so certain . . . No, they were right. This was definitely the right thing. Men just had not evolved to the point of sustaining a relationship.

Paul sniffed and raised his head, tilting it to one side in that high-minded way people assume sometimes.

'Sensitivity,' he declared, 'is not genetic. We'll hire a ballet dancer as a child-minder.'

'What about the Sumo wrestler?'

'We can have a Sumo wrestler and a ballet dancer,' he pronounced grandly.

* * *

As Bruce removed his flak jacket, he actually winked at me – which was a bit much. I mean, we'd all got the point. OK already, we know you're a Camel man among Camel men.

He undressed slowly, unbuttoning his khaki shirt and running his hands over his chest, just in case I'd missed it. The hair, babe, the hair – symbol of manhood, emblem of virility.

'Right, babe, let's get this show on the road.' And he lowered himself to the bed with the vaguely patronising reassurance that he'd try not to hurt me. Try? Hah.

Nothing happened. I waited. Still nothing happened. He was silent. I was still.

I waited a bit more. Men didn't like to be hurried. Perhaps he was gathering the impetus to leap. The Siamese leapt instead, curling between us on the bed. He was silent. I was still.

Suddenly he did leap, burying his face in my bosom and leaking tears from screwed-up eyes, little sobs breaking from his muscled chest.

'It's just that when I think of my own little *laaitie*, you know? Of never taking my own little guy down the Congo. I just don't know that I can go through with this.'

'Perhaps the next one shouldn't be told,' I suggested.

The name problem, when I brought it up again, was suddenly as nothing. So much for impediments. This whole baby thing seemed to have developed a momentum of its own.

We repaired to the Bassline for a recce, passing the men who hawked wire sculptures on the pavement, past all the trendy men with shaved heads and consciously ugly glasses, and the suited ones with bellies, and all the faux bohemian men . . .

All I could see now were Progenitors-in-Prospect. Short-sighted men, tall men, men with bow legs and, boy! There was a predisposition to heart attacks if ever I saw one.

The jazz club was filled mainly with genetic catastrophes. Except for the man who played guitar. There was no doubt that he was blessed by breeding. I was just noticing the shadows under his cheekbones, and the way those little pecs or specs or biceps or whatever danced as he stretched over his guitar. Paul leant over and pointed out the creativity of that little riff he'd just played.

'I have a violin for Aaron,' he whispered. 'He can start when he's three.'

I rolled my eyes and told them to bugger off. I wasn't going to get very far with them hanging around. 'Now just remember, ask him . . .'

'I know what to do,' I said.

But Mark's sister Megan turned up before they could leave, supported by her crowd of over-confident just-about-twenty-somethings. How is it, I asked Paul, that just-twenty-somethings are always more confident than I ever was, or let's be frank, than I am now? They were all hanging over Mark and tripping over their platforms to kiss him effusively in that overly flirtatious way young women affect with gay men. Paul hissed that charmed lives always resulted from a combination of long legs and short imagination. And tended to be marked by that white-faced, kohl-eyed look. 'Bad genetic sign,' he said.

Megan asked why we were there, in a tone which

suggested her slight embarrassment at hanging out in the same place as those who were so lacking in cool. Mark, who can never keep his ingenuous mouth closed, went and told her.

'Hey . . .' said Megan. She flicked back her hair and gave a quick, superior sniff. As they gazed at me, mouths a little agape – and one still in braces, dear God – I transformed into The Ancient One. I stammered that this was a life choice, not yet a necessity, and that I could still . . . you know, there was still time . . .

'I kno-ow,' they all chorused with their patronising little mouths moueing at me. 'But we think it's really cool, you know, like, for someone like you?'

Megan said she thought the guitarist just brilliant. 'I mean, it's so clever of you, you know? I mean, to pick someone like him in the new South Africa. So good for the child.'

'Why?' cut in Paul. 'Good eyesight?'

'No, like, I mean, you know . . .'

'Musical?'

'No-o.'

'O-oh, you mean because he's slightly tinted, darling? Well, the fact is, we picked him for aesthetic reasons. The child'll blend so nicely with our pumpkin-coloured walls.'

The upshot was that after gazing speculatively at the guitarist, Megan declared a little more recce activity to be required. And that she, being the selfless girl she was, would discover all there was to discover about him, and ask all the necessary, icky questions, so that I needn't see him more than the once.

'You don't want to risk a relationship starting,' she said

sagely, gazing at me in the expectation of gratitude.

'Well, it's a tough job . . .' muttered Paul, but Mark frowned at him.

'Don't say I never do anything for you,' said Megan as she took up a position just to the left of the dais, ready to accost the musician at his first break.

I settled into my relaxed new life with the Siamese, relatively certain that I was committed to nothing for at least three months. Oh, I still believed in the principle . . . But in the meantime, the fridge was always full of olives, and I began to read *The Alexandria Quartet*.

I'd forgotten, however, that the cycle moved faster for the just-twenty-somethings. I remembered this when I arrived home to soufflé, my temperature being taken at the door, and Megan announcing that Robert (his name – the last impediment fallen) was amenable and just perfect for someone like me.

As it turned out, the fates were all with me. My temperature was just right, I had not a zit in sight and so, at last, this was it. Finally.

There was plenty of time before the Bassline began swinging. Perhaps I'd just stop off for a cup of coffee on the way. Just to fortify me, you know? And of course a shot of caffeine was necessary if I was to be up all night. I hauled the book from my bag. It would be perfect to carry me through the first trimester.

'Given up on men?'

He was smallish and wore glasses. Absolutely not on, genetically speaking.

'Why?'

He sipped at his cappuccino. His face dimpled and . . . well, it kind of flickered with light and dark.

'Last time I gave up on women, I read *War and Peace*. But that's a bit clichéd.'

He joined me for coffee. He asked, I nodded. There was still plenty of time, and it was nice to have some company in the meantime.

We talked about, well, everything. Books and movies and clubs – he enjoyed the roof place, but generally preferred somewhere you could talk.

It was ten o'clock. Well, OK, probably better to skip the first set now, and get there for the second. Robert'd be more relaxed in any case.

We discussed women then – strangely he had no tone – and relationships. We switched to wine. It was important not to drink too much caffeine. I'm sure it couldn't help the fertilisation process and I'd just get jittery.

He was clever, and witty – in every other respect, of course, a minefield of bad heredity. But now that I'd given up men as a romantic option, I found I could enjoy this kind of man, just for the company. Oops, it was past midnight. Well, maybe it'd be better to get there just before the end. Then I could act decisively and not spend the entire night hanging about.

He was busy telling me how he preferred to defer the sex thing, and even then he liked to date, rather than move in together. Funny, when his face flashed with that strange darkness and then glowed with light, he had a mesmerising effect. Certainly nice to share a glass of wine with.

He ordered tequila. Well . . . that was confident of him. I liked confidence in a friendly companion, if it were balanced, you know? By . . . well, by . . .

'I just thought tequila would be fun,' he said. Fun, that was it . . . balanced by fun.

'But don't drink it if you don't want to . . .' And sensitivity . . . balanced by sensitivity.

'. . . I'll make sure you get home safely, OK? You needn't worry.' Protectiveness was important.

'It's just that I don't want this to end. You're . . . kind of special.' Oh yes, and charm. Charm was essential. It made me wish he wasn't so deeply into deferment.

Oh God, what was I saying? They'd all kill me. And Megan had gone to so much trouble. Paul'd made so many soufflés, Mark taken so many temperatures. Oh Jeez, it was already too late. The night was gone.

I stared at him and blinked. It must be the tequila. Those genetic shortcomings – what were they again? Um, eyes? But they were such nice eyes – they had that way of flaring with brilliance. His . . . his body? But he had such a nice way of touching as he talked. And those dimples, flashing with wit. Oh God, this was a disaster.

'Do you eat olives?' I asked.

'I don't mind them in my food. But I never eat them straight from the fridge.'

Val Corbett, Joyce Hopkirk and Eve Pollard began writing together with *Splash*, a UK bestseller. Their latest novel is *Unfinished Business*.

Val Corbett was a newspaper journalist in South Africa and London before switching to television. She produced several acclaimed programmes and became a director of a leading independent television production company. She is married to Robin Corbett MP and has a daughter and two stepchildren.

Joyce Hopkirk has been an editor on *Cosmopolitan*, the *Sun* newspaper, *The Sunday Times*, the *Daily Mirror* and the magazines *She* and *Chic*. She has twice won the Magazine Editor of the Year Award. She is married to Bill Lear, an executive of De Beers; they have a daughter and a son.

Eve Pollard worked on newspapers and magazines before becoming editor of the *Sunday Mirror*, where she won the Editor of the Year Award. She was editor of the *Sunday Express* when it won both the Newspaper of the Year and the Sunday Newspaper of the Year Awards, and is a regular broadcaster on television and radio. She is married to Sir Nicholas Lloyd and has a daughter, a son and three stepchildren.

Love, Lies and Other Delusions

Val Corbett, Joyce Hopkirk and Eve Pollard

Josephine leaned back against the seat of the taxi, closed her eyes and shivered, feeling his strong hands unhurriedly stroking her body. It was as real as if he were right there beside her, travelling through the rain-soaked streets of a dank London.

Her reverie was punctured by the shrill of her mobile and she wondered anxiously if he'd had second thoughts about coming into the West End from the airport for such a short time. But it was her best friend Nicola, at twenty-four one of the youngest reporters on a national daily. Most days they exchanged news and gossip at least once, if not twice. This time Nicci was calling to say she was being sent on the trail of a pop star who'd done a disappearing act before a sell-out concert and she wouldn't be able to buy food for supper that night.

'Just as well you called,' said Josephine. 'You'll never guess who's turned up out of the blue. Robert.'

'That bastard? What does he want?'

'To see me. He's on his way back to Cape Town. His father's ill.'

'You're not going to, are you?' Nicci asked, then answered her own question: 'You are.'

'What harm can it do? He's only going to be in London for a few hours.'

'Hang on, are we talking about the same Robert? The guy who made you stay at home every night for weeks, weeping, wailing and whining?'

Josephine was momentarily diverted. 'Wow, four alliterations. You're good.'

'Don't change the subject,' Nicci sighed. 'Well, at least choose somewhere noisy. And crowded. Yes, very crowded.'

'I've asked him to come to the editor's flat.'

'What the hell are you doing there?'

'She's been summoned by Him Upstairs and didn't want to cancel her architect. I'm the only one she can trust to be alone there, or so she says.'

'Great,' said Nicci. 'You can have a good snoop around.'

'Typical reporter. No, I'll try and deny my baser instincts. And don't worry about Robert. I intend keeping it light, friendly and *very* detached.'

'If you can.'

'I can.' She paused. 'I will. Don't worry, nothing's going to happen.'

'Attagirl. Call me later,' said Nicci. 'I want to hear every dot and comma.'

Josephine had grown up with Robert in South Africa; their families lived in the same neighbourhood. He had looked her up when she was working in Paris and he was back-packing across Europe. After a month of romantic walks along the Seine, leisurely meals in restaurants all over the city and hours of languorous lovemaking, she'd been confident when they said their goodbyes that this was not just a holiday romance. It was special. Robert departed to New York to work in a top advertising agency and she'd played it cool for three weeks before cracking. But her jokey fax had gone unanswered and Josephine had miserably congratulated herself on making the right decision not to pursue him any further. That had been six months ago, and since then there had been no word from him. Until this afternoon.

During their phone call, pride had prevented her asking him why he had taken so long to get in touch. She would know soon enough. Despite her brave words to her friend, Josephine wondered whether this meeting was wise. Nicci always told her she underestimated how attractive she was, with hair her friend described enviously as burnt amber but which Josephine had always thought of as simply and irritatingly red, and it was true that there had been several opportunities with men since Robert. But the fact was, no one had measured up and she couldn't resist the chance to see him once more.

Josephine had made sure she'd arrived at the flat in good time and was looking for somewhere to hang her umbrella when the bell rang. She told herself it could be the architect, arriving early too. But there was no mistaking the navy-blue eyes gazing down at her Robert. For a second they stared at each other before he pulled her into his arms. She resisted half-heartedly before relaxing into his body.

This was not going according to plan. She could feel his heart beating through his linen shirt and was about to break away, slightly nervous, when he bent over and began a slow, gentle kiss that brought back a rush of emotions. Pleasure. Need. Panic.

'God, I've missed you,' he said.

'Really?' she couldn't help asking. 'Then why didn't you phone?' Instantly she regretted the question.

He looked uncomfortable. 'Let's say I had some complications in my life I had to sort out.' He pulled her to him and kissed her again. 'And now they have been.'

Reluctantly she took hold of his hands and gently disentangled herself.

'I'll make some coffee,' she said, in what she hoped was her firmest voice.

Robert was walking around the hallway, his blond head leaning towards the watercolours that lined every inch of the walls.

'Wow, look at this place.'

He smiled at her, the dark shadows across his jaw adding maturity to his misleadingly youthful appearance, then he walked ahead of her into the living room with its floor-to-ceiling windows and the impressive view overlooking the Covent Garden piazza.

'You're such a success,' he said admiringly. 'This is great.'

'Well, actually . . .' she began but he, continuing his inspection of the room with its mix of antiques and designer furniture, did not appear to hear.

'Wait till I tell everyone back in Cape Town,' he said admiringly. Josephine closed her mouth. What was the harm in letting him think her dream had come true a couple of years earlier than it would? Robert was in town for such a short time and she and Nicci fully intended to work their socks off so that they too could afford a home like this, instead of the rather dingy duplex they shared in south London.

He turned from the window, looking at her in a way that made her insides do somersaults, then moved determinedly towards her.

'What about that coffee?' she asked hastily and opened a door she assumed was the kitchen. It turned out to be a cupboard. Robert looked at her enquiringly.

'See how organised I've become?' she said with a laugh, hoping it didn't sound forced.

'Very impressive,' he agreed, doing a quick survey of the neat rows of glasses and assorted bottles of alcohol. 'Come over here,' he said softly, holding out his arms.

'No, no. I'll make the coffee,' said Josephine, flustered, opening a door and finding herself confronting a water cylinder.

'Good size, don't you think?' she asked breezily and opened the adjacent door, only to find a white-tiled cloakroom. Desperate to cover up her mistakes, Josephine tried to keep her voice casual. 'Having the cloakroom here is really useful,' she said before at last finding the door that led into a diminutive galley kitchen.

Fortunately, Robert seemed distracted. The best ploy, to keep safe from temptation, was to maintain a distance between them, she decided. But as she filled the kettle he came up behind her, wrapped his arms around her and began nuzzling her neck.

'There hasn't been one day I haven't thought about you,' he said quietly, his breath warm against her hair.

Josephine turned to look at his tanned features, so sensitive, so concerned. This was madness. They were living on different continents and he was only here for a few hours. She flicked a switch to turn on the kettle and, to her embarrassment, heard the loud whirring of a garbage disposal unit. Disconcerted, she turned off the switch and was on the verge of explaining that she did not own the flat when he silenced her with another kiss.

After a few blissful minutes they broke for air, and it was then that Josephine realised how much she'd missed him, not just the physical excitement but the talking, the laughing, the closeness. She'd been hurt by his silence but now she could see how much he wanted her she felt more in control of the situation. She wanted him too. Why deny herself the opportunity to discover whether or not the magic was still there?

'Where's your bedroom?' he asked huskily. Between kisses she gestured down the hall towards the only door she hadn't yet opened, hoping fervently that this time she'd got it right.

Her boss's bedroom was out of character. Georgia favoured tailored suits and had a streamlined office, but this was a confection out of a Hollywood film. White muslin was draped from the four-poster, white calico swathed the windows and an all-white carpet was fitted wall-to-wall. The effect was breathtaking, and even Robert paused for a fraction in the doorway before lifting Josephine up and depositing her gently on the pristine white satin coverlet.

'Jo,' he groaned, 'you can't imagine how much I want you.'

'Me too,' she replied, fighting her desire to forget about reality as she began sinking under his lean frame, losing herself in the familiar smell and feel of him. God, she had missed him. It was when he started to unbutton her shirt that some section of her brain clicked into gear. What was she doing? This was the editor's bed, the editor's sheets. And the architect was due in twenty minutes. She attempted to free herself but he began kissing the side of her neck, trailing downwards towards her breasts, and once more her will-power collapsed. Well, she would have to take precautions. With a supreme effort she slid out from under him and said quickly, 'I won't be a second,' before dashing into the en suite bathroom to grab a couple of white bath towels.

Robert, stripping off his jeans, watched in amusement as she positioned the towels carefully over the coverlet.

'I never realised you were so house proud,' he said, before leaping on to the bed and holding out his hands to her. Slowly he began to peel off her clothes, punctuating his efforts with kisses while she murmured in pleasure. After what seemed a lifetime, he separated her from her shirt, bra, tapered black trousers and finally her bikini briefs. As they stroked, caressed and nibbled he whispered exactly what he intended doing to her next. God, this was even better than Paris! She was about to lose herself completely as Robert started to roll himself on top of her when over his naked shoulder, though half-glazed eyes, Josephine saw the door handle move. Frozen, suddenly obvious to Robert's caresses, she watched horrified as the door slowly opened. Framed in the half-light was the bulky figure of a man staring at them.

Josephine recognised him at once. It was Georgia's lover, his expression of surprise changing to one of indignation as understanding dawned.

'Patrick.' Her voice was a croak. 'What are you doing here?'

'I might ask the same thing of you,' he barked.

Robert hastily grabbed a towel and Josephine plucked at the bedspread to cover her nakedness.

'Josephine!' snapped Patrick. 'Come out here immediately. And you,' he gesticulated furiously at a stunned Robert, 'whoever you are, the sooner you get out, the better.'

Shrugging her shoulders in an apologetic gesture at Robert and fixing a towel sarong-like around her body, Josephine disappeared through the door. How would she explain her way out of this? Mortified, she followed Patrick into the living room and attempted to apologise, but he was apoplectic.

'Georgia said she trusted you. Is this how you repay her, by dirtying her bedroom with your squalid affair?'

A slow flush coloured Josephine's cheeks as she clutched her towel defensively.

'We didn't plan this, and there's nothing squalid about it,' she said levelly. 'Robert's catching a plane this evening and this was the only way I could see him and not let Georgia down.'

'You *have* let her down and I'll make quite sure she knows about it.'

Josephine was appalled. 'I admit I was wrong, very wrong, to take advantage of the situation like this.' She stopped, hearing the slam of the front door, and started to rise from the sofa.

'Stay where you are. I haven't finished yet.'

'But Robert's just left. I have to . . .'

'What's more important to you, young lady?' Patrick's voice was scathing. 'This Robert or your fucking job?'

Josephine stared at him with undisguised hostility but his gaze did not waver and she sat down again.

'I think I need a whisky,' he said, striding to the drinks cupboard. 'Want one?'

She shook her head, not trusting herself to speak, hoping like hell that Robert would wait outside for her.

To her surprise, after pouring himself a double whisky Patrick came and sat next to her on the sofa.

'Look, I'm sorry I came on so strong,' he said, his tone more conciliatory. 'I was expecting to see you here with the architect.' He sat up suddenly. 'That wasn't him, was it?'

'No,' she said sharply. 'That's a dear friend.'

He grinned suddenly and patted her knee. 'An extremely close one, from what I could see.'

Josephine stood up abruptly and went to sit on the sofa opposite.

'Are you going to tell Georgia?'

He didn't answer at once. Leaning an arm languidly across the back of the sofa, he crossed his fashionably trousered legs, at ease in these familiar surroundings.

'That depends on you,' he drawled eventually.

Her gaze was sour. 'Please don't tell me you're going to do this "I won't say a word if you're nice to me" routine. It would be so predictable.'

'I would've put it a little more elegantly, but that's about the gist of it.' Patrick grinned. 'I've always had a thing about red hair. My turning up here wasn't a coincidence,' he smirked, rolling the whisky glass meaningfully in his hands. 'I was rather hoping it would be me who would end up in that bed with you.'

Josephine glared at him furiously. 'What made you think I'd sleep with my editor's boyfriend?'

'I had a little clue. Can you deny coming on to me at the office party?'

She made no effort to conceal her astonishment.

'Yes I can. Nothing was further from my mind. My God, Georgia was standing next to me.'

'That's what made it so exciting.'

The slimeball, nearly twice her age, actually believed that some pleasantries and a few laughs constituted a path to something more. He couldn't be serious.

But he was. Without any further preamble he said, 'I suggest we carry on where you and your boyfriend left off.'

'Here and now?' she asked, trying to keep her voice steady.

Finishing the whisky in a gulp, he slapped the tumbler on to the glass-topped table.

'Why not? I'm in the mood and you must be a little frustrated, I would've thought.'

'And how do you think I could face Georgia afterwards?' she asked.

'Easily, if she doesn't find out.' He leaned towards her and instinctively she shrank away.

'I know how she feels about this flat, especially her bedroom. It's her fantasy, her dream. If I told her what you'd been up to in that precious bed of hers, you'd be out of your job in an hour.'

'But you'd have no scruples about us using the bed.'

'Listen, we both win if we keep our mouths shut. Give me what I want and you keep your job. Otherwise I'll tell Georgia. It'll be my word against yours, and who do you think she'll believe?'

He paused. 'So, young Josephine, what's it to be? Me or your P45?'

Patrick began unloosening his tie, looking at her expectantly and, she thought, with some degree of confidence.

The shit.

Well, he had asked what was more important to her – Robert or the job. She wasn't sure about Robert – there were too many unanswered questions – but as for the job, it had been difficult to get. She'd had no experience of journalism in Britain and if it hadn't been for Nicci's contact at *Woman's View* she might still be working in a bar while she filled in application forms. She had fitted into the position of assistant to the features editor as easily as if she'd been computer-matched. Her ideas, her enthusiasm and her sheer zest for the job had gained immediate approbation and at the regular brainstorming sessions she'd quickly caught the attention of the editor.

Now this sleazebag, who'd betray his lover for a casual fuck, was threatening her career. Ahead of her stretched a vision of fruitless interviews. Nicci would help all she could but she couldn't manufacture a job out of thin air and it wouldn't take long for the story to spread around their media village. Patrick would probably paint it blacker than it was, and what other editor would trust her then?

He was still looking at her lasciviously, as if he was aware of all that was passing through her mind. Suddenly she half-ran into the bedroom and quickly locked the door. She could imagine what he was thinking, a complacent smile on his face. Almost at once the handle rattled.

'Can I come in?' The voice was halfway between peremptory and seductive. 'Don't make me wait.'

'Won't be long,' she called out, and true to her word, a few minutes later, having smoothed the sheets, straightened the coverlet and replaced the towels, she unlocked the door and stepped out. Fully dressed.

He was plainly puzzled. 'What are you playing at?'

Josephine made no reply but walked swiftly past him towards the front door. Before he realised what was happening she was standing half in and half out of the hallway. She was taking no chances with a man who'd just downed a double whisky and had no scruples about coercing a subordinate. But she had to be careful what she said to him. After all, he had been Georgia's lover for two years.

'Patrick, you've read me wrong,' she said firmly, in a last-ditch attempt to salvage the situation. 'I'm sorry if you thought I'd been leading you on, but if I did what you wanted, don't you think we'd both regret it?'

'No,' he answered promptly. 'It can be our little secret and it need never happen again.' He lowered his voice. 'Unless it's really fantastic.' He paused. 'As, of course, it would be.'

She gazed firmly back at him.

'I couldn't be so disloyal.'

'It wasn't too loyal using your boss's flat for an afternoon fuck.'

'But it was with my boyfriend, not hers.'

'Come on,' he urged, 'stop being a prick-teaser. You know you want it as much as I do.'

A red mist descended on Josephine and she jettisoned her plans to try and placate him.

'I'm damned if I'm going to be blackmailed by you. Do what you want,' she shouted, furiously slamming the door behind her.

Trembling, Josephine found her way out of the building and looked up and down the street. There were dozens of people around but there was no sign of Robert. Why hadn't he waited? He'd probably be making his way back to the airport and she didn't even have a mobile number for him so that she could at least say goodbye. She walked to the end of the road and hailed a taxi. As it drew away from the kerb, she dialled Nicci's mobile.

The merest outline of what had happened that afternoon was enough for Nicci to appreciate the quandary in which her friend found herself, and they were quick to agree on the only way in which she could deal with her predicament.

'But the worst thing is that Robert didn't hang around,' Josephine wailed as a miserable postscript to her story.

'Of course he didn't, you dope,' retorted Nicola. 'Can't you see how it looked to him? If he thought that was your flat and a man comes in using his own key, what do you expect him to think?'

Light dawned.

'Oh God.'

Now she'd lost everything.

Josephine hoped Georgia would walk in before she changed her mind about what she was going to say. As she looked at the framed magazine covers lining the walls, the awards in the glass case in the corner, she thought sadly how she would miss this glossy, Technicolor world.

There was a flurry in the corridor and the editor was preceded, as she always was, by a cloud of the latest designer scent. She smiled when she spotted Josephine waiting in the chair opposite her desk.

'Did the architect take long?'

Josephine sat up. She had forgotten about him completely. Presumably Patrick had dealt with him.

'He hadn't arrived by the time I had to leave,' she said carefully.

Georgia sat down with a sigh. 'What a pain. It took me ages to pin him down.' She pressed the intercom button for her secretary and asked her to put a call through to the architect.

'Look,' said Josephine, 'you're going to be even more upset when I tell you what happened.'

Now she had Georgia's full attention, and as she recounted Robert's arrival, the mix-up about the flat's true owner and how they had found themselves making love, the editor grew more and more rigid with fury.

'In my bedroom? On my bed?' Her voice was ominously low and sombre.

'We didn't have time to do anything,' said Josephine hastily. 'We were interrupted because Patrick arrived.'

'Patrick? I told him you'd be there to let the architect in. Why did he turn up?'

'He didn't say.'

Her boss suddenly looked tired, showing every line of the forty-four years she acknowledged in the record books, not to mention the extra six on her birth certificate. Then, visibly settling back into her glamorous façade, she appeared to have regained control.

'I have to say I'm most disappointed in you, Josephine.'

The younger woman reddened and prepared to hear the worst. She had gambled and lost. Not only was she soon to be jobless, but once again Robert had disappeared from her life.

'Bedrooms are very personal places, and you abused my trust.'

Looking thoughtful, Georgia stood up and walked towards the window overlooking the busy West End square. For a moment the silence was broken only by the clatter of the fax machine in the outer office. There seemed little point in prolonging the agony, and Josephine was rising to leave when the editor turned round to face her.

'But there are extenuating circumstances. I can understand how it happened and I must say I admire your guts. You could've waited for Patrick to mention it but you were upfront about it and I appreciate that.' She smiled. 'Of course, Patrick would've kept your secret. He's very loyal, you know.'

There was a pause while the two women's eyes met. Finally the editor said softly, 'Let's make a pact. I won't talk about it, neither will you, and I'll make sure that Patrick doesn't either. It'll be just between the three of us. OK?'

Georgia's face, apprehensive and vulnerable, confirmed Josephine's vow that she would never reveal what Patrick had been planning.

Josephine nodded slowly, understanding.

After two weeks of waiting and waiting and waiting for Robert to telephone, Nicola made it quite plain she was weary of hearing the 'if onlys' and 'what ifs' from Josephine.

'Get a grip,' she said, as they finished a bottle of post-work Sauvignon. 'Whatever happened to Girl Power?' And, reluctantly, Josephine agreed to her help in composing an e-mail.

To: Robert Hutcheson
From: Josephine Simmons

It's time to put the record straight. That flat wasn't mine. Neither was the man. They both belonged to my editor. I'm currently only an assistant features editor but when you come back next time I hope to be higher up the ladder and, who knows, living somewhere similar. Of course it'll take me a couple of years.

From: Robert Hutcheson
To: Josephine Simmons

You don't have the time. I'm moving to a new job in London next month. Suggest you write my initials on every page of your diary from the 8th onwards so we can take up where we left off.

PS And this time, it'll be quicker if I make the coffee!

Sophie Parkin has contributed to two successful collections of writing, *Mothers by Daughters* and *Sons and Mothers*, as well as to many newspapers and magazines. She broadcasts on television and radio. She has two children and lives in London, as well as appearing live as an internet agony aunt, Dear Sophie, on AOL. Her first novel, *All Grown Up*, and latest novel, *Take Me Home*, are published by Review.

The Stench of Rotting Love

Sophie Parkin

L ife is full of hard stuff – concrete and granite, wire wool and bri-nylon, marbles and diamonds.

Sometimes you have to face what's hard and glide through it like an ocean liner with the thought of the *Titanic*'s fate buried in the back of your mind. There is always a chance you might sink. Then when you don't, and you're through to the other side, stoic but grin-laden, life starts to heap rewards upon you from out of the ether. Remember, it doesn't matter where it comes from, just grasp it in gratitude and keep going. Always answer back.

Dear Rob,

I have just received your letter, to my amazement and delight. Of course I remember our snog for five minutes in the back of the tent last summer at cousin Miriam's wedding. I can't say I often visit Newlyn but if you're ever in London, a drink would be fine. I'm afraid I know very little about art, except I know what I like, Matisse, Michelangelo, Moore, anyone else beginning with M. Doesn't Terry Frost come from

Newlyn? He was on *Desert Island Discs* on Friday and said the only record worth saving was 'Tea for Two'. Would you agree? Do you know it, do you know him?

At the moment I think my choice would be de-pressed, 'I Love You Porgy' by Billie Holiday, and I would play it every day and have my excuse for a fat weep.

Listen to me! Life and soul of the party, I'll put you off ever coming up. Don't worry 'it too will pass', as my gran used to say, and then I can show you the low-life of London or the high-life of Hackney (one and the same).

Yours sincerely,

Poppy X

Now where had those letters come from? Rob's one to me and the one I had posted back? I know I had to stretch myself to reply. Over the past two years I had begun to look like a favourite cashmere jumper put in the washing machine once too often, that the owner can't throw out because thank God it's that precious commodity, cashmere. Even my face looked shrink-wrapped, glistening with a pre-menstrual pore grease explosion; the spots would come next.

Two months back I had finished a year-and-a-half affair that was a straight road to downtown Pittsville, USA – no return flights available. Hauling my self-esteem back up the loose-gravelled Khyber Pass was proving gut-wrenchingly sore. Of course I hadn't finished anything. Anthony had just been coming home later and later until hardly at all. Then when he did appear, he would shout mouthfuls of defensive aggression, goading my anger into attack, and me, the dumb animal, fell for it like a pink Cadillac wrapped in a pink ribbon and with my name on the number plate.

You could smell a tangible rottenness off him, a mixture of watercress and chicken carcass left a month too long in the bottom of a jug of dead flower water, and yes, I still kissed him. Yes, I still wanted it to work because you begin thinking, after a year and a sodding half it damn well should work, or at least give a refund. Obviously it was useless, a dead, dying, angry thing. One night I was squeezed so hard that those tender words dropped from my mouth, pearls to the swine:

'Well fuck off, then! Leave! Go! Don't bother coming back. Fuck off out of here now!'

There aren't many other ways to say it. He got out of bed still only revealing his back – the part of him I knew best by that point – with its ageing, greying folds gathering in place of muscle, I pleasantly noted; he dressed and left. I cried myself to sleep.

A few days later and I had heard nothing back from Anthony, other than the reminder of his dirty knickers in the wash basket which I didn't know whether to throw or wash, but I heard plenty from my friend Jane. Jane says he's only gone and moved on to her estate, in with 'that fat cow Mona'. Mona isn't her real name – it's Lisa, of course – but her face is about as long and colourful as a piece of salt cod on the Caribbean stall on the Chats market. Mona worked at the local 'bike bar' for the new middle-class shag girls living round here chasing barrow-boy meat before they settle down. 'It's amazing how much space you can buy for the money when you move out of Notting Hill to East

London!' you hear them chirp in their Principles suits, off to work, catching the bus unladen by pushchairs and screaming kids.

I've lived here too long. Now that I won't be moving with the Anthony Charm School to any of the places (like Paradise) that he promised to take me, I'll be here even longer.

There was something not quite fair about being left with my kids in my flat after all those promises. When he left it felt like he'd glued my feet to the pavement, my heart nailed directly below.

Jane said, 'Sod him! Let's go out and have a shag. Shift the consciousness, break the lying bastard's spell. There's better out there, more available, bigger and harder, leaner and meaner . . .' Jane's a sensible girl, a little esoteric but I'd follow her advice to a canning factory. Not that her own life's sooo perfect, but then the cobbler's family is often the worst shod. And the way I see it is that she's so good at churning out for others, she gives the best stuff away and there's nothing left over.

So out we go, heels, lippy, Wonderbras, less lift-and-separate, more squash-and-bulge, but then we've each had two kids. Our bodies are proof of the ravages of too many bad relationships, Tesco's soft white thick slice and breast-fed babies.

Jane claims to have the perfect relationship. 'A good fuck when I need it and I always know where to find him, on site at the estate pub. Of course he's a total Neanderthal, but that's why they invented books.'

I'd say Jane was a typical single mother these days. We're too poor, we've worked too long bringing up our kids alone to have anything not on our terms, we think, and then we fall in love. Then all at once our lives resemble the pushchair seat after a day in the park: all piss and biscuits. But I've had it with falling in love. It's too expensive, it knackers you and inevitably fucks you over when you place your control panel in a man's hands. Men with a little power are dangerous, the whole sodding lot, megalomaniacs.

Jane's younger sister baby-sits for our brood. She thinks she's smart and she is, but she's got some awfully funny ideas. She's not going to be like us, she says, she's not going to get pregnant, she's going to study and work and not drink until she's got to the top of her corporate ladder, which is law. No men, until she's snug in her own barrister's chambers, then only when she's bought her house in Islington will she consider joining the human race. We look at each other, Jane and I, and try not to laugh at Chiffon's earnest, pretty face. Jane brought her up along with her own kids. It is hilarious, Thatcher's kids, Blair's teenagers. No difference. No more self-realisation than us at their age but they believe they've got the key because they won't let go of the steel-thin veneer of control, praying to the career god of work and money. At least we've got the kids and a laugh. No money, but plenty of laughs. Poor Chiffon, she'll have a job and not find a man until she's picked for her money and sports car, and when she wants a baby or security from what she saw as a man of promise, he'll be off in his Boxter faster than you can say Porsche, while she burns the midnight oil of work responsibilities. Will that make her any happier than us? Maybe.

'The problem is,' I said to Jane as we clip-clopped our high-heeled way to the bus stop, 'there's too much choice in the way we can lead our lives, and when nobody believes in God we're all living in free-fall.'

'You must be the only girl in Hackney who'd even think something like that.' She looked at me and laughed, but I continued seriously; 'And that is why everybody gets so bloody scared and ends up doing fuck all, or exactly as their parents did, and blaming why they're doing nothing on everybody else, or their parents.' It seemed simple enough to me, Chiffon just wanted some regular institutionalised safety. A fence built so she couldn't fall off the edge of the world.

'Very philosophical, but mind the dog dirt in front of you.' Jane caught hold of my arm to steer me clear as though I was blind. 'It wouldn't do walking into some posh West End club covered in East End shit now. Everybody would smell where you came from.'

'Thank you, Jane. I had no intention of daubing myself as a dirty protest,' but around here it's nearly impossible not to. The streets are so grey it almost makes you glad that there's a different colour on them. We waited at the bus stop for the number 22, our means of escape. I love that feeling, riding into town at the top of the bus right at the front, the whole evening lying in wait, stomach quivering anticipation. Six to eight hours later and you're staggering back on the night bus, jitters mixed with too much nicotine, a wide selection of alcohols, and every time the bus lurches you think you will too.

'Those highlights have worked really well,' I said to Jane just as the bus was turning the corner towards us. I had helped her do them courtesy of an old swimming hat and a Silk Cut to burn the little holes, just like you get in the hairdresser's, but the smell was rank.

'I know. Jimmy loves them, says I look just like Cindy out of *EastEnders*.'

'No you don't!' I say, outraged. We jumped on the bus and climbed our way to the top.

'I know that, but Jimmy can only compliment women by comparing them to his idea of what he thinks women aspire to, God help us.'

'Is he still seeing his wife?'

'Yeah,' she said in a tired, nonchalant way. 'But his real love's the pub, so I'm not exactly jealous, am I? I feel sorry for that poor cow, she's pregnant again, still working and with the other two kids, believing he's back with her. She actually puts up with all his crap. I s'pose I do too.'

'We all do sometimes. The things we do for a shag, eh!'

'I don't think I can be bothered any more. Anyway, it's too limp. I think I'll tell him to sod off. It's all right as long as you don't have to hear the stories, but they can't resist it. Eventually they start on the one about the long-suffering other woman, what she does for him because she loves him, and if you loved him you'd do it too . . . Have you got your mobile on you? I'll do it now.'

And she would too. 'No, I left it behind in case it got nicked. Hey, you could have this bus conductor instead.' I suggested helpfully as we paid for our tickets.

'You be good girls,' he said. 'I'm a married man.'

'Boo!' we jeered back, laughing as the bus threaded its way through Islington.

I know what Jane means about the story. You can take it at first, but when you start becoming part of the plot-line it's no good. Anthony was like that about his ex. One moment he loved me, the next I could never measure up to the standards of Candy. He was always yearning for what could have been. Sometimes he'd start to cry about how he'd fucked up the ending for everyone, disappointed his mum and dad, making the happy family fantasy impossible. He had a son – still has, Stevie – couldn't forgive himself for leaving him.

Anthony, Candy and Stevie. Anthony had jumped overboard when Candy was still pregnant, then he behaved like a bloody yo-yo for the next three years. After that, he found me. He can't give up his son, he says, and then wouldn't see him for months on end. When he did, he'd bring this poor excuse for a child over and not know what to do with it. Stevie would sit clinging to his dad like a cowering whippet or a starved koala, but get too close and he'd separate your fingers from your hand, and all the time giving you those mournful eyes. Eyes like that make you want to cry with recognition. We've all felt like that at some point, haven't we?

I tried to love Stevie. I like kids, so do Ruby and Lucy, my twins. They're at that age, seven, when they like smaller kids to condescend to as a teacher or mother, but none of us could take to Stevie. You didn't want to get near his face, what with all the flaky skin and scabs from his eczema that extended visibly across his scalp with the thinness of his hair.

Anthony had said. 'If you love me you will love Stevie as if you was his mother!'

I'm afraid I did. Love him about the same as his mother, which to look at him wasn't doing him much good. Poor kid. In other countries a sickly child like that would be put on a hillside to die. But I wasn't going to think about Anthony and Stevie any more.

When we got to Piccadilly, Jane and I hopped off to look at Fortnum and Mason's window, the Royal Academy posters and the book shops. With our coats done up we looked respectable enough to slip in and patrol the latest releases. All the promises of unread secrets wrapped in their glossy new covers. I love books.

Jane and I have been doing this college access course for two years but I left last month when I got a job on a magazine with the glimmering prospect of editorial assistant ahead of me. I'm going for the publisher's job, once I finish my evening course; she doesn't know it yet, thinks I'm just the office girl computer whiz, but I've got the girls to think of. It's not as though I'm doing it to spend at Karen Millen.

I have to keep reminding myself. The wonderful thing about being a single mum with no bloke about is all the time you get once the kids are in bed. The telly's turned off, cleaning finished, then you can hop into a hot bath, clean bed and good book, and get more of a response most of the time than from any man. The pity is when you feel like sex and a wank doesn't quite do the job, like stuffing a flannel into the plug hole when you've lost the plug. But there are a lots of pluses. No extras – cooking, cleaning, ironing, washing, nagging, crap telly other than what you want on. I have to keep telling myself these plus points like a mantra, otherwise I forget the shit and only remember the sex, and the good sex at that!

We made a note of all the books that looked worth ordering from the library, and went on across Eros to the Atlantic Bar. It's gorgeous and plush in there and the doorman says, 'Good evening, ladies,' and for a minute you feel like you're gliding down into an elegant thirties cruise liner. Cruise might be the right word once you see the Hugo Boss footballers and fashion PRs and designer-spanking Essex girls, not a label out of sight. I don't know how Jane and I would be categorised – second-hand chic maybe, if you're kind, I don't care – but if Jane says it's a good chat-up bar, it must be.

We pushed through, got a drink but nowhere to sit, till we wandered next door and shared a table with a bloke by himself. Jane had been saving the Anthony-goes-on-holiday story to cheer me up. She must have been gagging like a Monica on the bus.

'I bumped into Anthony this morning down the shops, he'd just come back from Cyprus. Had a holiday with Mona and his kid . . .' She feeds me these little crumbs non-chalantly, knowing I'd be hungry for more.

'Yeah? How does he do it? She must have paid, 'cos he hasn't had any work for months.'

Anthony is a professionally unemployed actor; a better-qualified leech. When I met him he was actually on *London's Burning* but he left 'cos he didn't feel 'fulfilled'! Which surprised me, because the work meant he had the money for the pub.

'Apparently,' Jane said, completely straight-faced, 'he had a horrible time. Well, it was Northern Cyprus where the soldiers are, Anthony said if we'd gone we'd have probably been raped.'

'I'll book for next year then, shall I?'

'Mona wasn't touched once except for Stevie's projectile vomiting into her suitcase whilst she was unpacking.'

'That's my boy! She wouldn't have liked that.'

'And as if that wasn't bad enough to ruin a romantic hols, Anthony, poor love, got a dickey tummy from the foreign food, and spent the whole time in the bog – which was just as well, 'cos it pissed down all week apparently!'

'Ahh, poor things.'

'They were only there for eight days and the weather was awful, except the first day and she got burnt.'

This hit the laughter button when nothing else had done properly for weeks. The more I tried to stop laughing, the more impossible it became, with the image of Mona, Stevie and Anthony suffering a horribly expensive time. Felt like balm to my wounds, divine, divine retribution. Do you believe in God?

Pulling back my honks of appreciation, I wiped the tears from my eyes. 'God, that feels better. I needed that. Thank you, Jane. You deserve another drink, whether it was true or not,' I said getting up.

'It bloody well was! I know, same again, Missus.'

'Absolutely.' I struggled through the bar throng, still chuckling, and thought, I must remember to tell Jane about the wedding snog letter . . . I was startled when I was asked what I wanted, not by the barman but the bloke off our table, now pressed close to the bar. I tried to give him money to pay for our drinks, but he said he wouldn't dream of it, he wanted to know what we were drinking. We seemed to be having such a laugh he wanted one too. I reckoned he was in his early forties, said his date hadn't appeared. I'm not sure I believed that part, since out of his corduroy pocket poked *Men are from Mars, Women are from Venus*. The rest of him was dark floppy hair, leather-patched elbows, glasses. He wasn't Jane's type, not convict enough for her, too old. I don't think I have a type any more.

Anthony was Steve McQueen hit the bad times. The twins' dad was Steve McQueen at the beginning, a student I picked up from the wrong side of the bar. No idea where he is now, but I think every day how lucky I was to have such a sweet-faced man, not around long enough to get bored with, fuck other women or for me to start hating. I understand why some women hit their kids after the dad has gone: they hold photocopy expressions that can sandpaper at your rawness. The twins look just like him, not me.

This bloke in the bar was called Simon. He looked like one too. Slim, weedy, probably goes to the gym but it never has any effect.

'I bet he has reading glasses, and his girlfriend's just left him for her personal trainer,' Jane whispered to me when he went off to the loo.

'Ahh, pity!'

'No, Poppy, not tonight, no pity! No public schoolboy rejects need apply tonight, he's probably poof material.'

'Something soft to sit on, modom?'

'Yeah, well, he's cramping our style. Next drink and we walk over to the gorgeous bar hunks.'

Being with Jane for the night is like enrolling in her private regiment for the evening: either agree or don't sign up. When Simon came back he pulled out some posh invitation from his pocket and offered it to us.

'Is that free drink?' asked Jane.

'Of course,' said Simon with a slight look of amusement. 'Come along as my guests. It's Hugh Wimpole's party for his new magazine.'

'Hugh Wimpole?' I said, impressed, because in my few months working, even I knew his name was big doody. Then I began to worry. About my half-bitten nails, shoes I'd forgotten to polish, that my legs were fat, all my clothes were charity shop, and that if we did go nobody would talk to me because of the ladder on my heel. All the normal neuroses.

Jane and I have a friend called Gemma who worked in a bar near the Chelsea football ground, and ended up marrying a player. Just like a real fairy tale, he took her off to live in a dream mansion in Surrey with her son, Kieron. She never worried about anything before, except how to pay the leccy; now she's lost, clinging to the bottle. New lives can bring fresh neuroses.

Jane looked at me, her eyes lit with mischief. Posh parties were just her line for a laugh, and I knew she'd changed our plans. 'All right,' she said, and we trotted off to apply new mounds of guck to our faces before leaving.

We arrived one on each side of Simon, and him with a hairline grin. The party was grand, a whole restaurant overrun with media babes and crumpled men, a lot of them so rich they couldn't be bothered to dress. The girls were immaculate. Too beautiful, too thin, too clever. Jane whispered, 'Barren bitches,' to me in the loos, to make herself feel better. There was a vodka sculpture (an ice sculpture that a waiter stood next to with shots of vodka to pour through into your glass, guaranteed freezing), a champagne fountain (made from stacking glasses) and lots of mucky food on trays (too much sauce), and everybody said darling and kissed twice. Simon was perfect, he introduced us to everyone and nobody was anything other than charming.

That's what good education's for. Nobody, not even the bouncers, turned and hauled us out shouting, 'Oi, you from Kingsmead, out!'

When the music started and Jane was shaking her funky butt like it wouldn't stay on, the boys were round her like a pot of honey. My, it was fun, it was like French perfume clearing the stench from my nose. Parties like that should be put on prescription.

At a certain point of insobriety, with the music slowing down, Simon leaned too close. He smelt expensive and I thought, fuck it, and let him kiss me. It had to happen sometime, break the Anthony seal with full disapproval. Rub his animal smell off me, his dog scent that had made me his bitch for far too long.

'Poppy, my girl,' I told myself, as though it was Jane talking, 'change the record, open the window before it seals up and you're never able to jump out of it again. If you don't I'll push you anyway!' And while all these words were falling around my head attached to the champagne bubbles, Simon said, 'How are you getting home? Where do you live, Poppy?' and I must have given him a look, because I never said a word but I could see his eyes brighten. 'Just hold on there, I'll get them to call a cab to Sloane Street,' he said.

'What's happening, baby?' Jane sidled up with a boy young enough to still be a mother's son.

'I guess I'm going home; someone else's home.' I hiccuped and giggled. A worse friend would have rescued me at this point, but Jane gave me a hug and a kiss and said, 'Don't worry about the kids. I'll see you at lunch, have a good time.' She didn't even refer to Simon as a soft stool.

The next morning I woke with a size ten hangover, fresh

coffee, Alka Seltzer and toast on a tray. Simon jumped back into bed and we had some ordinary sex followed by great conversation about words and books. He made me feel clever and funny, laughing at every joke I made. Even though the sex was rubbish, he was sweet and kind, solicitous in a nice way, ran me a bath that had me stinking like a king's whore, ordered me a cab on account and asked me for my phone number so he could take me out to dinner. He said he was a writer, but he's too rich unless he'd broken into somebody else's flat so many times he felt it was home. I don't care what he does really. I'm not sure I'll see him again. I could be his experiment, obsession, girlfriend, but none of that's the point.

The point is, he was the perfect Prince Charming, came along when I was comatosed by the evil Anthony, broke the spell with a night of luxury cotton-sheeted perfection to show me there are some gorgeous men out there, some as good as in books, some as good as books. Next week the painter snogger from Cornwall's appearing. He wrote me a few more letters, we've got quite the Charing Cross Road witty correspondence going. I spoke to Cousin Miriam and she said I must have been blind drunk not to notice he was the best thing filling the tent at her wedding, built like an advert. 'Just blind,' I explained. 'With only eyes for Anthony, but I've had the operation now, removed the cataracts.'

The other night our kids were playing out together and we were having a cup of tea on the balcony, chatting away, keeping our eye on them, when Jane said, 'The thing is, Pops, when it comes to men, you're forgetting. You don't have to introduce them to the kids, have them move in, reprint your life. Just have them on the side.'

I almost said, 'Jimmy still seeing his wife?' but I knew better.

'Hey, leery!' she laughed, reading my face. 'You can always teach them about sex.'

Jill Mansell worked for many years at the Burden Neurological Hospital, Bristol, and now writes full time. She lives with her partner and three young children in Bristol. *Mixed Doubles* was a recent top twenty UK bestseller and her latest novel, *Head Over Heels*, is available from Headline.

Popping Out

Jill Mansell

Lucy wasn't interested in having fun, particularly not the going-out-and-getting-groped-on-a-Saturday-night kind.

What Lucy wanted was the opposite of fun.

Otherwise known as . . . baby-sitting.

'It was a sunny morning in Greendale. Postman Pat looked out of his bedroom window and thought, I know, today I'll wear my pink dress, the one with the lace collar. So he put on his bra and pants and his high-heeled white shoes. By heck, thought Pat, it's about bloomin' time I shaved my legs –'

'This isn't true.' Alice, curled up next to her, dragged her thumb out of her mouth with a slurp. 'Postman Pat never wears a dress.'

'He does, he just doesn't go out in it. Nobody else knows,' Lucy explained. 'On his day off he wears girls' clothes and make-up and calls himself Patricia.'

'What about Jess the cat?' Alice's tone was challenging.

'Ah well, on Jess's day off, he dresses up as a dog.'

'That's definitely not true. Cats don't wear clothes.' With

a sigh, Alice slid off the sofa. 'If you can't tell me a proper story, I'm going to bed.'

Imogen reeled in five hours later, giggling.

'Luce, you're an angel. Sorry I'm a bit late, but I honestly didn't notice the time.' She collapsed on to the saggy sofa, kicking her shoes across the room and narrowly missing the television. 'We were just having so much . . . fun!'

'You said midnight at the latest.'

'Oh come on! You aren't in a strop, are you? There's wine in the fridge,' Imogen wheedled. 'Let's have a drink. You can sleep on the sofa.'

'It's two o'clock.' Lucy hated sounding grumpy, but her contact lenses were starting to chafe, and in all honesty what did Imogen expect? 'I'd rather just go home.'

The trouble with breathtakingly selfish elder sisters was they had no shame and didn't feel a bit guilty about putting you out.

'Never mind getting home.' Imogen bounced off the sofa. 'You're twenty-four years old, Luce, you want to get yourself a life.'

'I've got one,' Lucy protested when Imogen returned from the kitchen hugging two tumblers and a bottle of Romanian red.

'A bloody boring one these days. I don't know how you stick it! You should be getting back out there and meeting people.'

'Meeting men, you mean.'

'Why not?' Recklessly Imogen sloshed the vicious-looking wine into both tumblers. 'Meeting men and having adventures, that's what life's all about. Like tonight,' she went on, 'we had the most brilliant laugh at the club . . .'

Twenty minutes later, yawning like a hippo, Imogen stumbled upstairs to bed. There was a hole in her tights, a red wine stain on the back of her white skirt and a cigarette burn in the sleeve of her new black Lycra top.

'You have the sofa,' she mumbled over her shoulder. 'Spare duvet in the airing cupboard. See you in the morning.'

Lucy tipped the vile wine down the sink, in case Alice came down in the morning and thought it was Ribena. Then she picked up her jacket and let herself out of the house.

Two miles down the road a dark figure leapt out in front of her Mini.

'Oh shit,' Lucy breathed, automatically jamming her foot on the brake and realising at once that this was the wrong thing to do.

But what choice did she have, short of running him over? This was a narrow country lane and half of it was already blocked by the Volvo the dark figure had jumped out of. And he clearly had no intention of letting her get past.

Her heart hammering in her chest, Lucy hurriedly locked both doors and switched off her Celine Dion tape.

She felt sick as the man's face loomed up at the windscreen. He was mouthing something and making frantic winding-down movements with his hand.

Lucy lowered her window half an inch.

'Quick, please, I'm not a murderer, you have to help me.' He sounded agitated.

'I'll stop at the next phone box and call the police.'

To her horror, Lucy heard an unearthly wailing sound coming from inside the Volvo.

'It can't wait that long. The car's broken down and my

stepmother's having a baby. Please believe me, this isn't a trick –'

'I haven't got any money,' Lucy blurted out. 'And . . . and I've got herpes.'

This was a useful thing to tell potential attackers, apparently. It put them off wanting to have sex with you. She had read this in an article in *Cosmopolitan*.

'Oooh, *owww*, make it stop!' shrieked a female voice from the depths of the other car. 'Dino, *do* something, please!'

Trembling, Lucy wound the window down a couple more inches. She took a deep breath and yelled at the top of her voice, 'Are you really having a baby?'

'No,' the man gestured in despair, 'she's plucking her eyebrows.'

'Sshh,' said Lucy.

'Aaarrgh, I want to push!'

'Don't push,' Lucy bellowed back without knowing quite why. It was just what doctors always said on TV.

Scrabbling at the lock, she flung open the driver's door and leapt out.

'Ouch,' shouted Dino as the edge of the door ricocheted off his shin.

'Are you a doctor?' whispered the woman sprawled across the back seat of the Volvo.

'Well, no.'

But I've never missed an episode of *Vets in Practice*, thought Lucy. Being a couch potato had its advantages.

Dino, hovering behind her, said, 'I don't mean to be rude, but isn't herpes infectious?'

'What?' The woman looked as if she were about to faint. She gazed up in horror at Lucy.

'I don't have herpes, OK? My name's Lucy Webb' – it seemed only polite, under the circumstances, to introduce herself – 'and if you think you can make it across to my car, I'll drive you to the hospital.'

'Oh God, another contraction!' The woman screwed up her face and threw one leg over Lucy's shoulder. 'I need something for the pain,' she begged, panting furiously. 'Can't you do anything, please?'

Lucy, crouched uncomfortably in the doorway, thought of the couple of dusty paracetamol she probably had lurking at the bottom of her handbag. Spotting a pair of leather gloves in the door's side pocket, she pulled them out and thrust them in front of the woman's mouth.

'Here, bite on these.'

'Why don't I take your car,' said Dino, 'find a phone box and get an ambulance out here?'

'Got a torch?' Lucy glanced over her shoulder at him.

'Er . . . no.'

'Then you can't go. It's pitch black out here. Without the headlights from my car, I won't be able to see a thing.'

'OK, so we'll get Max into your car.'

'Who's Max?'

'Me,' gasped the woman, bracing her other leg against Lucy's hip. Her voice was muffled by the leather gloves but incredibly she managed to laugh. 'Maxine Santorini, pleased to meet you . . . but I don't think there's time to get me anywhere . . . *Ooooh!*'

'The head's coming, the head's coming,' Lucy squealed, almost toppling over backwards as Maxine Santorini's bare feet pressed into her with astonishing force. Aware of Dino still hovering helplessly behind her – typical man – she shouted over her shoulder, 'You have to help me.'

'Oh come on,' Dino protested, 'Max is my stepmother.'

The next moment, to her own amazement, Lucy felt herself cupping the palm of her hand over the emerging head. Warm, wet and slippery, it was just like the lambs she'd seen being born on TV. Carefully she rotated the head in the direction it seemed to want to go. Sideways, that was right, wasn't it? Yes, yes, to give the shoulders room to slide out.

'Huuurrghhh!' groaned Maxine through her mouthful of glove.

'Nearly there, one more push, you're doing brilliantly,' Lucy marvelled, overcome with awe and – oh yuk – an unexpected gush of warm fluid over her hands. 'Quick, get a blanket,' she instructed useless Dino.

Maxine pushed, there was a slurpy plopping sound and the rest of the baby slithered into Lucy's trembling out-stretched hands.

God, what now? Was she supposed to hold it up by its heels and smack it until it cried?

To Lucy's immense relief an indignant wail filled the car.

'Oh, my baby, my baby,' breathed Maxine, bursting into tears as well and holding out her arms.

'Here.' Dino thrust a bundle of something past Lucy. Catching a waft of Calvin Klein aftershave, she realised that it was the sweater he had been wearing. 'Wrap him in that.'

'I'm not wrapping him in anything.' Maxine, miracu-lously recovered, grinned as she eased her legs down from Lucy's shoulders. 'Because he's a her.'

'You'll need this as well,' said Dino, dropping his car keys into Lucy's hand.

She swivelled round to him, filled with indignation.

'I thought you said the car had broken down.'

'Swiss Army knife, idiot, on the key ring.'

In the dim light she saw his teeth gleam as he smiled at her stupidity. The other thing she couldn't help noticing was his tanned bare chest.

'Jolly useful,' Dino went on. 'You never know when these things will come in handy.'

Belatedly the significance of what he was saying sank in.

'Oh no. I'm really sorry, but I can't do that,' Lucy said firmly. 'You'll have to.'

'You've just delivered a baby,' said Dino. 'Don't be such a wimp.'

'If I have to cut the cord . . .' Lucy shuddered, glimpsing the blue-white coil out of the corner of her eye and feeling horribly queasy, '. . . I shall faint.'

'Go on.'

'I can't. You do it.'

'If I do it,' said Dino, 'I'll definitely faint.'

'For heaven's sake.' Maxine raised her eyebrows and whisked the penknife out of Lucy's hand. 'You're both hopeless. Here, I'll do it myself.'

'Yeeurgh,' Lucy and Dino murmured in unison as, with a faint crunching sound, the cord was sliced in two.

The cafeteria at the hospital was dimly lit and almost deserted. Lucy, her jacket tightly wrapped around her to conceal the fact that all she had on under it was her bra, sat opposite Dino. Luckily he looked stupid too, in her pink sweatshirt, which, as well as being way too small for him, had a picture of George Michael on the front.

'Present from my sister a couple of Christmases ago.' Lucy nodded at George Michael, feeling obliged to explain. 'She kept complaining that I never wore it. So I did tonight just to shut her up. I was baby-sitting. Nobody else was meant to see it.'

'I forgive you,' said Dino. 'Although there's still the matter of the Celine Dion tape in the car.'

Lucy, going pink, wondered if she could get away with blaming Imogen for this too.

Probably not, seeing as it had actually been in the tape deck.

'Well, nobody else was meant to see that either.'

He grinned across the table at her, dark eyes sparkling beneath hair that flopped on to his forehead. Lucy, experiencing a sudden urge to reach over and push it out of his eyes, sat firmly on her hands instead.

'It's four o'clock,' said Dino. 'Are you shattered?'

'I'm OK.'

'You don't have to stay if you don't want to.'

'I'd like to make sure Maxine and the baby are all right.'

She and Dino had been dispatched to the cafeteria while the doctors carried out their examinations.

'They won't have finished yet.' Dino rose to his feet. 'I'll get us another coffee.'

As he went, she admired his rear view. Excellent body, Lucy couldn't help noticing, terrific bum and legs. Oh yes, if Imogen were here now she'd give Dino a nine, no question. Maybe even a nine and a half.

Except Imogen wasn't here.

With a jolt, Lucy realised that what she really meant was *she'd* give him a nine and a half.

Only in theory, though.

Five more months to go yet.

'Would you mind if I kissed you?' said Dino, his tone conversational as he returned with two Danish pastries and the coffees.

'Um . . .'

While Lucy dithered, he lifted her chin and planted a kiss on her startled mouth.

Actually, rather a gorgeous kiss.

'Thanks. That male nurse over there was winking at me.' Back in his seat before she could draw breath, Dino ripped open a packet of sugar and emptied it into his polystyrene cup. 'So, no boyfriend then?'

Lucy was torn between indignation and astonishment. Had the kiss given her away? Was there, perhaps, some kind of physical difference between lips that regularly saw action and those that hadn't been kissed for seven months?

Oh my Lord, Lucy shuddered with embarrassment, do I have shrivelled-up, desperate, haven't-done-it-for-ages lips?

'Sorry, it wasn't meant to be a difficult question.' Dino sounded amused. 'I just thought baby-sitting, alone, on a Saturday night . . .'

Phew, that was all right then. Anything was better than having sex-starved lips.

'I was seeing someone.' What the hell, she may as well explain. 'We broke up seven months ago.'

'Why?'

'I found out he'd been seeing someone else.'

'How did you find out?'

'She came to the garden centre where I work and told me.'

'What did you do?'

'Threw a tray of potting compost at her, called her a few names.' Lucy smiled at the memory. 'Oh, it was all very dignified. My boss went mental.'

'Why? It wasn't your fault.'

'I know, but she was his wife.'

Pulling a sympathetic face, Dino offered her the cherry from his Danish pastry.

'And after that?'

'I decided to give men a miss for a bit.' Touched by his generosity, Lucy popped the cherry into her mouth.

'How long is a bit?'

'I promised myself a year. Twelve blissful, uncomplicated, man-free months.'

Dino shook back his hair.

'So what happens if you meet someone brilliant before the year's up?'

'I won't.' Lucy stirred her coffee with confidence. 'I've made sure of it.'

'How?'

'Easy, I don't go out.'

He looked stunned.

'No pubs, no clubs, no parties?'

'Especially no parties. Especially not on Saturday nights.'

'You just baby-sit.'

Lucy nodded happily in agreement.

'Just baby-sit.'

'And that way you're safe,' said Dino.

Her eyes narrowed.

'Are you making fun of me?'

'Wouldn't dream of it. You might tip a bucket of potting

compost over my head.' Dino's mouth began to twitch. 'Come on, drink up and we'll go and find Max.'

Maxine was sitting up in bed in a side ward, carefully applying mascara. With her blonde hair brushed and her mouth freshly lipsticked, the difference was amazing.

'Off out somewhere?' Dino grinned, gave his stepmother an affectionate kiss on the cheek and plonked himself down on the bed next to the perspex cot.

'I managed to get through to the hotel. Your dad's on his way down from Manchester. Business conference,' Maxine explained to Lucy. 'The baby wasn't due for another fort-night, we thought we'd get away with it.'

'Bit of an improvement here,' said Dino, nodding at the baby. 'Scrubbed up quite nicely. I must say, I prefer them with all the gunk washed off.'

'You're a lost cause,' Maxine said fondly. 'Hopeless. She's your baby sister. You're supposed to adore her, gunk or no gunk.'

'When she's fifteen, I'll be forty.' Carefully lifting her out of the cot, Dino wiggled his eyebrows at her in big-brotherly fashion. 'I'll be able to teach her how to drink and smoke and play a mean hand of poker. Actually,' he went on, sounding surprised, 'she's quite pretty, isn't she? What d'you think?' He turned the baby around so Lucy could see. 'Does she look like me?'

'She's much prettier than you are,' said Lucy, though this wasn't strictly true. Blinking and cautiously rubbing the corner of her left eye, she realised that her lenses were about to start playing up again. It was five o'clock in the morning and they had had enough.

'I'd better go,' she told Maxine. 'I just wanted to make sure everything was OK.'

'Come here.' Maxine held out her arms. 'Everything's wonderful, thanks to you. I don't know how we'd have managed if you hadn't come along.' She gave Lucy an emotional hug. 'My midwife in shining armour.'

'Well, midwife in a black bra,' said Dino as Lucy's jacket gaped open.

'And you can't just run away,' Maxine exclaimed. 'You must write down your address and phone number so we know where to find you again. My husband will want to thank you; in fact, we'd love you to be god-mother –'

'Aaargh, *no*,' Lucy cried out, stiffening in alarm.

'Oh well.' Maxine sounded disappointed. 'It doesn't matter, if you'd rather not.'

'I didn't mean that. It's my contact lens.' Lucy disentangled herself from Maxine in slow motion. 'I just felt it pop out.'

They hunted everywhere, in Maxine's hair, in her impressive cleavage, amongst the tangled bed sheets and on the floor.

'Bugger,' said Lucy, after ten minutes of fruitless searching.

'What is it with contact lenses?' said Dino. 'Why do they always have to be so difficult to find? Why can't they be fluorescent pink?'

'All my fault, for hugging you so hard.' Maxine patted her arm. 'Don't worry, the least I can do is pay for a new pair.'

'It's not that,' said Lucy. 'It just means I'm not going to be able to drive home.'

* * *

'Thanks,' she said as they pulled up outside Imogen's house.

'Don't mention it. Just call me your knight in shining pink sweatshirt.' Dino peered up at the bedroom windows. 'No signs of life. Are you sure this is OK?'

'It's five thirty in the morning, I wasn't expecting signs of life. Anyway, I've got a key.' Lucy held it up to show him. She was tired now, and Imogen's house had been closer to the hospital than her own flat. All she wanted to do was curl up on the saggy sofa and fall asleep.

'Right, well, I'll leave you to it then.' Dino sighed. 'I shall just trudge off down the road, find a petrol station, lug a can of petrol all the way back to the car . . . it can't be much more than five or six miles . . .'

'You're breaking my heart,' said Lucy.

He grinned.

'That's the general idea.'

'I thought there was something wrong with the car.'

'Actually, it was more a lack-of-petrol situation. But if Max finds out, she'll have my guts for garters.'

'Go on then, you can borrow mine.'

With only one contact lens, everything was fuzzy, but she saw his smile broaden.

'You know what? I think I love you.'

'I should think so,' said Lucy, climbing out of the car. 'Just don't forget to bring it back.'

'Make way, make way, woman with a hangover coming downstairs,' Imogen announced, clutching her head and clinging to the banister rail. 'I need tea, toast and hundreds of paracetamol. Lucy, wake up this instant and feel sorry for me, I'm *dying* here.' Her eyes lit up. 'Hey, did I tell you what a completely fab time I had last night?'

'You did,' Lucy murmured, knowing she was going to hear it all again anyway.

'God, you look worse than I do! Staying in and being a Nellie No-life must really take it out of you. And what's this?' Peeling back the spare duvet, Imogen gave the black bra a resounding *pinggg*. 'Have you been prancing around the sitting room again, pretending to be Madonna?'

Lucy peered at her watch.

'Where's Alice?'

'In the other room, watching TV. I've trained her well,' Imogen said smugly. She glanced out of the sitting room window. 'Where's your car?'

Imogen was a ruthless interrogator and Lucy wasn't up to twenty questions.

'Parked round the corner,' she said after a pause. 'Didn't want it getting stolen.'

'Oh. Tea?'

'Yes please.' Sitting up, Lucy discovered how much her shoulders ached from having Maxine's feet pressed into them. She called through to Imogen, now crashing about in the kitchen, 'OK if I have a bath?'

'Lucy? Get down here this minute,' Imogen bellowed up the stairs.

'Why?'

'*Just do it!*'

By the time Lucy had managed to wrap herself in a dark blue bath towel, Imogen had burst through the door. Seizing

Lucy by the arm, she dragged her through to the front bedroom.

'You said you parked your car round the corner so it wouldn't be stolen,' she hissed, practically squashing Lucy's nose against the chilly window. 'So who's this?'

The Mini was back. Dino, no longer wearing the embarrassing George Michael sweatshirt, was lifting a bunch of yellow roses out of the boot.

'Crikey,' said Lucy, 'I don't know. Car thief? Come to say sorry he stole it?'

'Lucy.' Imogen gave her a long, don't-mess-with-me stare. 'That is a very, *very* good-looking car thief.'

'Is he? You know what I'm like without my lenses.'

'Are you going to tell me what's going on here?' demanded Imogen.

'He's coming to the door and I'm all wet.' Lucy shook her hair like a spaniel. 'You'll have to go.'

'Hi,' said Dino. 'Is Lucy up yet?'

'She might be. Who are you?'

'Hasn't she told you?' He surveyed Imogen with amusement. Up close, she realised, he was even better-looking than at a distance.

'No she has not.' Imogen was torn between outrage and downright curiosity. 'Anyway, told me what?'

'Could you let Lucy know I'm here?'

'How can I,' Imogen cried out in frustration, 'when I don't even know who you are?'

Lucy, from the top of the stairs, said, 'It's all right, I do.'

Dino let out an appreciative whistle.

'Look at you, Cinderella in a bath towel. These are for you, by the way.'

As he held up the yellow roses, Alice appeared in the sitting room doorway clutching her Postman Pat book.

'Who's this, Mum? Lucy's boyfriend?'

'Lucy doesn't have a boyfriend,' Imogen replied through gritted teeth. 'Compared with Lucy, Postman Pat leads an action-packed social life.'

'Actually,' Lucy said mildly, 'you'd be surprised what Pat gets up to on his days off.'

Dino wisely ignored this. He kept his gaze fixed on Lucy.

'You were fantastic last night.'

'Oh come on,' Imogen squawked. 'What is this, some kind of wind-up?'

'In fact, better than fantastic,' Dino went on. 'Magnificent.'

Imogen wondered if it was possible to physically burst with frustration.

'What are you talking about? Lucy was here last night, baby-sitting!' Jabbing a frantic finger, she wailed, 'She slept over there on that sofa!'

'Look, I don't mean to be rude,' Dino said calmly, 'but could you stop interrupting? I've got something I'd quite like to say to Lucy.'

'But, but . . .'

'Mum,' said Alice, 'sshh.'

Dino moved closer to Lucy, who was clinging on to her bath towel for dear life.

'I'll never forget last night.' As he spoke, he pulled a small velvet box from the top pocket of his shirt. Dropping down on one knee, he held it out to her. 'Lucy, you've changed my life for ever. I want you to have this.'

There was an audible gasp from Imogen on the sofa.

'I want you to wear it always,' Dino went on, opening the box.

'Oh my God,' wailed Imogen, biting her knuckles. 'Does this mean you're *engaged*?'

'You don't know how happy you've made me. It's what I wanted more than anything.' Lucy turned the satin-lined box this way and that, admiring the way the lens glittered in the sunlight. As Dino rose and took her into his arms she breathed, 'Where did you find it?'

'Floating in Maxine's water jug,' he murmured back. 'How am I doing?'

'Excellent.'

'My father can't wait to meet you.' Dino's voice reverted to normal. 'He's booked a table for lunch at Black's.'

'I still don't get this,' Imogen wailed.

'Black's. Gosh,' said Lucy, because Black's was posh.

'Nothing but the best for you, after last night,' Dino told her with a dazzling grin.

'Stop it, just stop it,' Imogen exploded. 'This is my sister you're talking about. She never goes out, she never has any fun' – her voice rocketed up another couple of octaves – 'and she definitely didn't go *anywhere* last night!'

'Oh dear.' Sliding an arm around Lucy's towelling waist, Dino gave her an affectionate squeeze. 'Will you tell her about the baby, or shall I?'

Alison Joseph was born in north London and educated at Leeds University. She has worked as a local radio presenter, as a reader for BBC Radio Drama, and for Channel Four. Alison has three children and lives in London with her partner. The latest in her series of crime novels featuring Sister Agnes is published by Headline in spring 1999.

Topaz Dreams

Alison Joseph

'I thought citrus colours for the walls, you see,' Chloe was saying. 'And then I thought, if the lampshade was turquoise, but with fruit –'

'What do you mean, fruit?'

'Plastic fruit, lemons and oranges and stuff. The colours would be great.'

Stella had given up all pretence of working, and her word processor sat silently in front of her. 'Chloe, it'll look like an Italian restaurant –'

'No it won't. And then I told him I was thinking of covering our sofa in fun fur, bright yellow I thought –'

'And what did he say?'

Chloe stared in front of her. Her fingers clicked idly on her keyboard, typing one character, then another.

'He didn't like it, did he?' Stella leaned towards her across the desk.

'I mean, you'd think he'd at least try to listen to what I was saying.'

'Chloe, most blokes, given the choice between plastic lemons and fun fur and something more –'

'Boring –'

'They'll go for the boring, won't they?'

'But Stella, that bloke you went to bed with last week, what was his name, Tom, wasn't it, the one you said had his whole flat done up in black and white with touches of chrome, diagonal lines you said –'

'Chloe, that was a one-night stand. Diagonal black and white's OK for sex. But Andrew's different, isn't he? You're supposed to be spending the rest of your life with him.'

'We've just bought a flat together. It's not the same as getting married.'

'Isn't it?'

Chloe's fingers tapped against her keyboard again. 'Thing is, he'll like it when it's done. I told him so. I said, it'll all make sense, I know what I'm doing, trust me.'

'And what did he say?'

Chloe sighed. 'He said how about magnolia, with a touch of apple white.'

'Oh dear. It's worse when they've got views of their own.'

'I'm just not prepared to settle for apple white.'

'Did you tell him?'

Chloe shook her head. 'Not yet.'

Stella tapped on her own keyboard. 'It's funny, I don't think of you two having rows. Me and Max, we were always yelling at each other –'

'We don't have rows. And anyway, it's not just the flat. It's about my future. I need a portfolio of my designs, Stel. If I'm going to get anywhere, I need to show what I can do, what my ideas are like. Otherwise I might as well just resign myself to staying here and typing for the rest of my life.'

'You really think you can make a living on plastic lemons and turquoise lampshades?'

'I know I can. I've got so many ideas, Stella, all I need is the break, just one commission, and then it all works by word of mouth. That's what Chez said.'

'Chez your downstairs neighbour?'

'Yeah. He got his break into fashion from one person liking what he did. That's all you need, he says. I don't expect everyone to like what I do, but you've got to have ideas, you've got to be original. I just need one person to share my vision.'

'And it isn't Andrew.'

Chloe looked up from her screen. Then she looked down again, put on her headphones and started to type. 'My period's late,' she said.

At lunchtime they sat in the park with their sandwiches.

'How late?' Stella struggled with a mouthful of lettuce.

'Two days.'

Stella picked the cucumber out of her sandwich. 'This business idea of yours – ?'

'What about it?'

'You're serious?'

'Sure I'm serious. You see, if I start earning from it, I could go to college, learn some new techniques, business management . . . It's not just about decorating. It's – it's about my whole life. Why are you laughing?'

' 'Cos you're such an Aquarius-Pisces cusp, you are.'

'Meaning?'

'All dreams.'

'Where else do you start?'

Stella picked a crisp out of her packet and nibbled on it. 'Well, if you're a Virgo with Taurus rising, like me, you start from what's possible. And if what's possible is magnolia and apple white, then that's where you start.'

'And what happens to your dreams?'

'They come later. I s'pose.'

Chloe was shaking her head. 'You have to start with the dreams, Stel. You have to protect them. Dreams are fragile, see. You have to hold them at the front of your mind, else you lose sight of them.'

Stella ate another crisp, crunching noisily. They watched an old man, his coat tied with string, walking unsteadily through the spring sunshine, raising his can of beer at passers-by in some kind of private celebration. His dog jumped merrily at his heels as they receded into the distance.

'Stella?'

'What?'

'You know that guy you slept with?'

'Diagonal black and white walls?'

'Yes. Him.'

'What about him?'

'Was it fun?'

Stella turned to her. Her mouth was dusted with salt from her crisps. 'What do you mean?'

'I mean, was it fun, going to bed with him?'

'Course it was. I wouldn't have done it otherwise.'

'Oh. Right.'

'Shall we get a coffee from the takeaway place?'

They left their bench and ambled through the park back to the high street. In the queue at the coffee bar, Chloe said, 'Only – I thought – what you said about Max . . .'

'When?'

'Monday. Tuesday, maybe.'

'What did I say?'

'About no one comparing to Max.'

'Two cappuccinos to take away, please. Did I say that about Max?'

'Yup.'

'Oh, well, Max, different league altogether. Max, I mean –' She sighed. 'It's true. There's no one like Max.'

They took their paper cups and headed back to the office. The glass door at the main entrance dazzled them with sunlight. Chloe stopped. 'You see,' she said, 'I was just wondering why you – I mean, why you shagged that other bloke when you knew that Max was – you know . . .'

Stella looked at her. 'Max is over, that's why. And good riddance. And Tom, well, I met him at that bar, and he's nice, and he made me feel desirable, and no, he wasn't like Max, but you can't have everything, can you?'

'Can't you?' Chloe pushed at the heavy door, and they waited in the foyer for the lift.

'There you go again. Aquarius-Pisces cusp,' Stella said, as the lift door closed behind them.

Later their office fell silent from the endless clicking of keyboards, as Chloe went to get them some tea from the machine. When she came back, Helen from the next office was sitting on her desk, reading out a quiz from a magazine.

'OK, girls, listen –' Helen crossed long tanned legs under her short pale yellow skirt. ' "He forgets your birthday. Do you a) Scream and shout –" '

'Certainly do,' Stella said.

' "b) Determine not to remember his in future –" '

'Yup,' Stella said.

' "c) Remind him quietly but say it doesn't matter –" '

'Absolutely not.'

Chloe put three paper cups of tea carefully on the desk. 'Andrew forgot my birthday last month.'

Both women looked at her. 'And what did you do?' they asked.

'Nothing.'

Helen folded up her magazine.

'Max always remembered my birthday,' Stella said.

'So why did you dump him?' Helen picked up her cup of tea.

'You know why. As I said at the time, good riddance.'

Helen sauntered out of the office. Chloe put on her headphones and started to type. She was aware that Stella was asking her something.

'What did you say?'

'I said, did he really forget your birthday?'

'He didn't mean to. He was busy at work. He was really sorry.'

'It's not good enough,' Stella said, returning to her computer.

'He remembered the next day. He bought me that scarf, you know, that lovely gold velvet one, dead expensive it was.'

Helen reappeared suddenly. 'Someone just phoned for you –' She went over to Stella's desk with a scrap of paper. 'It came through to me.' She handed Stella the note, and went back to the door. 'Who is Tom anyway?' she said, before disappearing out into the corridor.

'Tom?' Chloe stopped typing.

'Tom?' Stella was staring at the scrap of paper. 'He phoned. Oh God.'

'Are you going to phone him back?'

'But – but he was –'

'Black and white diagonal lines –'

'Black and white diagonal lines. Exactly. And now he's phoned me up. They always surprise you, don't they?'

Chloe walked to the bus stop in the pink haze of an urban sunset. She wondered if Andrew would be home first. She wondered what to cook for supper. She saw the bus approaching and wondered whether to stop off at the supermarket. She wondered whether Stella would ring Tom. She wondered when her period would come. As she got on the bus, she wondered whether she could live with magnolia and apple white.

Stella walked in next morning, thumped her bag down on her desk and went to get a coffee. When she came back, Chloe was still typing. Stella sat at her desk. She lifted the cover off her computer and took a sip of coffee. Chloe didn't look up.

'Since you ask –' Stella said.

Chloe sighed and stopped typing. 'Yes?'

'I phoned him.'

'And?'

'I'm seeing him. Tonight.'

'Tom?'

'Yes.'

'Oh. Good.' Chloe started to type again.

Stella threw her a look, then opened the file on her

desk. 'Did you have a nice evening?'

'It was OK,' Chloe said, without looking up.

'Period come?'

'No.' Chloe was still typing.

Stella gave her another look, then started to type too.

At eleven, Helen breezed in. 'OK, girls, how about this one.' She flicked through the pages of her magazine, then sat on Chloe's desk. ' "You suspect that he's seeing someone else. Do you a) Ask him outright b) Start flirting with one of his friends to make him jealous c) Go through all his pockets for clues –" '

'All of the above,' Stella said. 'Speaking from experience.'

'Sorry I spoke,' Helen said, folding up her magazine again. She was wearing a short green linen skirt and matching strappy sandals. 'And what's wrong with Chlo?'

'Nothing,' Chloe said, taking some papers out of a file on her desk.

'It was like that with Max,' Stella said. 'Suspecting him the whole time. Looking for clues. Didn't have to look far, mind you.'

'That's why you dumped him?' Helen checked her pink-frosted nails.

Stella nodded.

'I thought you said he was a sexy, wonderful, attentive lover?'

'He was,' Stella said. 'It's just he was a sexy, wonderful attentive lover to about ninety-three other women too.'

'Better off without him, then.'

'Mmmm.' Stella took an envelope from her desk and stuck a label on it.

Helen picked up her magazine. 'Oh well, girls, back to work.'

At lunchtime, the keyboards fell silent. Stella looked up from hers. 'Sandwich?'

'OK.'

They sat in the park, although the sky had clouded over and there was a sharp breeze.

'So what happened?'

'What?'

'You and Andrew? You've hardly spoken all morning.'

'Nothing happened.'

'So yesterday evening –'

'I just stripped some wallpaper, washed down the walls, sanded the woodwork, did a bit of undercoat . . .'

'All evening?'

'I like it. I find it soothing.'

Stella unwrapped her sandwich. 'Mozzarella and sun-dried tomato on walnut bread,' she said.

'Andrew's away on Thursday night.'

'Oh.'

'I said I'd do the painting then.'

'What colour?'

'We haven't talked about it.'

'You'd better decide before he goes away.'

'I know.'

Stella finished a mouthful of sandwich. 'Can't you compromise?'

'Between magnolia and citrus yellow? There's not much room for compromise, is there?'

'S'pose not.'

* * *

Chloe was alone in the flat. Andrew had phoned to say he was working late – 'We've got a team meeting, it'll take ages, sorry, love –'

She ran some sandpaper along the skirting board, enjoying the scent of the bare wood. She worked her way round the room, cleaning, scrubbing, making all the surfaces ready for painting. She stood up, barefoot on the bare floorboards, in baggy overalls and a large old white shirt that had once been Andrew's. She ran her fingers over the smooth plaster of the walls, looking out of the window at the rooftops spread out before her, other houses, other homes, other windows making bright squares against the night sky.

She went to a corner of the room and picked up a tester pot of paint. She opened it and smeared some of the paint on to the wall. There was a knock at her door.

'Kid, it's Chez,' she heard, through the door. 'Are you at home to visitors?' She opened the door, and there he was, tall and broad and enfolding her in a hug which smelt of expensive cotton shirt and Calvin Klein. He went out on to the landing and reappeared with a large cardboard box. 'Present for you. Why, sweetie, you've been painting. What's this one?'

'It's called Orange Blush.'

'Wild, kid. And this?'

'Sundance.'

'The names they give these things. And that turquoise?'

'Oh, Topaz or something. I thought I'd do some matching stencil stuff in it, but I was trying it out on the walls.'

'It's great. With the orange.'

'That's what I thought.'

'And dear old Andrew –'

Chloe was shaking her head.

'It's always like that. When I lived with Gavin, the rows we had. I wanted everything white with natural tones – it was the eighties, remember, sweetie – and he wanted black and purple, can you imagine, with mirrors. I really don't know what I saw in him.'

Chloe was laughing. She went into the kitchen and came back with a bottle of wine and two glasses. 'And what's my present?'

'Paint,' Chez said. 'I've been helping a friend, a new bistro thing he's opening, we did it up for him. The café's called Montezuma –'

'No –'

'Believe me. It'll do great, it's the *Zeitgeist*, kid. Salsa music, latin feel, wild décor. Fusion menu, kind of peasant Spanish combined with Caribbean. Can't lose. Anyway, there was loads of paint left over, I thought you could use it when your business takes off.'

'Whenever that is.'

He looked at her. 'Kid –'

'It's OK, really.' Her eyes welled with tears.

'Listen, kid, if Andrew doesn't see it your way –'

'It's not that –'

'Maybe your expectations are just too high.'

'He loves me.'

Chez sighed. 'Love, babe.' He shook his head.

'And I want to live with him. Really.'

'For ever?'

'What's ever?'

Chez smiled. 'Let me help you with these tester thingies.'

Later they heard Andrew's key in the door. 'Chloe? Oh, hi, Chez.'

'Have some wine,' Chez said. 'I'll get you a glass.'

Andrew went over to Chloe and kissed her. 'How's things?'

'OK.'

'You've been trying out colours?'

'Um, yes. Chez helped.'

'Sundance, Daybreak, Firework, Orange Blush –' Chez handed him a glass of wine. 'This one's Lime Crush – and what was this – I liked this one –'

'Topaz Dream.' Chloe giggled.

'Mmmm. Don't you just love it?'

Andrew wandered around the empty room, his wine glass in one hand. 'And what was this?'

'Oh, that.' Chez raised his eyes to the ceiling in disapproval.

'Magnolia,' Chloe said.

'You two have got to work this out, don't you think?' Chez sat down on the floor.

Andrew smiled. 'We'll be OK,' he said.

Chloe got off the bus near her office. It was a bright spring day. The sun flashed against the glass of the city. As she went through the door of her building, she thought about the colour of spring sunshine, the silvery grey of the morning streets, the dark suits of the hurrying commuters.

Stella was already there. Chloe got two coffees from the machine, then went and sat at her desk. Stella didn't look up.

Chloe switched on her computer. 'Well?'

'Well what?' Stella clicked her mouse furiously.

'You saw him?'

'Who?'

'Tom.'

'Yeah.'

'And?'

Stella looked up. 'It was OK.'

'More than OK?'

'Yes. It was nice.'

There was a clatter of heels at their door, and Helen came in. 'OK, girls, how about this one?' She was wearing a pastel blue suit in light wool, and she perched on the edge of Stella's desk. ' "He asks you to do something in bed that you're not happy about. Do you a) Tell him to get stuffed b) –" Oh dear. Look at you both. Wrong moment, maybe?'

'Stella saw Tom last night,' Chloe said.

'And?'

'Oh, you know.' Stella shrugged, tried to smile.

'Is he nice? What's he like? What does he do?'

'He's nice. Dresses well. Works in computers.'

'Good-looking?'

'Yeah.' She shrugged again. 'OK, you know.'

'Will you see him again?'

'Dunno. Yeah. S'pose so. He said he'd phone today.'

'Great. Let's hope this one's faithful, eh?'

Stella was blinking back tears. 'Yes,' she said.

'Not like Max,' Helen said.

'No,' Stella said, tears welling in her eyes. 'Not like Max at all.'

* * *

Later Chloe said, 'What are you going to do?'

'I don't know.'

'What is it about Max?'

Stella looked up from her computer. 'You remember when I met him? We were at that party, you remember, I didn't want to go, you'd dragged me there, you said it would cheer me up.'

'Yes.'

'And I walked in, and I knew no one, and it was on that new estate behind Tesco's . . . And I was just thinking of leaving, and then he arrived. Standing in the doorway, oh God, I'll never forget it. All six foot three of him, wearing that shirt, and those jeans, and the shirt was undone, just at the neck, but it was enough . . . and he looked at me, and it was like . . .' She closed her eyes, breathing fast. 'Oh God, Chloe, there's just no one like him. Sometimes I think, maybe he'll walk back into my life and he'll tell me things are going to be different, he'll tell me I'm the only one he wants –'

'You wouldn't believe him, though, would you? Men like that don't change.'

Stella sighed. 'No. I wouldn't believe him. But – I've been thinking about it, Chloe – maybe sometimes you just have to take a chance.'

'I thought you Virgos were practical –'

'Sometimes I imagine him just walking in here and just, you know, opening his arms, and smiling at me with that smile, that kind of glowing, lighting-up-the-world smile . . .'

'I thought it was only us Aquarius-Pisces cusps who lived on dreams –'

Stella sighed.

They sat, staring at their screens. After a moment Chloe said, 'So, Tom?'

Stella looked up. 'There's no point me going to bed with someone to get over Max if all it does is make me realise how much I want Max. Is there?'

'S'pose not.' Chloe pressed her Return key a few times. Stella got up, took a file out of a drawer, sat down again. 'And how was yesterday evening?'

Chloe smiled. 'Chez came round, we've covered the walls in colour, all the tester pots I had, it was fun . . .'

'And Andrew?'

'He's OK.' Chloe opened her desk drawer, closed it again. 'My period still hasn't come,' she said.

'Your period's late?' Andrew placed two plates of pasta on the kitchen table, then sat down opposite her.

'Yup.'

'How late?'

'Only a day or two.'

'Is that – I mean, what does that –'

'What does it mean? Nothing, I hope.'

'Good.'

Chloe looked at him. Why good? she wanted to say. Why's it good if it means nothing? Why do you want it to mean nothing? You're sleeping with me, after all. She stared at him, saying nothing.

'Perhaps you should go back on the pill,' Andrew said.

'But I hated it.'

'I know.' He grated some more parmesan on to his linguine.

Go on, say it, Chloe was thinking. A baby. Ask me, go on.

Does that mean we're going to have a baby? Do we want a baby? Do I want a baby? We could at least discuss it. Go on, she willed him, staring at him. Say it.

'You're very quiet,' he said. He looked up, and smiled at her. 'You look nice in that top.'

'I'm going to do the painting,' Chloe said. 'While you're away.'

'Oh. OK. What colours have we agreed on?'

'We haven't.'

'No. I'll miss you,' Andrew said.

'It's only one night.'

'Chloe –' Andrew got up from the table. 'Don't do anything too – too mad, will you? We've both got to live with it.'

'That's just the problem.' She flashed him a glance, sharp with anger, but he was over by the sink, washing some grapes.

'So, apple white it is, is it?' Stella seemed more cheerful.

'Dunno. Yes. S'pose so. We've both got to live with it. He said.'

'Period?'

'No sign.'

'Morning sickness?'

'Don't.'

Stella put a cup of coffee down on her desk for her.

Chloe sipped the coffee. 'Did Tom phone?'

'Yeah. I said maybe next week. What's the point, though? I know what I want, and it's not him.'

'And I know what I want, and it's not apple white.'

'Do you love him, though?'

Chloe was silent. 'The thing is, I can't imagine life without him,' she said at last.

Chloe sat on the bare floorboards, alone. The windows were open, and she listened to the sounds of the evening, the traffic rumble, occasional passing footsteps down in the street, music floating across the night air as windows were opened and closed again. She looked at her tins of paint, the citrus yellow, orange, turquoise. And then there were the new ones that Chez had left for her, yet to be explored.

What if I'm pregnant? she thought.

There goes my business, she thought. There goes my dream. That's why they're fragile, dreams, she thought, standing up and opening one of Chez's tins of paint. Because life doesn't make room for them. She stared into the tin. It was terracotta, a deep blood red. So, a baby, then. And magnolia and apple white. She opened another tin. It was black. Thick, inky, sticky black. We've got to live with it, Andrew had said. Don't do anything too mad.

She painted the wood areas first, watching the fine pine grain absorb the colour, watching it begin to glow with life, with dark, deep tones, taking up the light from the bare bulb in the centre of the room as the night wore on. Then another tin, splashed across the walls, fierce and cavernous, echoing the darkness of the night outside. And then the gold, dense lines drawn at angles across the room, changing the square corners into pyramids. She watched the first coats dry. It needs more, she thought. More of something. The *Zeitgeist*, Chez had said. Outside, the edges of the sky lightened into grey. Chloe stared at the bare lightbulb, and thought about a lampshade. She remembered the turquoise shade with lemons. No, she thought. Something else was required.

Later she heard a knock at her door. 'I know it's early,' Chez's voice said through the door. She let him in. 'You've been up all night,' he said. 'Forgive my nosiness. So have I.' He looked at her. 'And you've been crying,' he said.

The dawn light flooded the room.

'Wow,' Chez said.

'Andrew will leave me,' Chloe said.

'Thank God it's Friday,' Helen said, sitting on Stella's desk, crossing one foot over the other in their pink mule sandals. 'Half an hour to go, then freedom. Plans for the weekend?'

Stella was assembling a series of documents, clipping them together. Chloe was staring at her word processor.

Helen sighed. 'Remember when life was fun?' She got down from the desk. 'Tom phoned again?'

Stella looked at her. 'All the time.'

'It's so tiresome.' Helen flicked some dust from her short pink skirt. 'They always want what they can't have. The best way to get rid of him is to fall madly in love with him.'

When she'd gone, Stella looked at Chloe. 'When was he due back?'

'Lunchtime.'

'Maybe he went straight to the office.'

'No. He'd have dumped his bag first. He's been home. I know he has.'

'Maybe he'll forgive you.'

'Stella, you haven't seen it. Even Chez was shocked.'

'Maybe he's waiting till you get home.'

'No. He'll have gone. I know him. I know Andrew.' The

words seemed to hang in the air. I know him, she thought. And now I've ruined it.

'Dreams, you see,' Stella said suddenly. 'No point chasing them.'

Chloe nodded. Outside they could hear a commotion, shouting, footsteps striding along the corridor, a voice saying, 'I know she's in here –' and then their door flew open. Stella stared in astonishment. 'Max –'

He opened his arms, and smiled at her with a kind of glowing, lighting-up-the-world smile.

'Thing is, I've been thinking about it,' he said, as she got up from her desk. 'Maybe sometimes you've just got to take a chance.'

Stella grabbed her bag and her coat. She turned to Chloe, smiled, shrugged, then fell into Max's arms and allowed him to lead her away.

Chloe sat, staring after them. She put the cover on her computer, picked up her jacket, and went home.

Andrew's bag stood in the hallway like a reproach. There was no other sign of him. Chloe went into the room. The paint had dried, and she ran her hands over it, feeling the layers of colour, the smooth wood around the window frames.

Chez knocked at the door, and she let him in. He had a friend with him. The friend was dressed all in black. Chez hugged her. 'He meant it, then?'

'He's gone,' Chloe said, biting back tears.

'This is fantastic,' Chez's friend said.

'Chloe, meet Charles.'

Charles offered his hand in a formal way, and she shook it. 'This is amazing,' he was saying, staring around the room.

'So black, and red. So . . . primeval. Aztec, even, kind of sacrificial . . . raw, gutsy . . .' Charles was walking around. 'And the lampshade, where did you get that?'

Chloe looked up at the strips of gold velvet.

'So immediate,' Charles was saying, reaching up and touching it. 'The rough edges, like someone just ripped it up and twisted it round that wire . . . Such feeling. I'll take the whole lot.'

'Um –' Chez took Chloe's hand. 'Charles is opening a chain of shops, men's fashion . . . He needs a look for them.'

'I've found a look for them,' Charles said. 'I've found The Look for them. Let's go out and drink champagne.'

Chez looked at Chloe. She shook her head.

'Chloe's a bit low just now,' he said to Charles.

Charles shook her hand again. 'When can you start?'

'Um –' Chloe looked at Chez.

'Have you got other commitments?' Charles asked her.

'Um, no. No,' she said. 'None at all. I can start as soon as you like,' she said.

After they'd gone, she sat alone in the room again. She stared at the black and gold, the terracotta draped in curves across the angles of the room, the lampshade with its ripped velvet.

It is beautiful, she thought.

And my period came.

No baby after all.

Just some work, instead. Some proper work.

She heard Andrew's key in the door. He walked into the room, and she looked up at him. They stayed like that for some moments. Then he knelt on the floor next to her and reached out his hand, and his fingertips brushed her face.

Daughter of the writer Emanuel Litvinoff and Cherry Marshall, Vida Adamoli was born in Nottingham, brought up in London, and has lived most of her adult life in Rome, catering to the needs of an Italian husband and two sons. In Italy she worked as a film translator and editor, notably with Bertolucci, but mostly dedicated herself to the art of shopping, shouting, cooking *al dente* pasta and not minding her own business. She's brought these skills back to London and the Elephant and Castle, where she now lives and writes full time. Her latest novel *Housework*, is published by Review in spring 1999.

Fiorella la Bella

Vida Adamoli

Nineteen sixty-eight was the last year the village perched high on a jutting headland between Rome and Naples belonged to itself. Less beautiful places along the coastline had been colonised, but because of its relative inaccessibility San Rocco was overlooked. This castellation of whitewashed buildings with small, recessed windows and doors, shutters painted blue or light green, had been clinging to its rocky promontory for centuries. Some of the streets were steep staircases, others narrow winding corridors. They formed a honeycombed maze leading through low arches and tunnelled walks to the blind, hidden corners where marauding Turkish pirates once had boiling oil poured on their heads. All the walls were feet thick, the plaster moulded with no sharp corners. Buildings curved and flowed into each other, making everything an essential part of the structural whole. It was a world of its own, a life folded in on itself, a clenched stone fist.

Then an up-and-coming director used the village as a location for part of a movie he was shooting. At the same time the holiday section of a national newspaper featured it as an unspoiled gem. The heraldic reverberations were immediately picked up by those who wanted to avoid the usual Mediterranean tourist traps. Fringe actors, would-be writers, eccentrics and the alternative, adventurous young came flocking. Those with money rented apartments festooned with purple bougainvillaea and balconies overlooking a glittering expanse of pellucid sea. The less affluent settled for dark and airless grottos (previously accommodating mules or vats of wine and oil) that dripped condensation and turned bed linen and clothes green with creeping mould. In other words, San Rocco had been discovered. Its charmed isolation was violated forever.

Up until then the beach had been a place of work, not recreation. It was where fishermen kept their boats and mended their nets, where the catch was brought in, where linen was washed in the icy eddies of a freshwater stream and spread on rocks to dry. Villagers also used it as a cure for certain ailments. Signora Piera, for example, buried her fat, varicosed legs in the hot sand for half an hour or so each day; others did the same for rheumatism. But with the influx of outsiders things changed. Suddenly there were gaudy beach umbrellas, transistor radios and half-naked bodies offered with sacrificial ecstasy to the scorching sun. Warnings to be careful of overexposure were rarely heeded. As Kristina – a blonde Valkyrie who found her way to San Rocco from the Swedish island of Gotland – said, 'I'm not here to worry about burning, for goodness' sake! The sun is my awakener. I'm a flower blooming after a long Arctic night.'

There were two rival establishments renting out deckchairs and umbrellas, selling beers, soft drinks and ice creams and preparing food. They were both run by families who had lived for poverty-stricken decades on squatted land bordering the beach. Each year the original wooden shacks expanded further as toilets, kitchens, extra storage space and so on were tacked on. The more popular of these was Leone's. This was because he was young, welcoming and in the early years gave credit (also his mother's mussel soup made with white wine, garlic and parsley was pure ambrosia). Leone was the eldest of nine siblings, the others being Fiorella, Leonardo, Pietro, Giovanni, Matteo, Marco, Gino and Patrizia. They were tall, well-built and, for the most part, handsome. This was especially true of Leonardo, who looked like a movie star, with lustrous eyes, a perfect nose, full, sulky lips and a crown of burnished copper-coloured curls.

By contrast their father was small, bent, toothless and prematurely aged – as, indeed, was his wife. At first it seemed a genetic miracle they had managed to produce such well-favoured offspring. But in fact, their physical aspect was simply a mirror of the poverty and struggle that had been theirs until summer visitors arrived to change their fortunes. Even with money flowing in, however – and more of it with each passing year – they found it hard to alter their ways. The mother railed against the extravagance of changing her wood-burning stove for a modern gas cooker. And the father continued rising each day at dawn to put in long hours on his two acres of land.

This heartless and stony patch was situated between the beach and the coast road. To irrigate it water was hand-pumped from deep wells and distributed by a system of hosepipes that ran along the narrow paths and bamboo windbreaks that crisscrossed the terrain. The main crop was tomatoes, but spinach, onions, garlic, lettuce, courgettes and broccoli were grown, too. There was also a small olive grove, lemon and apricot trees, a few goats and a dozen or so scrawny hens. It was Leone's father's proud boast that until the youngest, Patrizia, was born the family had never eaten anything he had not caught, grown or bartered for. During the holiday season the only one who could be spared to help him was Pietro. Giovanni ran the kiosk, Marco and Matteo waited tables, Leonardo was in charge of the umbrellas and Fiorella worked in the kitchen with her mother. Gino, eight and an aspiring drummer, was allowed to spend much of the day bashing away on his oil-can drum kit in the middle of the tomato patch. Patrizia, six, also was left to play. Leone, all smiles, charm and efficiency, dealt with complaints and kept everything together.

Fiorella, the second eldest, was tall like her brothers, with a long face accentuated by the headscarf she tied peasant-fashion over her hair. Whereas they were handsome, however, she was plain, heavy-limbed and moved as though weighed down by perpetual lethargy. Of all the family she was the one most fascinated by the summer *habitués* whose spending had transformed their lives – especially the foreigners, with their guitars, gypsy-style clothes and loud, exuberant kids. The one she particularly noticed was an American called Jasper. He had been in several Andy Warhol movies and because of that behaved as though he was a star. What Jasper liked most in life was to dazzle, and his favourite way of dazzling was the seduction of young girls. In San Rocco his quarry were the overexcited arrivals from northern Europe, for whom he strutted his sexy, supple body and leonine mane of sun-streaked hair. He set them up and waited for them to fall. And fall they did, dropping their knickers with such alacrity the air vibrated with the eager twanging of snapping elastic. They would learn later that the charming surface (he was also a great storyteller and clown) hid the heart of a narcissistic and ruthless Pan.

In 1973 Jasper became one of a handful of foreigners who now lived in the village all year round. Occasionally he disappeared to Berlin to work in some underground movie or other, but most of the time he just hung out. The older villagers regarded him with disapproval, although some of that was dissipated when he successfully climbed the greased pole during the May *festa* to claim the smoked ham tied to the top. His clique of supporters were waiting to grab him as he slithered to the ground. They hoisted him on strong shoulders and carried him off in whooping triumph. Children showered him with paper streamers, teenage girls gave him shy, giggling smiles, men stopped to pat him on the back and say, 'Bravo, *americano!*' Fiorella was there with her brothers, wearing her best flower-sprigged dress. She, too, smiled, waved and shouted, 'Bravo!' Jasper returned the wave from his lofty perch, then impulsively reached for her hand and kissed it. The brush of his lips on her bare skin sent an electrical charge shooting up her arm. Her cheeks flushed and her heart missed the proverbial beat. And at that moment her fascinated admiration blossomed into a full-blown crush.

A few years earlier a jukebox had been installed on the long, bamboo-roofed veranda adjacent to the drinks kiosk. That year it was playing Stevie Wonder's 'You are the Sunshine of My Life', Lou Reed's 'Take a Walk on the Wild

Side', the Stones' 'Angie' and Donny Osmond's 'Young Love'. This music – not the Italian hits – drew Fiorella like a magnet. Every day, when the lunchtime rush was over and the clearing up done, she slipped off her apron and ran to put them on. And it was then – swinging her hips and singing along with words that charmed and excited her but which she couldn't understand – that she felt the fizzy elation of being eighteen with everything still in front of her. At these moments she could believe that life wouldn't always be an endless succession of boring chores. That another world existed where girls were as free as boys and could do what they wanted. Jasper, who spent much of his time on the veranda drinking beer and playing cards, had no idea what was in her head as she did her solo bop. He just knew she was enjoying herself. 'Go for it, girl,' he would say, encouragingly. 'Give it everything you've got.'

From the looks Fiorella was giving him the day after his triumph Jasper knew he'd scored another hit. Bedding her was out of the question (local girls still regarded virginity as their most precious asset), but it amused him to flirt. So he started addressing her theatrically as Fiorella la Bella, blowing kisses when the father's back was turned, bringing her the occasional posy of wild flowers and waltzing her up and down the veranda to the strains of 'Young Love'. This tongue-in-cheek attention transformed her. The lethargic heaviness evaporated and her plain features lit by happiness were almost pretty. Meanwhile, Fiorella was desperate for someone to confide in. She chose Zoe, the only foreign regular in whose company she felt relaxed. Standing together at the water's edge, watching Zoe's two young boys splash and scream, she gave blushing voice to all her high romantic feelings. She also had a million questions to ask. How old was Jasper, for example (twenty-nine), what sort of girls did he like (Zoe was tactfully vague there), did Zoe think he wanted to live in San Rocco forever? On the rare occasions when Jasper wasn't mentioned, Fiorella talked about her dreams for a different sort of life. 'I want to live in a big city,' she told Zoe. 'I want to be surrounded by cars and noise and bright lights. And I'll spend every last penny I earn going round the shops!'

Jasper's courtship of Fiorella lasted a little over two weeks, then he departed for Germany (rumour had it to appear in a porno movie). For a while Fiorella was so miserable she didn't even play her jukebox songs. Then she made friends with a family from Turin, which revived her spirits somewhat. She chatted with the wife, played with the kids and gave them all special attention on the occasions she waited at table. Before leaving they presented her with a ceramic brooch and asked if she wanted to take over from their au pair, who would soon be leaving. As well as a small salary – which seemed big to Fiorella as, unlike her brothers, she received no pocket money – she would have her own room with TV and en suite bathroom. On top of which, Turin was a Big City!

Her determination to accept this wonderful offer caused a family crisis of mega proportions. There were daily rows with her mother, often during the lunchtime rush, and screaming confrontations with her brothers, too. Her father expressed his wrath less vocally. On his return from work he sat in his chair on the veranda, silent, unapproachable and grim. The dark shadow cast by this bleak monument to parental fury had a cowing effect on all his strapping sons.

Only little Patrizia seemed unconcerned. 'You know what,' she said chattily to Zoe one day. 'Papa says if Fiorella goes to Turin he'll never take her back. Not even if she comes crawling on hands and knees.'

Fiorella, however, was clearly undeterred by this threat, because she left before the summer was out and stayed away for five years. People tactfully refrained from asking how she was faring, or even mentioning her name. After a while it became a question of out of sight, out of mind, and most of the regulars forgot she had ever existed. Then in 1978 she reappeared. She was much slimmer, bony almost, and her hair was dyed red and cropped as short as a boy's. The real surprise, however, was not her radically altered appearance. It was the moon-faced toddler with chocolate-brown eyes who clung to her thighs and called her 'Mamma'.

The official word was that the child was the fruit of Fiorella's failed marriage to a no-good Torinese. But the truth – eloquently expressed by the bitter and unforgiving back turned on her – was that little Andrea was a bastard whose existence trumpeted the shame and dishonour now staining the family name. For this Fiorella had become a pariah. She was given no work (Pietro's wife and sister-in-law had replaced her in the kitchen), nobody talked to her and she even had to take her meals alone. She bore this savage ostracism with a penitent's stoicism. Her days were spent reading magazines, chain-smoking contraband Marlboros and making listless sand castles for her small son. Occasionally she listened to the Bee Gees on the jukebox, 'Stayin' Alive' and 'Night Fever', or Timmy Thomas's 'Why Can't We Live Together', but she no longer shook her hips or sang along. Zoe, who still spent her summers in San Rocco, was not the only one who attempted to be friendly and show they were on her side. But Fiorella did not respond. There was an aura of hurt and distrust now that surrounded her like a wall.

Cora was the person who tried hardest to be friendly. As an unwed mum-to-be she considered herself Fiorella's natural ally. In reality, of course, they had nothing in common. Cora, a sexy starlet from Holland, had been impregnated by a married film director of bedroom comedies. Not only was she unfazed by the scandal their liaison had caused, she welcomed it. For she was the first to recognise that attention from the paparazzi had done more for her professional visibility than any of her so-called acting roles. This attitude was reflected in her defiant refusal to shroud her belly in maternity beach wear. Instead she let it balloon triumphantly between bikini bra and bottom like a golden-brown seedpod straining to burst.

It did not take the paparazzi long to track Cora to the village. And when they did they used a telescopic lens to snap her canoodling with her squat, balding lover on Leone's veranda. The resulting photographs were published in the largest-circulating gossip magazine under the heading: 'While Cora and Fabrizio Await the Birth of Their Love Child, the Betrayed Mother of His Five Children Weeps Alone.' The main picture showed Fabrizio leaning over a table to give Cora a lingering kiss. In the background, clearly recognisable as they stared at the couple with pointed interest, were Leone and his father.

Within hours of the magazine's arrival at the newsagent, everyone knew of Cora and Fabrizio's wickedness. But even infamous celebrity has a powerful magic, and for a while the villagers were sufficiently dazzled to suspend disapproval. More dazzled than anyone, however, were Leone and his family. Not only was their veranda and section of beach featured in a national magazine, but the head of the family and his firstborn son had also been anointed with instant fame. A framed copy – screaming title and all! – was given proud place above the till on the kiosk wall. Cora was deferentially fêted and fussed over while Fiorella looked bleakly on. The irony was cruel.

Cora left to prepare for her Big Event just before the storms that mark the passage from August to September. These meteorological extravaganzas are invariably preceded by several days of mounting electro-magnetic tension. During this time the air compacts, heat densifies and tempers detonate along a fractious edge. Hot, gusty winds whip up high, foam-crested waves, enticing kids and able-bodied adults alike to body-surf until salt water streams from every gasping orifice and brains throb in dizzy rhythm with the crashing breakers. The storms themselves are of a primordial ferocity. The huge basin of glowering sky echoes to the deafening boom and crack of thunder. Wild forks of jagged lightning slash through the shuddering stratosphere to unite heaven and earth. The surface of the sea turns a heaving, churning, seething black, below which the frenzied suck and pull of currents reworks the gently rippled bed into a landscape of steep cliffs and swirling vortexes. Violent squalls give birth to funnel-shaped waterspouts which spin across the mist-shrouded horizon like ghostly imprints of a whirling dervish's ecstatic dance. And when the rain finally comes it falls in blind, heavy sheets that turn the sand into gullied mud banks and make fast-flowing rivers of the village streets.

Zoe was caught on the beach later that summer in just such a storm. Leone had sensibly closed shop so she ended up sheltering under a jutting edge of corrugated roofing at the back of the kitchen. Pressed up against the wall, listening awestruck to the magnificent roar, it sounded as though the universe had sprung one gigantic leak. After ten minutes or so a figure appeared round the corner and dived for shelter next to her. It was Fiorella. She was soaked to the skin and her hair, plastered around her face, looked like a fluted red bathing cap. '*Ciao*,' she said, fishing a wet and crumpled packet of Marlboro from the back pocket of her cut-off denims. 'Want one?' They smoked in silence while the deluge continued to rage around them. When it was over they walked to the top of the steps that led from the veranda to the beach. 'What happened to that *americano* friend of yours?' Fiorella asked. 'The one who climbed the greasy pole and got the ham?'

'Jasper?'

'That's right, Jasper,' she laughed. 'Funny. I'd forgotten his name.'

It was only halfway through telling her that he'd died of a heroin overdose that Zoe remembered Fiorella's big crush. But Fiorella didn't seem upset. She just nodded, lighting a fresh cigarette from the stub of the one she was smoking. 'I lived with a musician who died of a heroin overdose,' she said in a neutral tone. 'He shot up the night before we were due to fly to New York. "It's the city of all cities," was the last thing he said to me. "You can shop till you drop there." In the morning he was lying stiff and cold beside me.'

'God, that's dreadful!' Zoe exclaimed.

Fiorella shrugged. 'Who's to say he isn't better off? After all, life's a shit – no?'

While Zoe was trying to think of a suitable response a child started crying. It was a thin, insistent wail coming from the family's sleeping quarters out among fruit trees at the back. As she monitored the sound Fiorella's expression softened, then she smiled contentedly. 'Andrea's teething, otherwise he's as good as gold,' she explained, flicking her smouldering butt into the air. It traced a brief, glowing arc before plummeting to earth. 'We'll be moving to Rome this winter,' she continued. 'If I can get a job, that is. But even if we stay here a while longer, it doesn't really matter. I'm never bored now, you see. That baby's far and away the best thing that's ever happened to me.'

Then she turned and walked quickly away. The sound was lassoing her heart and reining her in.

Carole Matthews was born in Merseyside and worked as a secretary before retraining as a beauty therapist. Since then she has worked as a television presenter, has written for a wide range of magazines and ran her own practice specialising in aromatherapy. She now lives in Leighton Buzzard with her neglected husband and a seriously spoilt cat. Her novels *Let's Meet on Platform 8* and *A Whiff of Scandal* are published by Headline.

Cold Turkey

Carole Matthews

I can't stand turkey. OK, so it's a reasonably priced white meat, versatile, low in fat and, supposedly, good for the heart. I have no quibble with that. Particularly. It's just all the other crap that goes with it. The cranberry sauce, the Brussels sprouts, the chipolata sausages wrapped in streaky bacon, the cheap crackers, the gaudy party hats, the waiting by the phone alone on Christmas Day in the vain hope that your married lover might be able to sneak away from the bosom of his family for a rushed two-second call. That's what I really can't stand.

I'm thirty years old, intelligent (questionable given current situation), financially solvent (also questionable after pre-Christmas spending frenzy) and gainfully employed as a human resources manager for a multinational corporation. It's just my own resources I have trouble managing. I have hair that wouldn't look out of place being swished around in a L'Oréal advert, porcelain skin and cheekbones to die for. So why am I staring at a pale, miserable face in a holly-festooned mirror, that looks back at me mournfully like the Ghost of Christmas Past? Because, on the down side, I have legs like Will Carling, a propensity to chain-eat Toffee Crisps in stressful situations, and it is already twelve o'clock and the aforementioned married lover hasn't troubled British Telecom with his custom once.

It was the same last year – that's the stupid thing. And the year before. I could go to my parents. My sister's there this year, having left her husband for the man at the Bradford and Bingley who decided after three weeks that he couldn't live without his children and returned, suitably penitent, to the marital bed. There's a lot of it about.

We all get on well, my family. We don't usually try to kill each other over the Queen's speech, we all like to watch the Christmas edition of *Only Fools and Horses* (even to the point of laughing at the same jokes) and we all marvel at the fact that my mother sticks religiously to the hideous time-honoured tradition of cooking a ham just for Boxing Day (which no one ever eats, of course). So there is no need for me to be this sad old bat, with swollen red eyes and tear-stained cheeks, looking fretfully at the turkey sitting patiently in the roasting pan, which, even though it was the smallest bird that Waitrose could offer, still looks like something that has wandered out of *Jurassic Park*.

I have a pile of peeled potatoes languishing in a pan of salted water. Carrots. Parsnips. The ubiquitous Brussels sprouts. You name it, I've got it. Christmas pudding, brandy sauce (carton of), assorted nuts (and I don't even *like* nuts), dates, Turkish Delight and all the other unnecessary little indulgences essential to make Christmas tick. You see, this year he said that he would come to me. He would try *very hard* to come to me. He would find a reason to nip out at an opportune moment, skipping the traditional family lunch that is being shared with in-laws, out-laws, wife, kids, cats, dogs and, no doubt, the festive hamster that his youngest son has brought home from school for the holidays. Feigning some disaster that had befallen his accountancy firm (fire? flood? famine?) he would rush from his home to my waiting arms and eat Waitrose turkey breast with me. And do you know what the really sad thing is? Even sadder than the raw meat, the uncooked potatoes and the ton of prepared Brussels? The sad thing is, I believed it.

The weather is bleak. Not a white Christmas – a grey, anonymous day marks the birth of the most enduring idol in history and the start of another round of family rows that will take until Easter to sort out. The sky is the colour of a school skirt and it looks seriously cold outside. I need fresh air, though, however bracing. Besides, how much longer can I sit by my flame-effect gas fire and pretend that I don't care that the phone is staring silently and knowingly at the back of my head?

My coat is warm and offers the comfort of weight that the arms of a lover should be providing. I walk my usual route towards Battersea Park, and the tall, solid columns of the defunct power station look down at me questioningly and say, *What on earth are you doing alone on Christmas Day?* With a hollow little shock inside, I acknowledge that I feel as powerless as they now are, and if I gave them an answer, I realise it would sound pathetic. I grip my bag of stale bread too tightly, my mind going over old ground as surely as my feet are. I am bright, I am bubbly, I am a very popular woman. (Have I told you this before? Hard lines. My mother tells me often enough.) So why am I putting myself through this torture? I love him. Is it so difficult to understand?

The seething mass of humanity that give this ragged piece of ground its buzz and colour are conspicuous by their absence. I know where they are. They're all at home snuggled in with their loved ones, stuffing their faces with turkey. I can hear my lonely steps echoing on the crumbling concrete pavements and I pretend I don't care. The boating lake is half-frozen, littered with crisp packets and empty Tango cans, and the ducks sit on the ice looking cheesed off. I rustle my bag of stale bread at them encouragingly and they stare at me with disdain. Perhaps they hate stale bread as much as I hate turkey.

There is a man at the other side of the lake, next to the boats abandoned bottom-up for the winter. He too is clutching a paper bag and making duck-like noises, which convince me, but clearly not the ducks. I walk closer to where he is standing, which surprises me because I'm normally a complete wimp when it comes to strangers.

'Quack, quack,' he shouts enthusiastically at his reluctant dinner guests.

He looks up at me and smiles. It is slightly crooked, but open and friendly. I smile back, a little shyly perhaps.

'Hi,' he says.

'Hi.'

He dips into the bag and pulls out his offering.

'*Pain au chocolat*?' I am impressed.

'Fresh too,' he offers. 'Supposed to be this morning's breakfast.' He rips one into small pieces and throws it on to the water, temptingly close to the ducks.

'You weren't hungry?'

'No,' he says sadly. 'I wasn't.'

The ducks scramble to their feet and waddle across the ice, their feet slipping on the smooth surface which robs them of their natural grace. I guess we all lose our footing when the ground is unfamiliar. Like ducks out of water.

'I wonder if their bottoms get cold,' he queries, 'sitting on the ice like that.'

I shrug. 'I expect so.'

'They look about as miserable as you,' he says kindly.

I laugh, and a little happy bubble pushes inside my pain. I look at the stranger. He is tall, very, with brown hair flecked with auburn which would catch the sun if there was any. His eyes are greeny-brown and they match his coat, which is long and a bit Dr Who-ish. He has the look of a hungover leprechaun, slightly cheeky, with red-rimmed eyes beneath eyebrows that are permanently raised as if in surprise. He would look better if he wore sunglasses.

'You don't look so great yourself,' I tell him.

He smirks. 'I guess not.'

I open my bag and frown into it. 'I don't think they'll eat this now you've indulged them with French delights.'

He takes a couple of steps towards me and I see that he has been crying. 'What is it?'

'Stale Hovis.'

'Staple diet of a duck,' he assures me.

'Staple diet of a human resources manager too,' I assure him.

'We could give them the bread and eat the *pain au chocolat* ourselves,' he suggests. 'We wouldn't want them growing up spoiled and not appreciating the value of money.'

We throw the bread to them together, tearing it into shreds to make it easily digestible. His hands are warm and soft when they accidentally brush against mine and they make me shiver inside. Retiring to the terrace of the shuttered café, we sit on the few plastic chairs that remain at the mercy of the elements, eating the greasy, calorie-laden bread in silence. When we are finished and have licked our fingers, he holds out his hand.

'Stephen Kelly,' he says as I take it and note that it is faintly sticky with sugar.

'Tara Lewis,' I say, returning the compliment.

He turns his body further towards me, but gazes out across the lake.

'So, Tara Lewis, why are you alone feeding the ducks on Christmas Day?' he asks.

'Because,' I pause, swallowing the lump that has come to my throat, 'I have a married lover,' I answer. 'Who promised me he would come, but hasn't.'

The corners of his mouth turn down in sympathy. 'That's terrible,' he says, his soft Irish burr deepening slightly.

'Why are you doing the same thing, Stephen Kelly?'

He looks back at me. 'Because I had a married lover too. Until yesterday.' There is a smile on his lips that doesn't match the sadness in his eyes. 'I didn't quite get the Christmas present I expected.'

'I'm sorry,' I say.

He studies his feet. 'I'm not sure if I am.' Suddenly, his smile warms and he glances up. 'I expect you've a cupboard full of nuts and dates and Turkish Delight. Little things to make your lover's heart glad?'

'Yes,' I giggle, feeling embarrassed.

'So have I,' he admits.

'The *pain au chocolat* were for her?'

He shakes his head. 'I doubted it even as I bought them.'

We watch the ducks settle back on the ice, fluffing their feathers up and lowering themselves gingerly. They might be cold and miserable, but at least they're not turkeys.

'I have pans full of peeled veg, and,' I nod at our feathered friends, 'a distant cousin in a roasting tin.'

'What will you do with it now?'

I grimace, thinking of how much it all cost, how long it had taken me to shop, how silly I feel now. 'Bin it,' I say with venom. 'I hate turkey anyway.'

'It seems a waste.'

'I couldn't eat it. Unless . . .' I laugh at my own stupidity. 'No.' It's the sort of thing people say in afternoon soap operas, the heroine going girly and coquettish, and here I am doing it too.

'What?' Stephen is frowning.

'Well, unless . . .' I will stay here stammering forever if I don't blurt it out. 'Would you like to come back to my place and we'll eat together?'

The permanently surprised eyebrows rise even further.

'Unless, of course, you've made other plans. You will have done, of course. It was silly of me to ask . . .'

'I've no plans,' he says in a rush. Then he breaks into a casual smile. 'Except that Julia Roberts said she might pop round, but I'm sure she wouldn't mind finding me out.'

'Not this once,' I agree.

We stand and shake the untidy flakes of *pain au chocolat* from our coats.

'It's not far,' I say.

'Shall we take a lap of the pond?' he asks. 'Then we can pretend we came here for a purpose.'

'I did come here with a purpose,' I protest.

'What?'

'Running away from my misery.'

'That's not a purpose,' he informs me with a grin. 'That's a reaction.'

'It feels good to be outside,' I say.

'With someone to talk to.'

'Yes.' I smile and watch my own breath hang on the air. 'It's as if the cobwebs are being blow from my fuzzy brain.' He walks closer to me as we complete our stroll round the dirty, desolate pond and it doesn't phase me at all. It's nice, he feels sort of safe and there's no need to watch over our shoulders in case people we know might spy us in places where we shouldn't be. 'The turkey awaits,' I say and we set off home.

The heat in the flat is oppressive after the sharp day outside. The sort of heat that steams up your glasses when you come inside – if you wear them. Stephen doesn't wear glasses, but he unwinds his scarf and abandons his coat with an alacrity that says he is steaming up inside. I throw open the windows, letting the cold air refresh the room so that I won't become fugged again, and take our coats out into the hall.

When I come back, Stephen is walking round the room, casually examining the contents of my life, and I'm surprised that I don't resent the intrusion. He stops at the bookcase. 'James Joyce,' he says, looking impressed.

'It's not mine,' I explain, feeling self-conscious. 'I read the Jeffrey Archers on the tube.' I indicate my pile of well-thumbed paperbacks that have been pushed to one side of the top shelf to make room for my lover's preferred choice of literature.

He wanders to the CD player and flicks through the discs. 'I guess you're the Simply Red and not the Bach.'

'You guessed right.' I couldn't help but smile. 'And the George Michael.'

He picks up the photograph next to the phone. 'Is this the absent lover?'

'Edward,' I confirm.

'Half-man, half-real-life Hollywood hero,' he says, his mouth tightening in what might be disapproval.

I flush. It's a photograph of Edward on holiday in the Caribbean and he has a deep mahogany hue and looks much much older than me. Which he is. Stephen is right, it has a vaguely unreal quality to it, sort of Kilroy Silk meets *Thunderbirds*, or an advertisement for a male hair dye that says *Hate that grey*? *Wash it away!* It used to be my favourite photograph of him. We've never had one taken together. This is all I have. 'He's very sophisticated,' I say, feeling anything but.

'He looks great,' Stephen replies, sounding unconvinced. 'I'm sure he adores you.'

Our eyes meet and we acknowledge the fact that if he did adore me, Edward would be here right now. I look away, and as I do, a slight jolt goes through me. The little red light on the ansaphone is winking seductively at me.

'I have a message,' I say, and make a mental note that my heart is playing *do-wah diddy-diddy dum diddy-do*.

'Shall I make myself scarce?'

'No, no,' I insist, with a careless wave of my hand. 'We're

not the billing and cooing type,' I reply, wondering for the first time why we aren't. 'There's some red wine open in the kitchen and the glasses are in the cupboard above it. Why don't you pour us a glass?'

My fingers hesitate as I switch the machine to Play. What if Edward has called to say he's on his way round? What will he think if he finds Stephen here? It would be unfair of me to ask him to leave now. The machine clicks and whirs into life and eventually throws my mother's voice out into the room.

'I hope you're out having fun,' she says in a warning tone. 'Don't be alone. Come over. Your sister's here. We've got plenty of turkey. It's your mother,' she adds, in case I was ever in any doubt.

Stephen has already switched the cooker on and is mixing Paxo in a bowl by the time I join him in the kitchen. It's clear from the expression on his face that he can tell I've been crying. Only a few measly snivelled tears, but crying nevertheless. His look of complete understanding and sympathy turns the tap on in my heart again.

'Here.' He hands me a glass, holding my fingers over the stem, his own gentle pressure urging me not to clench too tight and shatter it. The wine is luxurious, deep red. Rich, dark, the colour of love. Penfold Bin 28 Shiraz, Edward's favourite. 'Chin up,' Stephen says, tilting my face and running his thumb gently across my skin.

My chin falls and I cry some more. Stephen pulls me to him and wraps his arms round me. They are strong and supportive even though he is still a stranger to me. Someone I have just met in the park. His jumper is soft against my cheek and smells of cinnamon and stale smoke and ink jet printers.

'I've been there,' he says softly. 'I know what you're going through.'

I think his *pain au chocolat* woman must be mad to have left him, but it doesn't seem appropriate to voice it. I wipe my eyes on the kitchen roll he hands me and sniff attractively as I push away from him. 'Let's give this bird some grief,' I say with conviction.

Stephen leans back on the cupboards, crossing one long leg over the other. He puts down his wine glass decisively. The leprechaun's eyes twinkle in my strategically angled spotlights and they gaze directly at me. He bites his lip nervously. 'I have a confession to make.'

'Do I really want to hear this?' I ask cautiously. I have learned to my cost that honesty is not always the best policy.

'I think it's best.' He twists his hands together. 'Before we go any further.'

'OK,' I say nonchalantly and notice that my stomach has clenched.

'I'm a vegetarian,' he says.

We stare at each other open-mouthed.

'I am too,' I confess.

We both smirk like naughty schoolchildren caught stealing Jammy Dodgers until I start to laugh, at first tentatively and then uncontrollably, and it is such a long-forgotten act, this unfettered hilarity, that it makes my cheeks ache with pure pleasure. Stephen joins in, guffawing maniacally, clutching his sides as I do, until the tears stream down our cheeks. Then we cry the laughter away, the serious tears of the emotionally drained, and I cross the kitchen so that he can hold me some more. We stand entwined until the heaving, racking sobs leave our bodies and we are spent and sensible once again.

'What a pair,' he says lightly, to cover our embarrassment.

'Are you hungry?' I say, relying on the British propensity to substitute food for difficult scenes.

'Starving,' he replies.

Stephen says he is sure he has seen Ken Hom do something exciting with Brussels sprouts, so we chop the languishing vegetables into tiny pieces and stir-fry them, flinging in a jar of yellow bean sauce that was lurking at the back of the cupboard for good measure. I throw in a handful of the cashews (also Edward's favourites) with a flourish and a bitter little smile. There is some fried rice in a margarine carton in the freezer and I defrost it in the microwave. The abandoned turkey eyes us dolefully.

We observe some festive formalities by eating at the table, cosily set for two. I light the romantic fragrant candle as an act of pique and we crack our Christmas crackers, groan at the feeble jokes and admire each other's purple paper hats, which are obviously far too big. The relaxed atmosphere only falters slightly as we toast absent friends with the remains of Edward's Shiraz.

The Christmas pudding and brandy sauce sit heavily on top of our stir fry, but we plough our way stoically through it and even squeeze in a Mr Kipling mince pie on top out of politeness. We nurse cups of freshly ground coffee from the cafetière wearing a Santa's suit to keep it warm, and talk of our lives. An hour has gone by before I know it and, as I glance at the clock, I realise I haven't thought of Edward once.

The afternoon melts into evening and I turn on the lamps

to ward off the darkness and light some more candles, giving the room a mellow glow and the scent of Joyeux Noel (whatever that is). Stephen insists on washing up and takes his duties seriously, donning bright pink marigolds and reindeer apron before starting. I lie on the sofa, swirling a hefty measure of brandy in a glass, shoes abandoned, wiggling my toes in my tights and massaging my stomach, which strains in an uncomely fashion against its Lycra bondage. The knot of tension which has been a permanent and unwanted feature throughout my relationship with Edward has gone and, though it may well just have been squished out of the way by sheer weight of food, I feel it is in no small part due to Stephen's company. He whistles tunelessly as he washes up, clanking the dishes together with cheerful abandon. I want him to be finished soon, to come and sit with me, telling me some more of his silly wandering stories, heavily laced with Irish blarney.

My wish comes true after five minutes' wait. He flops down beside me on the sofa, brushing his hair back from his face, plumping the cushions and feeding his hips under my feet with the comfortable ease of a life-long friend.

'Happy?' he says.

And the strange thing is, I say yes.

We listen to *The Christmas Album* (Bing Crosby, Judy Garland, Ella Fitzgerald), a selection of songs destined to make you wish Christmas was how it used to be and not the commercial, fraught mess it is now. Bought, of course, with Edward in mind. Although it's pleasantly soothing, it is his type of music, not mine, and I consider how little we really have in common. The most obvious thing being that only one of us is free. Free? Am I really free, tied into this triangle that stretches eternally before me?

Stephen's head lies back against the sofa, his eyes closed, humming to the music, a pink alcohol-induced flush to his cheeks. My insides glow and I smile at him without meaning to. As if sensing my mood, his hand reaches out and massages my ankles. It isn't a sexual touch, just comforting, but it sends a thrill through my body nevertheless.

The telephone shrills just as Bing tells us he's dreaming of a white Christmas, just like the ones he used to know, and makes us both jump. Stephen's eyes shoot open and we both sit bolt upright as I rearrange my skirt, feeling ridiculously guilty. By the time I have mustered my scattered thoughts, the ansaphone has cut in.

'It's Edward,' a croaking voice says in hushed tones.

A needless introduction, just like my mother's (what a terrifying thought), and I can picture his hand cupping the mouthpiece, his eyes darting fearfully over his shoulder. I perch on the edge of the sofa and listen, for some reason reluctant to speak to the love of my life.

'Look,' he continues, whispering earnestly, 'I can't talk for long. It's going to be impossible to get away.'

Why does this not surprise me?

'I've got a terrible cold, Luke's gone down with tonsillitis, the mother-in-law's pissed and the fucking hamster's escaped and chewed through the Christmas tree lights.'

Stephen laughs at that and I grin back.

'I'm sorry,' Edward says flatly. 'But you know how it is.'

I know only too well. I walk to the wall and pull the telephone plug out of its socket a touch too fiercely, cutting Edward off in his prime. I wonder if he would have remembered to wish me a happy Christmas.

Stephen stands up, uncomfortable now. He puts his half-drunk brandy on the coffee table, careful not to clink the glass. 'Look,' he says, shifting from foot to foot, 'this must be difficult for you.' He shrugs uneasily. 'If you want to be alone, I'll leave. I've enjoyed it. It's been the best Christmas Day I've had for a long time. You've been very kind.'

'I think I've been very selfish,' I say. 'Keeping you here when you probably had a million other things to do.'

'I can wash my hair any old day of the week.' He flicks his fringe back for effect and makes me laugh again.

'You're very silly.'

His eyes look troubled. 'I don't want to overstep the mark.'

'What mark?' I tease.

'*The* mark,' he says, the twinkle returning.

'I want you to stay.' I'm astonished at how brazen I sound when I'm attempting to be sincere. 'You can help me to finish the leftovers.'

'Cold turkey?' he asks.

I nod in what I believe is a hopeful fashion. Cold turkey. 'Something like that,' I answer.

'Cold turkey can sometimes be the best thing,' Stephen advises.

'Even for vegetarians?'

As Stephen pulls me to him, I notice the mistletoe stuck with Blu-Tac above the kitchen door. 'Even for vegetarians,' he says.

On the CD player Judy Garland urges us to have ourselves a merry little Christmas. And somehow I think we might.

Tyne O'Connell was born in Brisbane and educated by Catholic nuns. She has lived all over the world – in Bedouin camps, penthouse apartments, beach huts, resorts and inner-city lofts – before finally settling in Mayfair, London. Surrounded by toy-men who know their way around an espresso machine, she's happily within tottering distance of all her favourite Bond Street shops. Her articles have appeared in *Marie Claire, Cosmopolitan, She* and *Ms*, and her latest novel, *What's a Girl to Do*, is available from Review.

Bad, bad girls!

Tyne O'Connell

My boyfriend picked up all his friends in cyberspace. He claims that he met most of them at university but I don't buy it for a minute. I've seen them *en masse* and in action and they definitely came from a 'people most likely to further your career' chat room.

Before you get the wrong idea about James though, let me make one thing clear: he's adorable. Seriously, hair-ruffingly, hold-on-to-your-clitoris-girlfriend cute. He's also loving, thoughtful, fun to be with, oh, and witty, natch. We've got masses in common, especially in bed. It's just his friends I hate. One friend in particular.

James likes to meet 'the guys', as he calls them, after work. We both work in the City, only after six, I like to flap my arms about as hard as I can and fly off to destinations other. Not James: he likes to hang out in all those Lads R Us bars around Liverpool Street Station, drinking designer beer from the bottle and talking about things that most people would have to double their dose of Prozac to survive. Stuff like micro-economics and inflation rates and naked options (don't get excited, it's a type of trade).

Actually, the truth is, I wouldn't really mind the lost evenings if it wasn't for Rupert.

Rupert is every girlfriend's worst nightmare, a total counter hon, as Nancy Mitford would have said. He works in futures, and as far as he is concerned, I don't have one with his mate James – period! He actually says that too – *period!* And it makes my ears curl. Rupert has made it his life's work to get James to realise that I am too 'girly'. I ask you, *moi*? Girly? I don't think so. Well, maybe a bit.

OK, so I see a pair of Jimmy Choos and I go weak at the knees and start speaking in tongues, and I admit, I do get a bit overexcited about this season's latest look, and sometimes I've even been known to take an afternoon off to – wait for it – *shop*!

In Rupert's mind this makes me an absolute airhead. Forget my meteoric rise in the City and my fierce determination to succeed in my career. As far as Rupert is concerned, it's only a matter of time before I break and throw in my job as a banker to become a lady who lunches or a baby machine.

This concept does actually terrify James, I know it does, he's said it does. His biggest fear is that he'll marry a girl with no life of her own, a girl who'll want to scatter cushions around the living room and go gah-gah at the thought of a wallpaper swatch from Colefax and Fowler.

'Wait till you move in together,' Rupert's started saying (James reports back). 'She'll start talking about giving up work to take care of you, and then she'll spend all your money on doing the place up and having lunch with her girlfriends while you bust a gut. Before you're thirty, she'll have saddled you with kids you never wanted, she'll have breasts down to her waist and if you try to get rid of her, she'll slap you round the bank balance with the ugliest damn divorce lawyer in town.'

Get the picture?

When Rupert talks about my career, he puts it in inverted commas. He does this in a faintly amusing sort of way so that everyone laughs, but it really pisses me off. Besides which, it's untrue: compared to my friends, I'm positively driven. I may not wear shoulderpads and I wouldn't know a two-piece suit if one jumped out at me in Harvey Nicks, but if we have to speak in clichés, that's me. Superbitch. I want to make shitloads of money. So sue me.

'Men are different from women,' Rupert tells me. 'They're just not aggressive enough to survive in the City. I'm not being sexist or anything, Alice, that's just how it is. You girls simply lack that killer instinct.'

I tell him that where he is concerned my killer instincts are alive and positively kicking. Unfortunately I see Rupert more than I'd like because he works for the same investment bank as me, only – wait for it – I'm his superior. Everyone at work has noticed that Rupert pro-actively dislikes me, hates me even. And it's not because of anything I've done either. Not because I tipped beer down his suit or stuck gum in his hair or told a girl he was chatting up that he had herpes, because I did all those things after he'd come out of the closet and outed himself as my worst enemy. I did all those things and more, but only after he had revealed his intention to make James 'see sense'.

James just laughs at Rupert's dislike of me. 'He's jealous,' he says. 'It's pathetic,' he says. 'You should feel sorry for the guy'. But somehow I'm not as comfortable with Rupert's jealousy as he is, and not the slightest bit sympathetic.

For a while I took my mother's advice and tried to make an effort, but after a few months of making myself entirely miserable, I got a brain and started taking Albert, my hairdresser's, advice. Hence the gum in the hair, beer down the suit, herpes rumour, etc. Albert just kept coming up with meaner and meaner ideas. He was having so much fun at one point he even stopped charging me for blow drys.

Rupert is like a time bomb ticking away on the outside of our relationship; he was probably going to blow at some point but with a bit of luck James would be over him by then. At least that was the way I felt before I got the phone call that morning, the phone call that was going to change everything. One minute I was rubbing sleep from my eyes, and the next minute three mad Australian girls from my Antipodean childhood were screaming down the phone. 'Surprise!' they squealed. 'We've just turned up out of the blue to destroy your life! Where shall we start our trail of destruction, your personal life or your career?'

Well, maybe they hadn't phrased it exactly like that. I think their precise words were something like 'Quick, break out the drugs, the men, the debauchery. We decided to drop in on you *en route* to the South of France, we've landed at Heathrow. Shall we come to your work or your flat?' But whatever their exact words were, it amounted to the same thing: my best friends in the world were going to bring me down.

I put down the phone and watched my relationship with James flash before my eyes. They couldn't have turned up at a worse time. James was turning thirty that weekend and his family were throwing him a huge party at Pharmacy, a trendier-than-formaldehyde restaurant in Notting Hill.

After three months of serious dating and sex, I was finally going to meet his folks. Normally by now I'm working out how to drop a guy, but this time meeting his parents actually mattered to me. I was keen to make the right impression. James had assured me that they would love me, but then he'd said the same thing about his friends.

Everyone he knew was going to be there, including my boss Alf Rutchet, who's just conceded that not all women are going to run off and have babies at the drop of a hat. And there lay my problem. My friends are a networker's nightmare. Their idea of a career drive is taking a cab to a party where there might be lots of eligible bachelors.

Love them as I do, they are the Antipodean equivalent of Tamara and Tara only with the volume turned up, heels a bit higher and cleavage a bit lower – and tans. Rupert was going to have a field day.

We'd all met in Sydney where I did my last two years of high school. These girls were bad, bad girls, the sort of girls my parents paid me to stop hanging out with. Being in their company was like watching one of those multi-TV-screen complexes at the Virgin Megastore. Either you buy the CD or you get a migraine, it's that simple.

It wasn't that I didn't love them like mad, course I did. We'd smoked our first cigarettes together, done *How fat are your thighs?* quizzes in the locker room when we should have been cutting up frogs in biology. We'd even dated the same guy once. But the thought of becoming respectable career women had never crossed their minds for a nano-second. They had given me the nickname Miss Shoulder-pads in the last year of high school, owing to my determination to be an A-star student. Kathy eventually became an out-of-work actress, Danielle was into New Age healing, Debbie, the successful one among them, became an anorexic – sorry, model.

But they were just marking time. All three of them imagined a future whereby some polo-playing media tycoon would whisk them off and install them in a penthouse apartment in New York/villa in the Bahamas/suite at the Ritz Carlton, in return for which they would reproduce said polo player's genetic line. In a nutshell they were not the type of girls I could hold up to validate my strong-minded determination to pursue a career at the expense of scatter cushions, babies and the like.

Anyway, I put the girls out of my mind and forgot about them on the way to work, only to walk out of an important and gruelling meeting with my boss at around ten to find Danielle, Debbie and Kathy, in all their sex-kitten glory, at my desk with all their baggage.

I dropped the pile of papers I was carrying and stood there in horror, my lower jaw swinging around my knees like a pendulum. They were all gathered around Rupert, giggling like there was no tomorrow. I should also mention that Rupert's naked foot was in Danielle's lap. He turned when he heard me approach and purred like the veritable cat with the cream. The war was on and now my own girlfriends had become the finest weapon in his arsenal.

'It was only reflexology,' Danielle explained that night back at my flat. I tried to make her see that Rupert was my mortal enemy and, as such, an unworthy candidate for her healing powers, but they all yelled me down. Kathy flicked some vodka from her glass at me. Rupert, they declared as one, was v. cute. Ouch!

I could not believe it. I put my hand down my throat and started pulling out my intestines but they didn't appear to notice.

'Alice, he's *so* hot? How do you keep your hands off him? God, he looks just like Ewan McGregor,' they chorused.

'Ooooh, does he take heroin?' squealed Debbie. She's always liked a bloke with a dark side.

'He'd better not. I'm not going to have sex with him if he's a needle sharer,' Kathy announced primly, rearranging her leopard print G-sring.

The thought of Rupert – buttoned-up, short-back-and-sides, never-stray-from-the-path-of-conservative-values Rupert – injecting heroin with a bunch of Scottish criminals paralysed my brain.

'No one is having sex with Rupert,' I told them firmly. 'Don't you dare suggest it even.'

'Why? Has he got diseases?' Kathy asked, checking her flatter-than-flat stomach in the mirror.

'It's nothing to do with diseases, although he might have, I'm not sure, but anyway it's a rule.'

'What?' Debbie asked, looking at me like I'd sprouted a spot on my nose.

'A rule. You know, girls don't sleep with friends of friend's boyfriends.'

'Crap,' they all said as one. 'Friends of friends' boyfriends are fair game.'

'The fairest game of all, in fact,' Danielle decided, trying on one of my new pairs of shoes.

We argued the point for hours but to no avail. They all

agreed that while James was off the menu, Rupert was very much the *plat du jour*.

I tried to explain to them that Rupert was the enemy of all girls with a social conscience and that it was their duty to crush him like a serpent under their heels. I tried to get them riled about the 'women aren't as aggressive as men' slur, but they just shrugged their shoulders. 'He's probably jealous,' they suggested.

I folded my arms and gave them a v. severe look.

'Chill out!' they urged, pouring me another vodka.

'Look,' I told them, 'the thing is, James thinks I'm a career girl and I don't want him getting the wrong idea because of you guys.'

'What's so bad about us?' Danielle pouted. She was wearing one of the frocks I'd bought in the last season's sales, a size too small for me. She looked fab in it, natch.

'You can have that dress if you promise to hate Rupert,' I bribed her.

'Not till you tell us what's wrong with us; besides, it doesn't fit you.'

'Well . . .' I hesitated, wondering how I could break it to them easily. 'Don't take it personally, but it's just that sometimes, only sometimes, mind, you come across as only interested in shopping, sex, holidays and clothes.'

They all started flicking vodka at me then. 'Oh, and you're not interested in any of that, Miss Shoulderpads?'

I blinked. 'Well, all right, I probably am, but I don't want James or his friends to think that's *all* I care about.' Then I told them all about how Rupert was trying to make me out to be an airhead.

'And you think, what? You're not an airhead?' Debbie teased.

'I just don't want you to give him the wrong idea about me.'

'But you figure we will?' they asked.

'Well, yeah, basically I do,' I squealed as they all pounded me with the sofa cushions. 'Hide the cushions,' I screamed, fighting them off. 'They can be used in evidence against me as a symbol of my desire to nest and have babies.'

Debbie shoved a cushion up her T-shirt. 'I know what. Why don't we tell him that we're all up the duff?' She started strutting around the room.

'I'm not doing that,' Kathy said, shaking her head as she wandered back into the kitchen for more booze. 'Then Rupert might be put off sex with me.'

I told her again that under no circumstances was she allowed to have sex with Rupert, which she said was v. unfair indeed, given that the only up side of your girlfriends getting boyfriends was that it widened the sphere of sexual conquest.

But I was resolute and shook my head like a true fascist dictator. It was Rupert or me, I told them, they had to choose between us.

The choice must have struck some sort of colonial chord in them because next second they were all ganging up on me and tickling me. 'Just because you're English doesn't mean you can lord it over us Antipodeans, Miss Shoulder-pads!' they cried.

After that, they hung me out of the window of my apartment and demanded I sing 'Advance Australia Fair'. It took me ten minutes before I could even remember the tune. I mean, who knows the words to someone else's national anthem? Especially one that had only been invented for, like what – a minute? In the end they got me to agree that they should come to the party at Pharmacy. They said they would be on their best behaviour. And I drank some more vodka in an effort to believe them.

When they finally collapsed with jet lag around ten, I curled up on one of the massive white sofas I was still paying Mr Conran for and read an Australian magazine that one of the girls had brought over. James rang just as I was reading an article on how swapping your old friends for new ones could be v.liberating.

'Rupert tells me you have some friends staying with you.'

I sank further into the sofa and wondered if I could just slip down the side and live amongst all the lint and lost coins and sunglasses forever. Rupert had got to him; my life was over.

'Why didn't you tell me they were coming?' He sounded kind of strained.

'They're just here for a week,' I told him. 'They're, um, here for an Expo in Earls Court.'

'A what?' he asked. That would teach me to lie off the top of my head. What the hell was an Expo anyway? 'It's something to do with sales conferences and product demonstration,' I told him, imagining the girls clucking around customers in their little black dresses and kitten heels. 'They're very committed career girls,' I assured him.

The old adage about when you're in a ditch, stop digging, didn't occur to me until I put the phone down. Insanely I had agreed that we should all go out to dinner the next night at 192.

Bad, bad girls!

He asked if he could bring his brother and Rupert. I said, why not, as my life was over anyway, but he only laughed as if I was joking.

192 exceeded my wildest fears. Debbie started the eyes rolling with an in-depth discussion about Harvey Nichols as a cultural hotspot of the world. I tried to nip her off at the pass with a remark about the latest British art sensation at the Tate. But Kathy got me in a brain-lock with a blow-by-blow account of how she'd snogged Damien Hirst once when he was in Australia hunting sharks. Which, while sounding v.unlikely to me, seemed to impress Rupert no end. I tried to get an edge on things by opening up the discussion of the Asian debt problem. Danielle and Debbie thought I was being ironic and wet themselves laughing. Then they reminded James and his brother about the time I'd spent my first month's pay cheque on a pair of Manolo Blahniks only to soak them in daiquiri the first time I wore them. James was gripped and urged them to tell all, while I tried to drown myself in my risotto.

'I didn't realise you were such a *mad* shopper!' he said, looking at me curiously.

I was ruined.

Finally Saturday arrived. The girls had drunk a vatload of mango smoothy cocktail things with lashings of vodka (the excuse being it was good for the complexion) before we left the flat. I had swallowed a handful of camomile tablets and then, just to be on the safe side, rolled up two pairs of knickers and used them as shoulderpads under the jacket of the two-piece suit I'd bought specially for the occasion. I had decided I needed all the career props I could get that night.

At the party itself the girls got things grooving with a loud conversation about how the best way to discover your G-spot was to stick a load of polo players down your pants.

'Very lively girls, your friends, aren't they, dear?' James's mother intoned meaningfully just as I was sticking my head in a Valium display cabinet. She was a nice woman, in a pinched blonde-highlights sort of way, but I could tell she didn't approve.

'You've been peculiar all evening,' James complained when I tried to steer him away from the table where Danielle was demanding that his father and my boss strip to the waist for some Reiki therapy.

'Peculiar, me? No I'm just worried about work,' I told him earnestly, hitching up one of my shoulderpads that kept slipping down my sleeve.

He looked at me oddly. 'Maybe you should take a few days off?' he suggested. 'You know, chill out a bit. Maybe you're working too hard?'

'I love working hard,' I told him desperately.

Later on, at the bar, I gave the girls a ticking-off and told them that they were destroying my chance of happiness with James.

They all told me I was being ridiculous. 'He loves you *because* you're mad!' Danielle reasoned.

'I am not mad,' I insisted stoutly.

'Course you are, we wouldn't have travelled around the world to see you if you weren't!'

'Well, I don't want James to know I'm mad,' I told them firmly, just as his mother sidled up looking all beige and disapproving.

'What was that about James, Alice?' she asked.

Bad, bad girls!

'She doesn't want him to find out that she's mad,' Kathy explained as she fell about giggling. His mother said something about checking everyone was OK and scuttled off.

'He probably knows you're mad anyway. I mean, not every girl wears rolled-up knickers in her jacket,' Debbie pointed out.

'I wish you would stop saying I'm mad. James doesn't like mad, his friends don't like mad and nor do his parents. My boss *certainly* doesn't like mad. They all like boring.'

'That's because they *are* boring,' the girls chorused.

'Except for Rupert,' Kathy added defensively. 'Rupert's not boring at all. Oh, look, there he is!' she cried. Then she made a little squeal like she'd just swallowed her rape alarm and waved furiously.

He waved back and started to make his way over through the crowd.

'It's probably because his friends are so boring that he likes you being mad,' Debbie persisted.

'For the last time, I am not mad,' I yelled. Everyone in the restaurant turned.

'Mad, bad and dangerous to know. How's things, Alice?' Rupert asked silkily as he ran his hand up Kathy's back. 'Nice, er, shoulder lumps,' he said, giving them a squeeze. I thought it was v.disloyal the way the girls fell about laughing.

Despite all my warnings and threats to put Immigration on to her, Kathy went home with Rupert that night. I got into such a major funk about it that I was a perfect bitch for the rest of the night. James came back with me but he ended up going to bed on his own.

I waited up for her, natch.

She returned to our Notting Hill flat around dawn.

'And what time do you call this?' I demanded hotly, jumping up from the sofa.

I realised straight away that something was wrong.

Debbie wandered out in her hot pink G-string and matching bra. 'Thought I heard you come in. I can't sleep, I'm still on Sydney time.'

'Why didn't you stay the night?' Danielle enquired, joining us in her black Dolce Gabbana underwear. The set she'd nicked from me, actually.

'He snores.'

'How do you know if you didn't stay the night?' she asked.

'I can tell, he's the type,' Kathy stated pointedly.

'Oh!' we all said knowingly. 'It's like that?'

She nodded. 'And he's small.'

We waited expectantly as she slumped on to one of the really expensive Macintosh chairs I regretted buying because they leave a mark on your bum when you stand up.

'How small?' I asked hungrily.

'He had such a lot of trouble getting it up,' she explained, wrinkling her nose.

We giggled.

'But he did manage to get it up finally?' I checked.

'He probably had it up all evening,' she admitted. 'I just didn't realise it was up because it was so small.'

'What's going on?' James asked, walking out wearing nothing other than his Calvin Klein skin-tight boxers. He looked so adorable standing there rubbing his hair, and a quick glance at the girls showed me they were thinking the same thing.

'Rupert snores,' I explained, trying to hide the triumph in my voice.

'I've heard him,' he said, looking at me and winking.

'He couldn't get it up,' Debbie added.

James sat on the arm of the sofa and put his arms around me.

'He could get it up, but it was just so small he needn't have bothered,' Kathy reflected, miming a pair of tweezers with her hand. She turned to James. 'Did you know it was that small? Why didn't you warn me?'

He shook his head, bemused.

We demanded a blow-by-blow account. Kathy dished – and how!

I looked over at James at one point as Kathy was outlining Rupert's bedside manner, sparing us *no* forensic details. Basically, Rupert's penis lost a proverbial inch every minute it spent in our collective imagination.

'To cap it all,' she said, standing before us with her hands on her hips, 'he had floral sheets! Can you believe it? Floral sheets, Laura Ashley no less. He said his mum bought them. The guy's a drongo.'

I could see James was loving every minute of it. By the time she wound up her story he was nibbling my ears. 'What's this?' he asked pulling one of my shoulderpads. I groaned as he held it up for all to see – a rather greyish pair of cotton knickers.

'It's her shoulderpad,' Kathy explained as I went every shade of crimson. 'All career girls wear them.'

His parents, I am pleased to report, loved me. His mother's a bit of a feminist in her blonde highlights, interior design sort of way. She likes my modernist approach, she told me. I think she's referring to my serious determination not to tie her son down with children before his late thirties.

I am also pleased to report that my boss and James' father both loved their Reiki massage. But the best bit is that James has told me he loves me – wait for it – because I'm mad!

Rupert, well, Rupert is Rupert. I doubt that he'll make it as best man but we've drawn an uneasy truce. He's stopped going on about the difference between men and women and I've dropped the herpes jibes. Last week at work he even told me he admired my toughness in closing a deal.

Shoulderpads, who needs them?

Cynthia Rosi was born and educated in Seattle, USA. At the age of twenty she moved to London and has lived in the UK ever since. She now lives in Bedfordshire with her husband, Paolo, and two young children. Her suspense novels, *Motherhunt* and *Butterfly Eyes*, are available from Headline.

Quiero Ba ... Ba ...

Cynthia Rosi

Under a far and blue sky in the circle of summer, Sante
looked right-left-right down the lane and took Jake's
hand, leading him across the road into a field of wheat.

The path they made as she tugged him into the field
wasn't really a path, because the wheat flattened by her bare
feet and his workboots sprang back up. But still they would
be able to follow two parallel lines, a pair of toy train tracks
carved in a swaying carpet of grain, back to the road when
they finished making love.

This farmer's field was the first time they could be alone.
The beach was fit for talking and kissing and swimming
only, for smearing on sun cream, for reading 1980 issues of
Cosmo and *Vogue* which Jake's mother kept at the beach
house out of frugality, until those issues were collector's
items.

So when Jake and Sante could, they escaped from the
family duties of laying the table, helping his mum crack
crab, from Jake's two sisters and their husbands, and from
the strip of sand in front of the beach house staked out with
the debris of a vacationing family: a rubber dingy, a cracked

diving mask, a snorkel with a red plastic ball in its top, a bottle of suntan lotion with sand in the nozzle, a Donald Duck towel with a mouse-nibbled hole.

The first three days of their two-week holiday at the cabin in Devon, Sante and Jake trekked up and down the beach looking for some secluded spot in the driftwood. 'There!' Sante would point, and they'd crunch along in sand leavened with oyster shells to a pile of whitened logs. Sante felt let down – the logs were always so much *shorter* than they'd looked from a distance. Jake kissed her. They crumpled to their knees, kneeling and hugging on a mat of dried seaweed and crackling kelp. But as soon as they lay down, and Jake pulled up Sante's T-shirt and took her nipples in his teeth, Sante went cold. She looked up at the blue sky, straining to listen for approaching feet.

Sante knew Jake's mother had staked herself out in the beach house's wooden deckchair reading Jeffrey Archer and eating Dorritos. But in Sante's mind's eye she watched Jean walking along in her hot pink shorts, slingbacks clicking with each step, swinging a net bag weighted down with shells and stones, stopping to peer over the log with her heavy-lidded eyes. Those skinny lips would tense into a frown, the ash-blonde curls set into big springs would shake 'No!' and Sante, flat on her back, her areolas glinting in the sun with Jake's saliva, would be forced into the humiliation of collecting her holdall and books and dirty washing and taking the next bus back to London.

Jake's parents were holy-rollers. They didn't believe in pre-nuptial sex.

A cave in the red cliffs near the point became their next hope, but it turned out to be shallower than its shadows advertised. And the five-foot-high standing stone Jake used to hide behind when he was a kid wasn't tall enough or wide enough to shelter two teenagers who were willing to make love just about anywhere, even standing up.

'We're trespassing, you know,' said Jake as they walked deeper into the wheat, belly-high for Sante, hip-high for him. 'The farmer might shoot at us.'

'Nah,' said Sante. 'Don't be ridiculous.' But she imagined the farmer, red-faced and burly, glowering at them from the height of his tractor seat. The thought made her walk faster. 'Nobody would do something like that. You'd have to be crazy. Anyway, you got a better idea? What else can we do?'

'Why couldn't we just've stayed on the beach? That was a good spot behind those logs.'

'I get sand in my crutch.'

'Oh.'

'Jake, do you think what we're doing is wrong? Do you think it's wrong to have sex before you're married?'

'Do you think it's wrong?' Jake liked to judge other people's opinions before expressing his own, to make sure he fitted in. But Sante hadn't discovered that about him yet.

'It feels good,' she said. 'More than good.' When he popped her cherry that hurt. But the kissing, the feeling of skin on skin, of malleable warmth . . . Making love was like discovering Belgian chocolate ice cream for the first time, plus when she was five and she'd snuggle in her father's arms and he'd scratch her back, plus when her sister used to brush her hair after taking a bath, and when Sante came first in the hundred-metre hurdles for her school. When she hugged Jake and closed her eyes she dived into how her skin felt.

'Well then,' he said.

They kept walking away from the road towards a stand of beech trees in the distance. Finally only a seaplane on its way to Dawlish could also see them. The buzz of the plane made Sante stop and look up. She imagined an impossible scenario: of the farmer and the pilot being friends and the pilot rousing the farmer on a ham radio. It gave a rush to her heart so that she could feel it pounding. Jake stopped too and looked up.

'What's wrong? It's only a plane. C'mon,' he said. Sante felt silly.

They walked for what seemed like five minutes but was probably less before she tugged his hand.

'Here,' Sante said and sat down, pulling him. She tucked her blue ruffled skirt between her legs and wrapped her arms around her calves. She wriggled her toes topped with a fine silver dust of sand which licked up over her instep and towards her ankles. This summer she went barefoot. She wanted to walk silently while her feet felt cool, oily floorboards, sharp oyster shells, hot pavements, the cold shallows of the surf. The squishiness of the field and its sharp points of broken straw.

Jake sat cross-legged in Levis and boots and a navy polo shirt, not because he was a working man, but because that was what all the boys wore that year. The fashion of a short, cropped haircut meant Jake's gloriously silky blond curls (his mother had kept them in a pageboy when he was a toddler, and called him Little Lord Fauntleroy when he refused to eat his tea) had been shorn along the sides. He kept his fringe on top of his head by running a hand over his hair, but the curls dripped on to his forehead when he concentrated. This gave Sante a yearning that gripped her stomach in a fist. It compelled her to stop whatever she was doing – revising maths, watching him under the hood of his Astra – stand on tiptoe to grab a fist of curls, pull those blue, blue eyes and crooked nose close to her face and nip his chin between her teeth.

They stayed still in the wheat, cupped in a mat of straw and a circle of stalks straight and tall and slender with almost a full ear of grain, listening to the wind rustle and whisper. Streaks of sun slanted through the stalks and warmed Sante's bare knees in bars the golden-brown of toasted marsh-mallows. Jake sat in shadow.

Sante didn't pay attention to the mole on his neck, or the way the skin on his forearms pouted pink with an early sunburn, or his small ears and long toes and feet baby-clean as he pulled them out of those thick-soled black boots. Jake pulled the shirt over his head, and lying down undid the buttons of his Levis, wriggling out of the jeans to expose a matted blond fuzz, as frizzled as burnt hair, covering his legs, his stomach, his chest and genitals. No, those she already knew. Sante listened for the buzz of the farmer's tractor. She heard the shiver of wheat.

Sante made a pillow with the calves of his boots, their black soles facing out, piled his shirt on top and scooched over to sit on the stretch of his jeans. She tucked the front of her skirt up under the waistband and fanned the back of it out, so Jake had somewhere soft to rest his knees, so they wouldn't get criss-crossed with the markings of straw. She lay down and opened her thighs to let him kneel there.

Smiling down his crooked nose, he unbuttoned her blouse.
With a hand on each hip he pulled off her panties.

'Take this off.' He snapped the elastic waistband of her
skirt. 'And your shirt.'

'But what if . . .'

'Who's going to see?' He sat back, naked and cross-legged,
on the ankles of his jeans.

Sante pulled off her skirt and blouse, folded them and
added them to the pillow pile. Then she lay down again
and he lay on top.

She paid attention to the bristles on his chin, licked them
with her tongue, bit the tiny hairs on his chest with her
front teeth and tugged gently, sucked on his shoulder, his
neck, wove her fingers into the curls on his crown and kissed
him as delicately on the mouth as sipping butter from a
winkle. He kissed her neck and took a breast in his hand
and its nipple in his mouth. Then he squeezed her breasts
together and nibbled both nipples.

When they finally slammed into each other, again, again,
again, she held her head up to watch the magic of how he
disappeared inside her each time. At the end, she looked up
at the sky. It seemed to her the inside of a blue shell, so
close. And then he lay on top of her, filling up a space inside
that six months before she didn't realise existed in quite this
way.

He pulled out and propped himself up on his elbow. She
sat up cross-legged, taking his *petit mort* in her thumb and
forefinger, wobbling it back and forth like a piece of licorice.
He smiled. She grabbed two fistfuls of blond chest hair,
pulled him close and kissed him.

When Sante put on her skirt, her blouse, shook the hay

from her long black hair, and Jake had dressed, they stood up. She stared at the ground where they'd lain and found their expedition had made a little circle. She felt newly washed. As though she'd been scrubbed with handfuls of sand and thrown in the sea.

Holy clean.

Sante listened to Jake's heavy footfalls thud down the wooden steps of the bed and breakfast and lost the noise at the front hall. She stared at her files of interview notes and reports, then at the fountain pen in her hand. They felt inanimate without Jake in the room. Slabs of dead tree with black ciphers on them – that was what papers were. Useless. She couldn't concentrate with his anger hanging in her ears.

Sante got up and pounded down the stairs and out the hall door. She caught up with him striding through the field behind the house up towards the woods, and grabbed his hand.

'You saw sense,' he said.

'Shh! Look at the fox!' she exclaimed in a whisper, stopping and pointing, but also to get her breath back. Getting back into shape after having James had been no problem but she could never shake the fat from being pregnant with Nicholas. Or the stretch marks, those crooked fingers of brown which fanned over her tummy underneath an enlarged belly button. Her pincushion, her woman's little paunch of fat.

The single fox on the edge of the field hesitated for a moment, its red coat silhouetted against the blue of the sea. Jake continued to clomp along. He jerked on

Sante's hand, pulling her behind him, and the fox bolted into the secrecy of bracken. Sante stared at the back of Jake's head, at the wavy grey strands beginning to dull his blond hair.

'What'd you do that for? That was mean,' she complained.

'Stupid fox. Anyway, they're pests.'

'They're beautiful!'

'To farmers they're pests. You're being sentimental. If I had a shotgun I could've got it.'

Sante's reply would have been: 'Like you'd really know from staring at accounts all day,' but they were supposed to be enjoying their holiday in Devon while James and Nicholas attended camp.

'I know you're mad at me for wanting to get in some extra work, but this is the only time I've got. Otherwise I'm looking after the boys, or at the office, and at night I'm too tired after making dinner and cleaning up.' Sante's voice went up in a whine at the end. She noticed it and didn't like it. It was a sound that went with frustration.

Jake didn't say anything. He dropped her hand when they came to climb over a humping rock, thrown up out of the earth by two crashing plates and covered with a carpet of lichen. Sinking soft it felt under Sante's hands, a living Wilton rug, hooked and clawed into the crags.

As they rested at the top of the rock, Jake said: 'Let's have sex.'

Suddenly, for Sante the bright blue sky seemed too far away. In her turtleneck and jeans and gum-soled shoes she felt exposed.

The shelter of the great beech trees which ringed the

rock, of the oak with its spring leaves the size of squirrel ears and a translucent crashing green in the spring sunshine, those were no shelter. He wanted sex. As bald as an equation. Stimulation plus more stimulation equals orgasm. Sante saw it in her head as something almost mathematical: $S + MS = O$.

For the first time she felt revolted. Revulsion down to her stomach so that it turned into dull nausea. It frightened her. She'd never felt this way. She wondered what would happen if she turned and walked herself through the woods down to the coast road, letting him tend to his own needs.

Instead, she sat on the spot. She picked at the moss and picked at her thoughts.

'I don't want to.' She felt she had to explain but couldn't think of a good reason, and felt fear. She saw her refusal as another equation, this time with the hysterical answer of mistresses and divorce. 'It's because . . .' she faltered, and plucked three strands of moss – two short, one a longer spike. They looked like a saguaro cactus from their honeymoon trip to the Grand Canyon, that spine with its arms sticking up. She bent the arms down into little O's, unconsciously making the phallus and its two eggs attendant. Sante saw what she'd done and let them pop up.

'Why?' he demanded, and rightly so, a husband righteously asking why she denied him his right.

What she said next seemed to her like pathetic bargaining, the whingeing of a tied goat, the whimpering of a staked dog. Turning and walking into the trees and ferns would be more honourable. She whinged to buy time, to try to bring light to her own sadness, to light a candle on this brilliant day.

'I need affection. I need cuddles and kisses. Snuggles.'

'We can do that,' Jake said, puzzled.

'I want them sometimes to not lead anywhere.'

She sounded to herself like an article in a women's magazine and remembered reading *Vogue* at the beach-house, flopped on her stomach in the warm sand, kissing Jake when she turned a page. How many times had she read this conversation and smiled, a bit smug? But she had no other words. Unless she spoke a different language. How would she say: 'I want to be kissed, not screwed,' in Spanish? *Quiero* – I want – plus the verb 'to be kissed' – *ba . . . ba . . .* something. Screwed. Well. That was entirely beyond her GCSE language skills.

'I shouldn't have to coax you,' he said.

I should just leap up and fuck you senseless. I know that. Like I used to! Those words made Sante feel sad and shrivelled up like an old crone with the spirit of an old crone and her impatient desire for solitude.

Sante had no words for reply. The smell of the funk of lichen. The clean, spicy smell of rocks, the salt smell of the beach. These she could describe. How the blackberry vines under the oak trees looked like hoops of barbed wire, how an oak leaf, brown and fit to crackle, was impaled on a bramble's spine. How the rock felt, jagging up under her hips, how she felt a bone on each bottom cheek poking out, which always led her to think in the distance of the O of her pelvis. But for Jake she had no words. If it was big enough to cry over she would do it. But tears stayed in her stomach. She had no tears.

Sante couldn't see her way out of this fog of sadness, see to the great eye of sun. So in the end she kneeled. She bent her head over his risen phallus and nodded to the task of desire until it was finished and the seed with its taste of lemons overflowed itself and spotted the ground.

But while she nodded her indulgence and the smell of distilled urine filled her mouth – not the sweet smell of sweat tangled in thick and curly hair, a warm smell to bury her nose in for comfort and closeness, but the sharpness of public lift corners – the lump rose from her stomach to her throat in an almost-retch.

When she stood and uncrinkled the kinks in her bent neck and the pain in her knees from hard rock, she inhaled deep the sweet grass and sea salt before saying: 'Shall we dig clams for dinner? We'd better get back before the tide comes in.'

Jake had gone out to the pub. Sante sat in the room with her papers spread in front of her. She'd regained a little concentration since the day before and sunk it into the task of work. This was the third night running he'd disappeared downstairs to go out with his new mates, coming to bed in the early hours full of beer and their opinions.

'What's wrong with you, Sante? What's got your knickers in a twist? I'm letting you work, am I not?'

'Am I *not*,' she sneered at her fountain pen, and felt surprise at the sound of her mocking voice dropping the words into the room like pennies on to floorboards. Sante put down the pen and went to the mirror. She'd tied back her black hair to be off her shoulders, and because it needed a wash. Her face, plain in the mirror, stared back at her.

She'd only just begun to realise it was a pretty face, with good cheekbones and a strong chin, a face that, as it edged toward thirty, improved with each year.

Why has it taken so long for me to know my own face?

Sante took out a stick of black eyeliner and stroked it under one eye, then the other. Jake didn't like make-up. She'd always gone boyishly bare-faced for him.

Why have I listened? Why have I been so eager to please?

Sante picked up the papers from the floor and stuffed them into a green folder with her pen. Then she stripped off her leggings, T-shirt, knickers and socks, and stepped naked into the shower. In the clean of steam she soaked and soaped, rubbing her slippery hands over her body, over the body she'd always thought of as Jake's. Sante soaped her stomach, its little post-baby paunch, her arms, her thighs and breasts, and a key inside her turned. It opened a possibility she hadn't seriously considered for nine years: there were other men beside Jake.

Marriage doesn't have to be permanent.

Who'd said that to her? A blindingly obvious statement in today's world. It came from Sally, her boss's PA. *You say 'yes' to your marriage every day, and on the day you stop saying 'yes' you open the door to 'no'.*

'No,' Sante said in the shower, testing the word. It didn't bite. She didn't seize and fall over. 'No, Jake. No.'

Anyone watching Sante dress, especially if they'd known how she felt, would have thought she dressed to pull. A blue and black batik sarong that made her hips slink, a black body, dangling silver diamanté earrings, strappy sandals. She took care to unvarnish and repaint her toenails blue to match, and filed and buffed her fingernails before painting on a fresh coat. Then she applied all the make-up in her bag: eyeliner, mascara, lipstick, eyeshadow. That was all she owned. Sante stood dressed in front of the mirror with her black hair hanging loose to her shoulders and turned her body side-on. She felt so huge at times, as if her breasts, stomach, thighs, arranged themselves in rings of blobs like the Michelin man. But the woman who stared back *didn't* expand into the whole room. She was petite.

Why doesn't he tell me I'm not fat? Why have we both stopped noticing that I'm pretty? Even exotic with this black eyeliner. What's happened?

Sante picked up her keys and a ten-pound note, tucked them into the little pocket of her sarong, walked downstairs and out into the seaside night.

In the sky, ragged clouds blotted out patches of stars. At a candy-floss stand on the promenade Sante bought a white-chocolate Magnum and ate it, shucking her shoes to walk on the beach, dangling the straps of her sandals in her other hand. She trod close to the waves, her bare feet tickled by the tiny cold stones, pricked by shells, licked by the beating water. Although she was a lonely woman on a lonely beach, her only lamp the half-moon glittering shards in the waves, Sante didn't feel afraid. Completely self-contained, self-reliant. Like a she-snake she'd hiss at any approaching man.

She walked for maybe a mile in the night, climbing the steps up to the sea wall when she ran out of beach, the Magnum long eaten, her feet still bare. She wouldn't put on her shoes, even though sometimes sharp pebbles made her wince and it felt awkward for her heels to be flat. Bare feet and rebellion, bare feet and innocence, bare feet and freedom. Bare feet and that long-ago summer when she'd walked in the waves, refusing to wear shoes as if she sensed a future bound and shod, strapped in, contained. She walked slowly, every footstep a deliberate act of faith, an incarnate wish for a future of freedom even if that freedom meant being bruised and cut.

The promenade's electric bulbs guided her back: the dodgems, the Ferris wheel, the kiddies' tea-cups that spun on arms of light. Sante grabbed a fistful of coins from her pocket and bought a book of tickets. By the second ride on the dodgems, she had thrown back her head to squeal with the rest of them over the blare of a thump-thump bass, crashing into a group of teenage boys. She caught the smell of something good, a years-ago smell, and realised it was *them*: Brut and boy-sweat and full-strength cigarettes. A poignant smell that made her wish she could be someone else. *Sixteen's body with twenty-eight's experience would be nice.*

By the end of the evening Sante had spent her money. Another Magnum, all the rides. Only one left: a giant slide that dropped straight down for six feet before bottoming out in a hard curve. It frightened her.

Sante climbed to the top and placed a burlap sack under her bottom, squishing her knees together so as not to show her knickers, settling her bony backside against the plexiglass. She peered over the edge at the long drop, the hard blue plastic decorated to imitate a waterfall with white swooshes, and slipped an inch forward. Her sticky bare feet shot out and stopped her. She scooted herself back. *I've done enough rides*, she thought.

I don't have to make myself do this.

Two teenagers from the dodgems stood at the bottom of the slide, another two climbed up beside her, sat down in their Saturday-night jeans and whisked away, yelling. Like lads on a playground they ran around to the ladder and scampered up again, boys in their newly-got men's bodies. One blond sat down next to Sante. 'Do you need some help?' he asked.

Sante shook her head.

'Do you want to get down? Shall I help you?' His child's tenderness, his boy-scout helping the lady across the road, galvanised Sante.

'Do it together, yeah?' she said.

He grinned. 'You first.'

Sante scooted forward. She fell off the edge, her stomach lurching to her throat, her black hair flying and brown legs splaying, landing with a bump in a heap. She laughed a belly laugh, deep-throated and doubled over, laughed out the badness of the day. When she got up, the boy stood beside her.

'Do it again?' he asked.

Sante knew from his face she could take the boy's offer as far as she liked. She considered it. A perfect ending to a perfect night.

'C'mon,' he said. 'Just one more go.'

Sante imagined what it might be like with this boy, all fire and vigour, a boy so young his Adam's apple stuck out, as yet unsettled in his throat. 'I'd love to,' she said. 'But I can't go backwards. I've got ladders of my own to climb.'

The boy raised his eyebrows. 'Don't fall.'

'I won't.'

Sante didn't want to face Jake, didn't want to speak the difficult words: *Today I said 'no'*. Would Jake listen? *Maybe*. Sante knew she had to get him to see her world.

She'd make him join hands. They'd fly off *this* slide together.

Emer Gillespie is a writer and actress and lives in North London with her dog, Otto. Her first novel, *Virtual Stranger*, is published by Headline.

Similar Tastes

Emer Gillespie

We sat on a table outside by the pavement. All the plastic bags were tucked up carefully under our chairs. I counted them before I ordered my first drink. Eight items altogether, including my handbag. Diane only had six. But she'd spent more than me.

I always find it easier to count them up before I've had a few. The last thing I needed on the way home in the taxi was a panic. You know, that frantic shuffle through the lot searching for my faux snake bikini, only to find it in the last bag underneath the turquoise top with frilly Spanish señorita sleeves.

I love designer sales. I only have to see the small advert in the newspaper, the one with a square black box round it so it catches your attention, and my heart begins to beat faster. 'Cash or cheques only.' That cramped my style a bit today, until I realised they were going to let me write as many cheques as I wanted to for consecutive dates – gives me enough time to organise my overdraft.

'Two halves of lager,' I said to the waitress when she came out to take our order. Good legs. Nice tan. A black leather elastoplast of a skirt stretched across her thighs, and high-heeled sandals. I bet you that helped with the tips. 'And I'll have a drop of lime in mine . . . Cordial, that is, not fresh, Fancy a drop of lime in your lager, Diane?'

'No thanks.'

The waitress went back inside. When she turned around I could see the streaks in her tan where she'd missed a bit. Let herself down with that. You have to be so careful.

We sat there in silence. I was pleased with myself. I'd done very well. I sat there mixing and matching in my head, planning what I was going to wear that night, imagining the look in Anthony's eyes when he saw me all dressed up and then not so dressed up, all the way down to my new tangerine silk bra and knickers. By the end he'd have that look in his eyes, you know, panting for it.

The waitress came back with our drinks. I took a sip of my lager. It was crisp, cool and sweet. The first mouthful is always the best.

'I like a drop of lime in mine,' I said to Diane. 'If I drink at lunchtime, it goes straight to my head. I find a bit of lime does wonders. It must be the sugar in the cordial. It helps keep me compos mentis.'

'Just so long as you don't lose your sense of direction.'

It took me a minute to get it. But when I did we both snorted with laughter. We cracked up right there outside the restaurant and laughed till the tears streamed down our faces.

I think it was the release of tension. Shopping does that. You have to hold yourself steady and keep your wits about you. No wonder you want to go a bit silly afterwards.

This bloke sitting at another table, Greek looking, he

started to laugh as well. He raised his glass to us and winked. Well, that only set us off even more, didn't it? We just looked at one another and spluttered. Lager and lime came fizzing down my nostrils.

I don't know Diane that well even though we work for the same company. She's in Sales and I'm in Marketing. We'd met twice before at different training conferences. So when I saw her last Thursday evening during the coffee break it felt almost like seeing an old friend. We smiled and said hello and then there was one of those awful pauses. I didn't know what to say. I mean, it was bad enough having to spend an evening listening to Further Microsoft Applications without talking about it at the coffee break – you come across as a bit of a prat if you do that.

It was when I was groping about for something to say that I noticed her shirt. It was just a white shirt. It fitted in perfectly with the uniform code. But there was something about the way it was cut. It was perfect. Not too showy but perfect, if you know what I mean.

I asked her where she got it. And she told me.

I was right. I always am. I can spot quality. It was Comme des Garçons. She'd got it at a designer sale in Brook Street the year before. I told her she was lucky, you don't normally get Comme des Garçons off-loading their remaindered stock in London. It must have come from some shop that was closing down or something. Now if it was Paris . . .

Sometimes when I think what it must be like to live in Paris. All them ateliers. Not to mention Comme des Garçons, Issey Miyake, Azzedine Alaia. I could cry.

So she told me it was the only one on the rail. I bet it washes well, I said. And she said it did. It was hardly off her back. Just a quick run through the machine, some spray starch and there it was.

After that we got talking and I found out she was an addict, just like me.

Designer sales – they're not like normal shopping.

First of all there's the anticipation. You usually know about a week before that one is coming up. So you've got something to look forward to. I lie awake at night and start thinking about what I need and what I might find.

Then there's the feeling of holiday. I usually try to take the day off or at least a few hours in the morning. Not that you can have a lie-in. Far from it. You have to be there early if you want to find something good.

Then there's that purity of concentration when you're actually in the sale. You have to keep your wits about you. You have to keep your eyes and ears open. You have to keep focused. All your cares and worries fade away. There's nothing else like it. I think of it as a kind of meditation. It's like performing keyhole surgery or like driving a racing car round a track, holding the wheel with nerves of steel, one lapse and you're buggered.

Finally there's crunch time, decision time. It's not as if you can think about it and come back another day. No. Let something out of your sight for one second and you've kissed it goodbye.

I've been in a tug-of-war before. I'd just put a pile of clothes on the floor so I could get undressed, and as I was pulling my T-shirt over my head, that moment of temporary blindness, someone was in on the rummage. 'Excuse me, that's mine,' I said. 'Oh,' she said, 'oh, it couldn't possibly be. I was just about to try it on.' So I pulled it off her. And she pulled it back. And all the time there she was, smiling away at me. I had to get the sales assistant to back me up. I wasn't going to let go of what was rightfully mine. Luckily I'd been up to the assistant before to ask about the price, and she knew I had it first. As I said, you have to keep your wits about you.

Altogether I find it quite a private experience. You wouldn't take just anybody along. Most people would be a distraction. I always think that if I had a sister it's the sort of thing we'd do together. But I don't. So when I heard myself telling Diane about this sale this morning and inviting her along, I was surprised. I wanted to bite my tongue and take the words back. But they were out and she'd agreed.

We met outside Oxford Street tube at seven thirty this morning and headed up Great Titchfield Street together, stopping only to get a couple of cappuccinos in a sandwich shop. We queued for an hour before they opened the doors. It was good we got there early. Behind us a huge crowd built up and trailed all the way down the street and round the corner of the building.

When we got into the showroom, we split up. We did all our choosing separately and once we'd found what we needed, we got together at the end to check one another over. It was nice to have someone to check out the bits you couldn't see in the mirror. I mean, you can't trust a stranger, can you? They might tell you something doesn't suit you and all the while they are waiting to nab it off the rail when you put it back.

Eight bags, I'd bought. All in all I was very pleased with myself. A good morning's shopping and I'd found myself a new friend.

When she got undressed I knew. She wears matching underwear. I mean, that's such a little thing but it makes such a difference. It says such a lot.

You do have to be so careful, don't you? You never know how well you are going to hit it off with people. Things can start out so well and then suddenly they say something and you realise you are not remotely on the same wavelength and you have to start backtracking, thinking how on earth am I going to get out of that girls' night out with you and your mates, or even, once, nightmare of nightmares, the plan to go on holiday with a promising girlfriend – until I found out that her idea of a good time was swapping Oasis CDs. That was embarrassing. We ended up not speaking ever again after that one.

With Diane the potential for embarrassment was huge. If we didn't hit it off there was the possibility that we'd still keep running into one another year after year at training courses.

We were both tired and needed the drink to perk us up a bit.

'Doing anything special tonight?' I asked her, just to keep the conversation going.

Truth be told, I wanted to tell her that I was. I wanted to tell her what I was doing, and how I was looking forward to wearing those new black leather trousers with the red silk trim. She'd bought the same trousers, only the trim on her ones was lime green. Come to think of it, our tastes were so similar.

'No, I'm not doing anything,' she said. 'Not this week.'

She sounded really down in the mouth about it. Far too down in the mouth for someone who accidentally hadn't planned anything. It sounded as if she was actively not doing something that she would have liked to have been doing – if you know what I mean.

'Working, is he?' I probed.

'No.' Her voice was hesitant. 'No, he's busy.'

'Night out with his mates then, is it?'

'No. What about you? Are you out tonight?'

She'd changed the subject so quickly I hardly saw her blink.

'Yes, I am.' I could feel myself smiling with pleasure at the thought.

'What are you doing?'

'We're going out for a meal. And then afterwards we usually go back to his place.'

'He's your boyfriend then, is he?'

'I wouldn't say that.'

And I wouldn't say that. For a start, he's too old. I don't know how you can call someone a boyfriend if he's past forty. When I think of him in my head I call him my lover, but that sounds too poncey to say out loud. Anyway, I don't usually talk about him out loud. He's my secret.

'That bloke over there,' she said, 'he's trying to catch your eye. He keeps looking over at you.'

I glanced at the Greek. She was right. He was leering away at me. He didn't have a chance. No style – mock J.P. Tods in maroon patent leather. Please!

'Let him,' I said. 'A cat can look at a queen.'

I finished my drink and all the time I was thinking of Anthony and that look he gets in his eyes when he's excited.

Let's get this clear. Me and Anthony, it's just a bit of fun for both of us. I met him at work. He had his eye on me for ages before he asked me out for a drink. We'd pass on the corridor and there would be that little soupçon of a frisson, as they say in Paris.

He's going through his divorce at the moment, so I'm breaking one of my own rules. I don't go out with men if they're married, recently married or recently bereaved. Not that I've ever had one who's recently bereaved, but I wouldn't if I did. I've got too much self-respect to live in the shadow of another woman.

Anyway, with Anthony, my guess is that he's been such a bastard to live with over the years that his wife has finally had enough and thrown him out. Married for years and all of a sudden he's not. Trouble, in other words. Doesn't know where he is. Don't go looking for true love in a dustbin, that's what I say.

I don't normally waste my time. Normally, I go for a relationship. You know, fun's fun, but if I can't picture him some day with my baby in his arms, then the writing's on the wall and sooner or later I'm off. Beside, Anthony's already got babies. And if a man will walk out on one family, he'll walk out on another. Common sense, that is. Mind you, to give him his due, as far as his family's concerned he does make an effort. Every other weekend he devotes himself entirely to his children. And when you read in the news-papers about what most men get up to that practically makes him a saint.

And he is fun. I've kissed a great many frogs lately and nothing magic has happened. At least with Anthony you know he's a toad from the start. You know where you are.

We always go out for a meal to this really nice Thai on Fulham Broadway – the first couple of times in the restaurant I wanted to split the bill but he wouldn't hear of it. Now I don't even bother to offer. Over dinner he tells me he loves me, which even if I don't believe him is always nice to hear. I like going there. I like having the chance to wear really nice clothes, to dress up and be appreciated. It's much better than ending up in a pub with some wanker my age who's more interested in talking to his mates about football and who'll probably end up being sick in the gutter and splashing me with vomit before the night's out.

Sex at the end of an evening with Anthony is just the price you pay. You know, like going around to your girl-friend's flat for dinner and helping her do the washing-up. We go back to his bachelor pied-à-terre. No ornaments, no photographs. It makes me feel quite sorry for him, in a way.

'You're my pussy, all mine,' he says as he's about to come. I can hardly stop myself from giggling in his ear.

I saw Diane watching me. She looked sad and I realised that I'd been smiling away to myself.

'Are you going out with anyone?' I was trying to draw her out.

'Sort of,' she said. 'Only things are a bit difficult.'

Well, there are only so many situations that can make things a bit difficult, aren't there?

'Is he married?' I said, homing in on the most obvious one.

'No. Nothing like that. I wouldn't go out with a married man!' She sounded shocked.

'What then?'

'Well, he's been married. He's getting divorced.' To begin with she was reluctant, and then all hesitation vanished, she was desperate to tell someone. 'He's a lovely, warm, kind-hearted man and his wife's being a bit of a bitch about his access to the children, you know. So every other weekend he devotes all his time to them.' She was gushing about him and her eyes had a warm glow.

I asked her how long they'd been together.

'About six months.'

'Longer than me. I've only been with mine for four months.'

'Is it love?' she asked.

'Catch me!' I snorted.

'Where did you meet?' I asked.

'At the office,' she squirmed.

'That's a bit close to home, isn't it?' I asked.

'He travels a lot,' she replied.

'Which department?' I asked idly.

'Sales.'

'Oh.'

I felt as if I'd been punched. I knew what was coming. I mean, we do sort of look alike, like sisters in a way. And we do have such similar tastes.

I finished my drink. There was no sign of the waitress.

'What ages are his children?'

'Eight and six.'

'A boy and a girl.'

'How did you know?'

'The only clever thing him and his wife have ever managed?'

The waitress came out and I called her over and ordered the same again.

Diane's face was white.

'What did you say?'

'I said it was the only clever thing him and his wife have ever managed.'

'How did you know that? Who told you?'

'It's Anthony Hamilton, isn't it?'

'Yes.'

Toads and toerags, they're all the same. Still, you've got to hand it to him.

'Does he take you to the Empire Jade?'

'Yes. Does he tell you he loves you?'

'Yes. Does he say you're his pussy, all his?'

'Yes.'

'And you think he's going to spend this weekend with his children.'

'Yes.'

We were supposed to get bitchy and tear each other's eyes out in a jealous rage. That's what you're supposed to do, isn't it? But I couldn't stop laughing. And after a while Diane joined in.

We ordered another drink. This time Diane joined me with the lime.

'Do you meet in Bishop's Bridge Park?'

'Yes. That bench down by the river?'

'Yes. Does he have spots on his bum?'

'Yes. Does he get you to put the condom on and tell you he loves the feel of your warm, soft hands?'

'Yes!'

We roared and hooted and spluttered with laughter.

The Greek gave up in disgust, paid his bill and left.

We got a taxi home to my flat. Fourteen plastic bags, two handbags and three hat boxes. Diane had gone a bit quiet so I kept up a flow of chat with the driver. Nothing much, just a bit of banter. Fortunately we reached home before I'd run out of one-liners.

It was half past two when we got back. Anthony'd told me he would call before he got on the plane back to London. The phone rang at ten past three.

Diane's face fell.

I answered the phone and pressed the loudspeaker button.

'Hello, beautiful,' he said. He always manages to sound as if he means it, as if he's missed me.

'I'm sorry I can't pick up. I've just done my nails. Tarting myself up a bit.'

'That sounds hopeful.'

'How's it hanging?' I teased. I told you drinking in the afternoon always makes me a bit reckless.

'It's hanging strong and long.'

I felt a tickle in my belly and giggled. Then I caught sight of Diane's face and winked across the room at her.

'What time shall we meet?' I asked him.

'Same time, same place.'

'Good. I was worried in case you couldn't make it.'

'Why would I not be able to make it?'

'Oh, I don't know. You might have grown tired of me. You might have wanted to spend this weekend with your children.'

'No, they're with their mother this weekend. I've told you, every other weekend I'm all yours.'

We got to the park half an hour early. I was wearing my new leather trousers with the red silk trim. Diane was wearing hers. If I say so myself, we looked ace. Like sisters. We do have so much in common.

I had a bottle of fizz left over from my birthday. We brought that with us. A bottle of champagne – with three glasses.

He saw me first, like I'd intended.

'Hermione!' he said, a smile lighting up his face. (I know, I know. My mum was reading something at the time.)

The sun sparkled on the river.

'Diane!' he said.

'Girls!' he said.

I have to hand it to him. His cool. He didn't lose it for an instant.

And you want to know what we did next?

Well now, you and I, we've only just met. I wouldn't want to give away all my secrets at once. Could be embarrassing, couldn't it? I mean, with new friends you have to be so careful.

Maybe I'll tell you some day.

Julia Stephenson was born and raised in Surrey. After leaving the Lucie Clayton College she had stints as a professional cook, a chalet girl and a housewife. When she is not writing, she enjoys travelling and moving house, and is a student of Buddhism and *feng shui*. Her first novel, *Pandora's Diamond*, was published in 1997 and her second novel will be published by Headline in 1999.

A Feng Shui Romance

Julia Stephenson

'Oh darling, you looked so beautiful at dinner,' said Oliver affectionately. 'Jeremy thought you were smashing, he described you as "that gorgeous blonde with legs up to her armpits". I was so proud of you.'

I snuggled up to him expectantly, mellow with compliments, fine wine, delicious food and the pleasant evening we had spend with friends, and purred inwardly as he stroked my hair and kissed me affectionately. I allowed him to guide my hand downwards where, as I expected, nothing was happening. You see, while Oliver's mind was willing the flesh was weak, and in our three-month courtship very little was happening on that front. It bothered him far more than it did me, as I was recovering from an extremely physical relationship with a drummer in a well-known rock band. We didn't have much in common but at least the sex was great. Whereas Oliver and I had loads in common but the sex was awful. Still, I wasn't really complaining. I hadn't had cystitis for three months, which was a great relief. But after three months of no action I was beginning to miss the physical side of life a bit. One could have a little too much of foreplay that never went anywhere.

'Shall we go to sleep now?' I suggested hopefully, thinking that if this was going to go on for much longer I might have to start hinting about Viagra.

'Oh darling, I do think you could make a little more effort with our lovemaking. Things are just taking longer than usual because I'm under so much stress.' Oliver's mad Uncle Rupert had recently died, leaving him a zoo which he was having some difficulty selling. 'If you could just be more patient.'

'I know you're under stress, darling. We've both had an exhausting week and I'm shattered too.' In this way I managed to keep his ego vaguely intact by shifting the blame on to myself. Oliver rolled off me with some relief and soon fell fast asleep.

Apart from the sex shortage, I loved staying with Oliver at weekends. After a busy week in London, battling with the suppressed anger of six million people, I would head down to the stunning house in Hampshire he had inherited from a relative. Oliver's relatives were always dying and leaving him useful things, like houses, titles and land. In nearly every way things were ideal. We had masses in common, we liked the same people and we enjoyed doing the same things.

I had the week to myself, which suited me very well because I'm an authoress. Most people hate being asked what they do, but I love being able to say, 'I'm an authoress.' You'll have heard of my publisher, Mills and Swoon. Well, I write for their sister company, Ritzy City, which is a sexier, upmarket version, aimed at glamorous thirty-somethings with high disposable incomes. The sort of books Bridget Jones would read and keep hidden under the bed when her friends come round. Well, we're not talking rocket science, I'm afraid. And maybe authoress is a bit of a *folie de grandeur*, because I've only written one book. You may have seen it; it's called *Ruffles at Dawn*. It has a picture of some black lace knickers and a drumstick on the cover and is the autobiographical story of the passionate affair I had with the drummer.

Now I was on my second book, but I was a bit blocked. You see, I only like to write about things that have really happened to me, I don't have enough imagination to make things up, but it was proving very difficult to write a passionate frothbuster when I wasn't getting any passion. You see, Oliver was the sweetest man and I adored him, he was my best friend, etc. etc. (you get my drift), and he was also one of the most eligible men in England, for what that's worth. He'd even asked me to marry him, which was very flattering. It was just this sex débâcle. Something *had* to be done about it, but what?

I decided to discuss the situation with my best friend Joanna. Joanna is an esoteric consultant, occasional Buddhist, soothsayer expert and part-time authoress. Her recent bestseller, *Women Who Don't Love Very Much*, had just knocked *Women Who Love Too Much* off the bestseller list. No wonder I had noticed an increasing degree of confusion amongst the *Ally McBeal*-watching sophisticated classes recently.

'I think you should see Roberto, my *feng shui* man,' she advised during a riveting tête à tête at the Seattle Coffee Company. 'My friends in Fulham call him the *feng shui* love god. He's particularly good on relationships. He does love spells.' She lowered her voice conspiratorially and I edged closer. 'Anouska, my friend who runs the Women Who Don't Love Very Much support group, fell madly in love with Tristram, her next-door neighbour, so she called in Roberto for an emergency consultation. He advised her to buy some red knickers, wear them when she was, get this, *mid-cycle*. Then she had to take them off and put a picture of Tristram and one of herself inside the knickers, face to face, then put then under her bed.' Ugh, mid-cycle; it made Anouska sound like a washing machine.

'So did it work?' The adjoining tables had fallen silent and I felt sure they would want to know. *Feng shui* was of great interest to the sophisticated Seattle Coffee Company *habitués* and love spells were obviously the Next Big Thing.

'Yes! They're getting married next week! If I were you I'd get him round to your flat pronto. Perhaps you should draw him a floor plan of Oliver's pad; he might have a lavatory in his sex corner or something disastrous.'

It was with some trepidation that I rang up Roberto immediately for a consultation. When I told him I was the authoress of *Ruffles at Dawn*, he was thrilled and said he had enjoyed it very much. I was amazed. I had never met anyone who had actually read the book apart from a few close friends, and most of them were lying. As it was so urgent he said he would cancel his next day's appointment and come and see me instead.

Roberto turned up punctually the next day. He was quite small and robust with short dark hair, as befitted his presumably Latino origins. He was quite ordinary-looking really, except for his eyes. They were green and strangely glittering and one had the strangest sensation that he could read one's mind.

'So tell me,' he asked, 'What is the one thing you'd like to change in your life?' I ummed and ahhed about writer's block but he got it out of me.

'That's not the only thing that's blocked, is it, Tabitha?' It was spooky. It was like he knew the problem already. 'This boyfriend of yours, what does he look like?'

I showed him a photograph I had recently taken. Roberto looked at it for a long time and then just said, 'Hmmm.'

'Well, what can you tell about him from his face?' I asked curiously. Joanna had told me that he was also an expert in the Chinese art of physiognomy.

'He has great material good fortune but he is lacking in Life Force.' He looked at me intently. I blushed but couldn't help being impressed. He put the photo down and smiled at me. Again I had the sensation that his glittering green eyes could see straight into my mind. I tried madly to think pure thoughts.

'Have you anything stronger than this?' he asked, looking witheringly at the cup of green tea I had thoughtfully provided.

'Alcohol?' I hazarded. I hadn't expected him to drink anything stronger than green tea. With his Armani suit and silk tie he wasn't a bit like I'd imagined.

'If you have any.' I opened a bottle of good wine and things began to loosen up. We were soon chattering away like old friends, and after a couple of glasses I confided that although Oliver and I were very close, I was hoping to inject more passion into our relationship. When we had finished the bottle Roberto set to work.

'This is a very good flat,' he said reassuringly, dashing into each room with a pair of divining rods and a compass.

'No geopathic stress, which is excellent. But your relationship corner in your bedroom is disastrous.'

'Is it?' I asked. That would explain everything!

'Yes. You need to buy a nice spider plant and maybe a cactus. And put up a picture of a battle scene, that'll inject a bit of action into your life. And a nice picture of yourself too.'

'What will that do?' I asked doubtfully.

'It'll help you have a good relationship with yourself. That's the secret of having a good relationship with your boyfriend.' I gulped. Roberto had been reading Louise Hay too; he must be extraordinarily enlightened.

He suggested other improvements – wind chimes in the hall, red flowers for inspiration on my writing desk – and insisted I repair the dripping tap in my ancestral wealth corner. He stayed all afternoon, which was amazing as my flat is quite small, and refused to let me pay him, suggesting that I take him out for a drink instead. I felt it would have been churlish to refuse as he had been so generous and given me all sorts of life-improving *feng shui* gadgets. He had even offered to take a photo of my home so that he could meditate over it.

So that was the start of my friendship with Roberto. We would talk regularly, go out to the cinema, have lunch. All strictly platonic, of course. I had a suspicion that he fancied me but I'm afraid any physical attraction was strictly one way. I just enjoyed his company. He was witty and amusing and the sort of person you could discuss things with in complete confidentiality. But the strangest thing was that the closer we became, the more I drifted away from Oliver. The *feng shui* improvements had done nothing to spice up our sex life. If anything it had deteriorated. Oliver had developed a disturbing habit of grabbing me in public places and kissing me, but in the bedroom these passionate overtures led to nothing but embarrassment on both sides.

The crunch came when he invited me to Devon to stay in his late mad Uncle Rupert's exquisite manor house with attendant menagerie. Fifty rather aggressive Manx cats and three wallabies roamed the house and grounds, while six incontinent sloths inhabited the conservatory. Oliver suddenly discovered he was allergic to cats, (very feeble, I thought), and spent the weekend trying to sell them to various Chinese restaurants in the area, who all refused because they didn't have tails.

Mad Uncle Rupert had left a clause in his will stipulating that the house and menagerie couldn't be split up. This was unfortunate because lots of people had made offers for the house but were put off by having to take on the animals. Apparently, sloths make a dreadful smell at the best of times, but their inability to control themselves made the conservatory a complete no-go zone. Mrs Button, the housekeeper, refused point blank to go near it. Oliver was in a complete state and got so stroppy and unreasonable that I just drove back to London on Sunday morning and left him to it.

'I just don't understand how everything else has improved but my relationship with Oliver has utterly collapsed,' I told Roberto on the telephone the next day. I was in a good mood as a rival publisher had just made me a wonderful offer to write the book I had always dreamt of writing: the true love story between my great-grandparents, who had lived and died on the island of Nantucket, just outside Boston. I had decided to drop my current novel,

Passion in the Midnight Hour, and go to Nantucket to do romantic research. And since I had placed a money plant, a bright light and a crystal in my wealth corner, my agent had rung and said that he had sold the film option of *Ruffles at Bedtime*, to an Icelandic film company. OK, I know Iceland doesn't exactly have a thriving film industry, but it's a start. Then my mother rang me from Boston to tell me that she had won $100,000 on the state lottery and that she wanted to give me a quarter of it. This meant I could now afford to write proper books and rent a glorious waterfront condo to work in . . . it was all terribly exciting!

'Did you put the cacti and the picture of the battle in the relationship corner like I suggested?' asked Roberto. I had had my doubts about these improvements but as I said, amazing things had been happening to me in all other areas of my life and I knew that Roberto, who had just begun filming his own *feng shui* TV show and had been rated in *Cosmopolitan* as London's most fashionable *feng shui* consultant knew what he was talking about.

'Yes I did. Maybe it was for the best, maybe we just weren't suited and the *feng shui* speeded up the process.'

'That's right. You see, it works on a very deep level. How have you been getting on with your wardrobe?'

Roberto had very helpfully *feng shuied* my wardrobe and fridge the previous week, encouraging me to throw all sorts of things away.

'You'll be very pleased, I've thrown out most of my clothes, like you suggested.'

'Would you like me to come round later and *feng shui* your underwear drawer?' he asked hopefully. I frowned. Recently Roberto had been becoming a little lascivious in his suggestions. There had even been talk of *feng shui* massages with special oils. Of course I had firmly discouraged such notions but Roberto was so self-confident and had so many women flinging themselves at him all the time (women are very keen on guru-like figures) that perhaps he couldn't get to grips with the fact that I didn't fancy him.

'That's an intoxicating idea, Roberto, but I've decided to go to Nantucket and write my epic novel. I'm going to rent my flat for two months and fly out next week. Isn't it thrilling?'

'Hmmm,' said Roberto doubtfully. 'You know Mercury's retrograde at the moment, it's a bad time to go anywhere. And as a water tiger you're better off in Europe. You should stay in London and write it here.' We couldn't discuss it any further because the dustbin men were banging on my door and complaining about the rubbish mountain outside. Apparently the council were insisting that I keep a skip on permanent retainer. I slunk upstairs feeling guilty. *Feng shui* was sweeping through Chelsea like wildfire and I dreaded to think of all the landfill sites that would now be overfilled as the Royal Borough chucked out its clutter. It was a frightening thought.

Unusually, because I tended to take Roberto's advice about everything, I disappeared to Nantucket to write my novel. I rented a small house on the beach, overlooking a lighthouse, and spent mornings in the local library doing research and the afternoons beachcombing, dreaming and moseying around the exclusive designer shops that studded the cobbled main town. In the evenings I would write, sometimes wandering on to the deck, where I would look out to sea and gaze at the dark topaz sky, wrapping myself in ocean spray, the glittering stars and my secret dreams.

It was easy to imagine how my great-grandparents had found enduring love on this glorious windswept island, its grand colonial architecture framed with grey slatted shutters and brisk white picket fences. In those days Nantucket had been a sleepy whaling island; now, in the nineties, it was a chic mecca to old-money America. Fortunately its wealthy inhabitants had ensured that the island had lost none of its sleepy charm, and one had the delightful feeling of having stepped back in time yet with all the advantages of the modern age.

But it was lovely to be back in London, I thought, two months later, as I emerged blinking from South Kensington tube station. It was August bank holiday and the streets were eerily silent. Everyone appeared to have fled the city, which suited me fine. I was just itching to switch on my computer and get down to work. Delving for my house keys, my heart sank. I had cleared my bag out on the plane and carefully put my keys into the seat pocket in front of me then promptly forgotten about them. Joanna had a spare set but she was spending the weekend at a health farm. I sat down on the steps and put my head in my hands. It was just *too* maddening. I'd have to stay in a hotel – if I could find one open. Then I had a thought. Roberto had said he was about this weekend; he'd rung only a few days ago and suggested we get together for a drink as soon as I got back. He'd just moved into a two-bedroom flat in Hampstead, which he was thrilled with. I dialled his number and to my relief he answered immediately.

'I've been such an idiot!' I wailed. 'I'm locked out of my flat . . .' I paused hopefully.

'Come and stay here, please! I've got lots of space!' He seemed terribly enthusiastic, as if me coming to stay was doing him a favour. I pulled my case down the road to my car – Thank heavens I still had the keys to that – and drove to Hampstead. Part of me wondered if this was a good idea, but I was really too jet-lagged to worry. Besides, after travelling for ten hours I must have looked sufficiently wrecked to deter him from all thoughts of *feng shui* massages and any other exciting suggestions he might have had up his sleeve.

I arrived expecting a minimal, perfectly *feng shuied* haven, but he ushered me into a tiny hall full of what could only be described as clutter.

'I bet you could use a drink, I've just cracked open a bottle of your favourite champagne.' I hadn't the heart to tell him that after six hours of free champagne on the plane it was the last thing I felt like. I longed to crash but knew I must make an effort to be sociable. He grabbed two grubby glasses out of the drying tray and pulled a bottle of champagne from the fridge. 'Come on through to the balcony and check out the view.'

I trailed after him, tripping over a crystal that was lying on the floor, and fell sprawling into a pile of wind chimes that made a violent clanging noise. I got up gingerly and followed him outside. He poured the champagne and we clinked glasses.

'Thank you so much, Roberto, you are my knight in shining armour. If it wasn't for you I'd be sleeping on the streets tonight, I don't know how I can ever repay you.' Oh dear. Wrong thing to say. We both knew there was a very simple way that I could repay him, but as far as I was concerned *that* was non-negotiable.

'I think it was probably just as well you were locked out of your flat tonight. I had a dream last night and I got the feeling that you are in some danger there.'

'What do you mean?' I asked anxiously.

'Perhaps I shouldn't tell you, but four stands for death in Chinese. In Hong Kong no one will live in a number four.'

I thought of my lovely flat and could have wept with disappointment. There was nothing for it. 'I'll have to move, won't I?'

'It might be a good idea,' said Roberto, fixing me with his strange green eyes. 'I just have the feeling that at the moment you need to take care.' I thought of how I had locked myself out of the flat and the way I had tripped over the crystal. Roberto was right!

'So did you fall in love with anyone in Nantucket?' he asked lightly.

'No fear! I was working too hard.' I thought nostalgically of the simple, uncluttered life I had enjoyed there free of emotional and physical dangers, and drained my glass.

'Would you mind if I crashed? I'm starting to feel a bit woozy.'

'Yes, this stuff's quite strong, a friend of mine sends it over from Italy. It's orgasmic.'

'Don't you mean organic?' I said firmly. Really, Roberto was obsessed with sex.

He laughed, eased himself off the sofa and showed me the bedroom. 'You can sleep in my room, I've changed the sheets on the bed.'

'Oh Roberto, I thought you had a spare room.' I felt terribly guilty. 'I can't chuck you out of your room. Where will you sleep?'

'I'll sleep on the sofa, it's not a problem.'

'No, I'll sleep on the sofa, I'd be much happier, really.' I thought of the tiny hard sofa and sighed inwardly. I was very sleepy.

He laughed good-humouredly. 'We could always share the bed. I promise I'll keep to my side. I'm tired myself so we'll probably both be out like a light.' I looked at the bed. It was made up in crisp white linen and had big, soft, lacy pillows that I longed to sink my head into. I'd shared beds with male friends before and nothing had happened. I felt silly for being so uptight.

'Oh, all right. But no talk about *feng shui* massages.' I went into the bathroom and turned on the shower, relishing the hot water against my skin. It was bliss to feel clean again after the long flight. I borrowed a dressing gown and went into the bedroom and grovelled around my case for my sponge bag. Roberto was sitting up in bed reading the *Feng Shui Times*.

'So how's your love life, Roberto?' I asked, removing my make-up. 'Met anyone nice since I've been away?'

'Yes, I have, actually,' replied Roberto mysteriously.

'Well, go on ... who is it?' This was most unusual. Roberto never admitted to liking anyone.

'She's called Skye and she's a Finnish *feng shui* consultant.'

'Hey, a match made in heaven,' I replied cheerfully, getting into bed alongside him. I felt a lot more relaxed about sharing a bed with him now. He was obviously madly in love with this other girl and had probably completely lost interest in me.

He turned off the light and we chatted desultorily. 'I hope Skye won't mind you sharing a bed with another woman,' I teased. It was rather companionable lying in this big cosy bed gossiping, after spending so much time by myself in America.

'She'd be very jealous. I don't care, though, she's beginning to get too possessive. When I tell her that you're staying she'll probably stop talking to me, which will be a relief.'

'Don't you dare bring me into it. The last thing I need is some ferocious Finnish *feng shui* consultant doing horrible magic spells on me, thank you very much. I'm going to sleep now, good n . . . *Ouch!* It's my foot, I've got cramp, Youch!' My right foot contorted painfully.

Roberto quickly burrowed down and started to pummel it vigorously. The pain immediately subsided. But he continued to rub my foot, which was beginning to tingle deliciously. I didn't object when his hand moved languorously up my shin and over my thighs. 'Great legs,' he murmured appreciatively and continued his exploration. I shut my eyes and allowed great waves of pure lust to sweep over me. Roberto was muttering something in Italian which added to the unreality of the whole experience.

I knew he had been wanting to do this for ages. He had been patiently building up to it for months, cementing our friendship and being so generous that if I just lay back and did nothing he would still think it was Christmas. So I just lay there, letting him do delightful things to my body and floating away with the delicious sensations that flowed through me. I was conscious of being utterly selfish and barely making any effort in return. Just being available seemed to be enough for him. He was so grateful despite my apathy in returning his efforts. I certainly couldn't be bothered to go down on him with the care and effort he was bestowing on me. I moaned with exquisite longing as he licked me in all the right places until, to my surprise – because I rarely come during oral sex (the orgasm police will arrest me for admitting that) and certainly not with someone for the first time – my whole body exploded with physical pleasure. Unable to wait any longer, I pulled him on top of me, and suddenly he was inside me, making me gasp and sending me into a rapturous world of my own, in which he was barely present. And then, exhausted and satiated, I lay back as he continued trying to please me, determined to delay his own satisfaction until he was quite sure that I had had mine. I shifted impatiently. I'd already come three times, which was more than during my entire relationship with Oliver. He must have read my mind, because he suddenly climaxed and kissed me with great tenderness.

'Phew,' I murmured appreciatively. 'Where did you learn to do all that?'

'This is nothing. It's only the beginning.' He pressed himself against me and I could feel what he meant. God, the man was insatiable!

'I've spent years practising Tantric sex. It means the man can go on for hours and hours.'

'That's nice.' I yawned, disentangling myself from his enthusiastic embrace and drifting off into a deep, relaxed sleep.

I woke up five hours later, wide awake and longing to get

up. Glancing at Roberto's slumbering form next to me, I winced. What on earth had I done? I'd had the best sex of my life with someone I didn't even fancy. Roberto stirred, opened his eyes and gazed at me adoringly. 'Come here, my beautiful blonde goddess.' I cringed. He was going to want to make love again and I couldn't face it. Last night in the dark, drunk with champagne and jet-lag, I had drifted into having sex, great sex admittedly, but my feelings hadn't changed at all. He pulled me towards him and began kissing me passionately.

'I think we should have babies together, don't you?'

'Yes, with my looks and your brains,' I joked, trying to lighten the atmosphere a bit. Babies! What was going on?

'Be serious. I went to see my psychic last week and she said we were very compatible.'

'Oh, what nonsense. If any of these psychics were for real they'd know what lottery numbers were coming up and make a fortune. She's just stringing you along.'

'Darling, don't be so cynical. She won the lottery last year, that's why she's living in an enormous house in Eaton Square and has a chauffeur-driven Bentley.' I was impressed. This woman must know her onions.

'Perhaps I should go and see her. Did she say anything else to you?'

'She said that you and I would go to bed.'

'Did she? What else?'

'I'm not telling you. But I might if you stay for a few days. I don't think you should go back to your flat today. Losing your keys was obviously a sign of protection.'

'Hmm.' I was bit spooked about my flat. I didn't want to go back there but I certainly wasn't going to stay with

Roberto a moment longer. I had a brainwave. I would ring Joanna at Rosewood Health Farm and ask if they had any spare rooms. That would solve my short-term accommodation *crise*. I really needed to rest; my immune system was under siege from the worry of unprotected sex with Roberto. Worry and stress are very toxic. Of course I wasn't worried about getting pregnant. Most of my friends are desperately trying to conceive, but the only proven way of getting pregnant in the barren nineties is to be sixteen and bonk an unsuitable boyfriend in the back of his Ford Cortina.

'Anyway,' went on Roberto, 'I've got to get up. I've got to do a consultation in an hour. Why don't you come with me? You can hold my compass.' I shivered. If I had to stay here a moment longer that wouldn't be the only thing I'd have to hold.

'I'd love to, but I think I'll give Rosewood Health Farm a ring and see if they can fit me in. I'm in desperate need of a detox.'

'Well, come and stay when you come back. Do we have time for a quickie before I go?' he asked optimistically.

'No we don't.' I disappeared into the bathroom, locking the door firmly. Delving nosily around the bathroom cabinet, I discovered a small box containing some exotic green contact lenses. They must be his spare set. Roberto's glittering green eyes were nothing but a sham!

'Bye,' called Roberto forlornly through the keyhole. He was presumably still unwashed, 'Ring me soon.'

As soon as the coast was clear, I slipped out of the bathroom and got dressed. Noticing I'd lost an earring I scoured beneath the bed, but found only a flashy pair of red knickers containing pictures of Roberto and me! My heart skipped a beat. Roberto was using the knicker sandwich trick on me, the scoundrel! And presumably he'd been wearing them himself!

I rang Rosewood immediately, booked their Stress Overload package and left a message for Joanna, who was having a seaweed algae wrap and was unable to come to the phone, that I would be arriving later. I glanced at the piles of *feng shui* books and magazines that were stuffed on to the bookshelves. Huh. Roberto had criticised me for my crammed bookcase and insisted that no new projects would come into my life. Physician, heal thyself! Out of interest I decided to check out his romantic corner before I left. This fell in the far right of the apartment and happened to be an airing cupboard. I opened the cupboard and on the back of the door found a photo of me and one of him next to a picture of a copulating couple. There was also a small bag of leather straps and silk scarves! I quickly packed up my things and scuttled down to my car. Who knew what other esoteric horrors I would find if I stayed a moment longer!

Three hours later I had arrived at Rosewood and prised Joanna out of the algae room to discuss recent developments.

'I think I'm turning into a mermaid,' she said, pulling a slippery film of seaweed from her long dark hair. 'God, I'm starving. You didn't bring any food, did you?'

I shook my head. 'There wasn't time. I had to escape from Roberto and his leather straps!'

'Ooh, how exciting! So what happened?'

'I slept with him by mistake and he wants to go on doing it. He might even want to be my boyfriend, I'm not sure.'

'What d'you mean, "by mistake"?' She unravelled some

more seaweed from her hair thoughtfully. 'He didn't drug you, did he?' I shook my head. 'Don't tell me you've been the victim of the red knicker sandwich trick?'

'Yes! It works. I'm the living, bonking proof that it does. The man's an out-and-out charlatan. He's great in bed, though.'

My phone interrupted us. It was Roberto.

'Hello, darling.' Darling! Things really were getting out of control!

'I called my psychic and she says we are perfectly matched. Isn't that great news?'

'Roberto, I don't think I should stay again. It was a mistake. A delightful mistake,' I added hastily.

'But you mustn't go back to your flat. I told you, you're in great danger there.'

'Well, maybe I'll sell it. You see, last night was a wonderful, um, interlude, but . . .'

'But the psychic says we're going to make love many more times.'

'I think I should be the judge of that. There is such a thing as free will, you know.' I was suddenly transfixed by the head of an elderly lady appearing and disappearing behind the partition of the conservatory where we were sitting.

'I've got to go, Roberto,' I said, mesmerised by the sight of the energetic apparition.

'It's Lady Rosewood,' whispered Joanna. 'She's taken up trampolining.'

Lady Rosewood was the owner of the health farm and ran the place with an iron rod. She had officially retired but kept her hand in, so to speak, by dispensing colonics with a certain brutal efficiency. She claimed to be Swiss but her true origins were shrouded in mystery. Rumour had it that she was in fact the daughter of a Bolivian tap dancer, but she had married the present Earl of Rosewood years ago and was now terribly grand.

'You're right to get away from Roberto,' Joanna went on. 'It sounds like he's really manipulating you.'

'It's my fault. I've been so gullible. I've been depending on him for advice about everything, like he's some kind of guru. And he's not, he's just a normal man.'

'You know when you went to see him before you went to Nantucket and he told you to buy all those droopy plants and cacti and insisted you get a picture of a battle scene and put up photos of single people everywhere? Well, I've been reading up about *feng shui* and those are all complete no-no's. He was obviously trying to sabotage your relationship with Oliver.'

'And now he's insisting that I sell my flat because it's a number four, which means death in Chinese, and I'm in danger there.'

'Rubbish. Your flat has got a wonderful cosy atmosphere. I've studied numerology. Four stands for earthiness and stability. It's a wonderful number. He's just trying to put the frighteners on you so you move into his place.'

I knew she was right. We were distracted again by Lady Rosewood drifting past in a kaftan, graciously acknowledging the greetings of her awestruck guests.

'Good afternoon, my dear.' I sat up nervously as she mysteriously materialised at my side. 'Sister wants to know if you would like plain or flavoured cottage cheese for luncheon tomorrow?'

'Um, er, flavoured, I th-think,' I stuttered nervously. It was like being addressed by the Queen.

'I do so agree, a much more interesting choice,' she murmured approvingly, and glided off towards the light diet room, where a queue had already formed despite the fact that dinner wasn't for another two hours.

The days slipped by in a dreamy blur of seaweed, aromatherapy, reflexology and absorbing yet sometimes disturbing conversations with the other guests. I switched my phone off and had time to think properly without distractions, allowing Rosewood to work its subtle magic on my body and spirit. I read widely from the extensive New Age library, sipped wheatgrass juice, attended revitalising Buddhist chanting sessions, dreamed deeply and slept soundly. I needed to gather my strength because the next few months were going to be very busy. Filming was soon to begin on *Ruffles at Dawn*, and I had to finish my Nantucket love story. My agent had left a message that a Mexican film company were bidding for the rights, and, if a film was made, would première it at the small but highly regarded Nantucket Film Festival. I realised I had become too dependent on Roberto, *feng shui*, astrology and expecting other people and things to give me answers when, according to Deepak Chopra, the solutions were inside me all the time.

Meanwhile, Roberto had been faxing me and leaving messages which I hadn't the strength to respond to. Still, the whole episode would make a great short story, maybe even a movie. But it was all a bit far-fetched. I mean, who on earth would believe it?

At the end of the week I threw my case into the boot,

switched on my phone and set off for London. It was a glorious sunny day and I put down the hood, loving the feel of the sun on my face and the wind in my hair. The phone rang and I picked it up with anticipation. It was Oliver.

'Darling girl, wh – have – been?' The line was terrible. I explained what had been going on, detailing my experience with Roberto and repeating myself several times because the line was crackling. Oliver wasn't remotely jealous – he loved this sort of thing and laughed uproariously. 'Well, now I've tracked you down, I was wondering on the off chance if you'd like to come to Canada with me. I'm told . . .' voice faded in and out, '. . . Viagra Falls – lovely this time of . . .'

Viagra Falls, Niagara Falls, ugh, it was all the same! Memories of our disastrous bedroom encounters seeped horribly into my mind.

'Do say you'll come,' he crackled on. I smiled, remembering Roberto and his silk scarves.

'Well, it's an intoxicating idea, darling,' I replied tactfully, 'but I think I'm going to be a bit tied up for the next few months . . .'